EVADE AND CAPTURE

CALLAHAN SECURITY BOOK 4

LORI MATTHEWS

WILD COYOTE PRESS

ABOUT EVADE AND CAPTURE

Spencer Gordon wasn't expecting the call from Kathleen Drake, a woman she'd spent years keeping safe as part of the Witness Protection program. The terrified woman begged Spencer for help. Taking a leave of absence from her job with Homeland Security, Spencer hurries to her friend's side. But the threat to Kathleen is larger than Spencer bargained for, forcing a call for reinforcements. She didn't count on being attracted to Kathleen's arrogant, annoying, and sexy as hell brother.

Searching for his sister has been a driving force for businessman and multimillionaire Jameson Drake. When a woman approaches him out of the blue claiming to know where his sister is, he has no choice but to go along. He'd imagined all kinds of wild theories about what happened to Kathleen but the truth is more shocking than even he'd ever guessed.

Forced to work together to keep Kathleen safe, Spencer strikes an uneasy alliance with Drake, wavering between wanting to shoot him, and needing to kiss him. Other than their mutual attraction, the one thing they do have in common is their desire to keep Kathleen safe. If only the mob didn't have a different agenda.

For my husband who never fails to make me smile. Thanks for all of your love and support.

ACKNOWLEDGMENTS

Thanks once again to all the inhabitants of my city – the one it takes to bring this book into the world. My deepest gratitude my editors, Corinne DeMaagd and Heidi Senesac for making me appear much more coherent than I actually am; my cover artist, Llewellen Designs for making my story come alive: my virtual assistant who is a social media guru and all-round dynamo, Susan Poirier. My personal cheer squad which I could not survive without: Janna MacGregor, Suzanne Burke, Stacey Wilk and Kimberley Ash. My mother and my sisters who told me to dream big. My husband and my children who make my hair turn gray but also make me laugh. And to you, the reader. Your emails and posts mean the world to me. The fact that you read my stories is the greatest gift ever. Thank you.

CHAPTER ONE

Spencer Gordon lowered the rifle's telescopic lens and swore. The spring sun was reflecting off the target's twenty-third floor boardroom windows, and the glint made it impossible to see who the hell he was in there with. She ground her teeth as she brushed blond hair out of her eyes. Her angle wasn't the best even without the sun, but now she had no way to know what was happening.

Glancing at her watch, she did a quick calculation. The glare would be off the window in a few minutes so it wasn't worth packing up and moving to the second location she'd secured. "Come on," she mumbled under her breath. Jameson Drake had called in his head of security for an emergency meeting, and she wanted to see the men. She may not be able to read lips, but she could read body language, and she needed to figure out what Drake was feeling. Was he upset, or was this just a routine meeting?

She inched forward toward the window and brought up the scope again. "Finally." The sun no longer shone in her eyes. She studied the boardroom. Drake was gesturing with his hands and pacing in front of the windows. He ran a hand through his hair, then turned abruptly and strode to the other end of the room.

Spencer smiled. Good, he was upset. That was a positive sign. Upset and off-kilter meant he was more likely to make mistakes. She needed him down in D.C. where she had the home court advantage. That would help her cause. Then he needed to ditch his security or she needed to make that happen.

She adjusted her scope and focused on his face. Stressed, for sure. Anxious, judging by the way his body moved. Visible cracks fractured his normally cool facade. She smiled again. Things were progressing. She had hoped he would've shown up in D.C. right away after the incident, but at least he wasn't ambivalent. That was her biggest fear.

An assistant opened the boardroom door, but Drake gestured to her to leave again. That was her number one hurdle, or at least one of them. The man was rarely, if ever, alone. People gravitated to him, like moons orbiting planets.

Watching Drake for these last couple of weeks had been an eye-opening experience. All day, people came and went from his office. Even when he was on calls, they would trickle in and out. During down time, women flocked to him and it didn't matter the age group. The man never seemed to have a moment to himself.

Spencer changed position in her rented office window. Charismatic was what they called him. Maybe. She'd form her own opinion when they finally met. He was attractive in that Cary Grant, George Clooney kind of way.

His eyes looked deep green in pictures, and his strong jaw made every woman look twice. Suave, urbane, and damn fine looking in a suit. Spencer knew guys like Drake. She'd grown up around them. He'd be a player with all the best lines, and he'd always know just what to say. That didn't appeal to her at all. She'd married a man like that, only to discover he didn't have any depth whatsoever. She had no interest in repeating the experience.

She turned to study the head of security. Blondish hair, younger than Drake. His hand gestures made it appear like he was trying to calm Drake down. Good luck with that. Riled up worked better for her. Still, Mitch Callahan and his brothers had already made a name for themselves in the security business. She'd been impressed by what she'd read. It didn't help her cause any, though. She would have preferred it if he'd had some average Joe running things. But beggars couldn't be choosers.

Her cell rang. She lowered the scope and looked at the screen. Eddie, her former boss. He'd been calling her at least once a week since this whole mess started. She clicked *ignore* and put her phone back in her pocket. She'd call him later.

Raising her scope, Spencer fiddled with the adjustment knobs, taking into account elevation and wind. Shooting Drake would be a last resort. She needed him to come with her without raising a fuss. It would be so much easier if he just agreed. But if he argued, well she'd shoot him and drag him along. He'd better not die. That would ruin everything. She needed him alive in order for this to work. If he wanted to die afterwards, well that was a different story. It wouldn't be great but it wouldn't be the end of the world.

CHAPTER TWO

"I need you to run this all by me again. You're going too fast and skipping all over the place. Start back at the beginning," Mitch Callahan said. He flipped open the notebook in front of him on the boardroom table.

"A notebook, seriously?" Jameson Drake practically sneered as he stared at his security specialist.

"Listen, computers are all well and good, but they can be hacked and bugged and whatever else, as you well know. When was the last time you heard of someone stealing a notebook? Sometimes old-school is best. Plus, back in my SEAL days, my buddies and I worked out our own code for things. If someone does steal my notebook, they won't be able to read it, or at least it will take a long while. So start at the beginning. Go slowly."

Drake's back teeth clicked as he locked his jaw. He had waited sixteen long years. He no longer wanted to be patient. He wanted this to be over. His chair spun as he jumped up to pace in front of the floor-to-ceiling windows.

Drake loved the Hudson River view from this boardroom. He usually found it soothing. He had taken great pains to make sure his offices reflected his taste, and not some designer. The carpet, a creamy beige with a slight pattern of darker brown running through it, muffled all sounds of footsteps. The wood furniture in different tones created warmth, and the overstuffed chairs made people comfortable, even if Drake himself did not.

He did not like chrome and glass. It was boring, overdone, and cold. He was considered cold enough by his staff. He didn't want them to work in an uninviting environment.

He handpicked his senior management, and he wanted them to be happy, not because he truly cared about their well-being, although he didn't *not* care. But, in reality, happy people became productive people. Productivity was the key. It was one of the reasons a high-end hot drink station could be found in most common areas in the office building, along with fridges stocked with the popular water brands and various healthy snacks.

On a typical day, his environment made him smile. He was at the pinnacle of his career and liked being on top. He'd worked damn hard to achieve his goals. Enjoying the fruits of his labor was paramount in his world. This view was one of the ways he perceived his success and, normally, he reveled in it, but not today. Today wasn't typical. Today he didn't notice the view at all.

"Last week, Friday to be exact, I received a message on my phone telling me the software, the one Dani designed, had a hit. A sixty percent match for my sister. At first, I didn't pay much attention. Four previous positives with much higher match percentage were reported, and they were all false."

Every single time, his hopes had soared. And every single time, they crashed again when he viewed the video of the person in question. He'd picked up the phone to yell at Dani when the false positives happened, but to be fair, she'd warned him mistakes would occur on occasion. He liked perfection in his world, and the errors bugged him more than he was willing to admit.

The software might never be perfect was what she'd said, but he had allowed his impatience to get the best of him, and they had installed the nearly perfect program on all of his servers. Now the software ran in every hotel he owned throughout the world. When he stopped and thought about it, that was millions of faces over many hours of video. He was shocked only four false positives had occurred so far.

"Where was I...?" He had gotten lost in thought, which happened more and more these days. This whole business with his sister had destroyed his concentration. He had started making mistakes, unheard-of previously, and his staff had taken notice. He sensed their worry and caught several exchanges of panicked looks. They weren't the only ones.

Drake cursed silently at himself. He drew in a deep breath. "Friday. I thought it would be another false positive, but when I viewed the picture, I knew it was her. My sister. The picture was a screengrab from the security video footage of one of my hotels in Washington D.C."

Mitch cocked an eyebrow. "You're sure it was her? Why?"

He stopped pacing and turned to face Mitch. "It's hard to explain. I'm aware that sounds weak, but it's true. The picture looked like her slightly, but I got my head of security at the hotel to dig out the actual video footage, and I asked one of my people here to make the footage as clear as possible. I had high-resolution cameras installed in all of my hotels specifically for this...project. The resolution is beautiful. When I watched the video, I just knew. The way she moved, the way she tossed her hair, the way she shot an impatient look at the bellman. It was my sister."

Mitch took a sip of coffee and then placed the cup back

on the table. "Drake, you haven't seen her in sixteen years. How can you be one hundred percent positive?"

He wanted to take Mitch's head off for doubting him. He'd destroyed men for less, but one look at Mitch's face revealed that he was just collecting facts, not doubting or challenging Drake. Mitch and his brothers were top-notch. He needed to trust in them.

He put his hands in his suit pants pockets. "Instinct. If one of your brothers disappeared for sixteen years and someone showed you a video, would you recognize them, even if they looked different?"

Mitch tapped his lips with his pen for a moment and then nodded. "Yes, I would. Okay, so you recognized her. What did you do?"

"I attempted to reach her. I called my hotel and had them connect me to her room, but she didn't pick up. I then asked the head of security to go knock on her door. He did, but she didn't answer. I got concerned. I asked him to enter the room."

Drake smiled slightly. "I don't think Mr. Yazley was pleased. I think he thought I had a personal relationship with this woman, and I was checking up on her. I thought he might refuse my request because he paused for a moment, but he gamely did as I directed, no questions asked." Exactly what was expected from his top staff. Do what he said and don't ask too many questions. They were paid handsomely for their loyalty.

Drake continued, "When Yazley opened the door, the room was empty. I asked him to go back and look at the security footage to see where she might be, and that's where it gets interesting. The only footage is of her crossing the lobby, checking into the hotel, riding the elevator up to her floor, but when she steps out of the elevator, she disappears."

"What do you mean 'she disappears'?" Mitch asked.

"Just that. She does not appear on camera. Anywhere on that floor or any other floor. We cannot find where she went."

Mitch frowned. "So, your system was hacked?"

He nodded. "It's the only explanation."

Mitch picked up his phone and started typing rapidly. He set the phone down again. "I asked Dani to run a diagnostic on the hotel. I told her you suspected you were hacked. She'll get back to us shortly. So what did you do next?"

"I asked Yazley to conduct a search. They checked every nook and cranny in the entire hotel but found nothing." He leaned his shoulder on the window and looked at Mitch. "She disappeared into thin air. Again."

Mitch leaned back in his chair. "Any ideas on how that happened? I mean, I'm aware that a person or persons unknown probably tapped into the security cameras around the hotel, but someone must have seen her."

"You would think that, wouldn't you? But I had my people do a thorough sweep of the building and asked everyone who was working at the time if they saw the woman, but no one did." Drake studied Mitch. "What are you thinking?"

"A few things. One, where did she disappear to? People can't really dissolve into thin air so she had to go somewhere."

Mitch held up two fingers. "Point two, why bother walking through your hotel only to disappear again? Why was she really there? Does she just want your attention?"

"Three, we need to look at cameras outside of your hotel. If we're lucky, CCTV cameras will be in the area, and maybe we can track her that way. There should be plenty of traffic cams although I have no idea if we can gain access. Legally, that is." Mitch paused and reviewed his notes. Then he looked up. "Why now? Why show up on your radar after all these years?"

Drake shook his head. "I wish I knew. From your questions, I gather you don't think it was just coincidence that she walked into one of my hotels."

Mitch grimaced. "Look, Drake, I understand how much you want to find your sister, but this sounds too much like a setup to be anything else. I'm sorry, but I would be lying to you if I said anything different."

Drake clicked his teeth together as he straightened up. "Let's go to my office." He strode out the boardroom door and down the long hall, passing several people on the walk and giving each one a nod, but his mind was elsewhere. Entering his office, he waited for Mitch to follow suit and then closed the door. He went directly over to the bar area in the corner and poured himself a large scotch. "You want anything?"

Mitch's eyebrows went up, but he shook his head.

"I don't need a nanny," Drake growled as he walked over and sat down behind his oversize ornate mahogany desk. Everyone had an opinion about his behavior these days. They could damn well keep it to themselves.

Mitch sat opposite him. "I don't care if you drink all day, but you need to keep your wits about you if we're going to figure this out."

He gave Mitch a hard look. "Have you seen me out of control even once since you began working for me? I'm not the problem. Just do your job and find my sister!"

"My job," Mitch retorted, "is to keep you safe. If we end up finding your sister, that's a bonus."

Fucking asshole, but he grudgingly admired Mitch. Not once did the man take any shit. Normally, Drake would have fired someone for speaking to him like that, but he'd come to rely on Mitch to tell him the truth whether he wanted to hear it or not. He let out a long breath. "You're right. So how do you propose we handle this situation?"

"First, we find out if there was any legitimate reason this woman"—Mitch glanced down at his notes to confirm the name she'd checked in under—"Petra Morrison, might have been at your hotel. We'll do a deep background on the name and see if we turn anything up. Then we find out if there was any illicit reason she was hanging out. Something stolen or someone killed. Any reason that someone might check into a hotel and then disappear again in minutes.

"My first guess would be sex, but she wouldn't have disappeared that fast. She went to too much trouble for just an affair of some kind. Hacking your hotel security system is no small task. We will check the outside cameras and the ones in the area. I'd like to bring in the whole team on this. There are a lot of questions, and we need to find some answers before we decide on a course of action." Mitch grabbed his phone and sent off another quick message.

Drake took a sip of his drink. "Petra Morrison is the name that was on my sister's fake ID. It was a joke between us. She picked Petra because she hated the name Kathleen. She thought her name was boring. Morrison because we grew up on Morris Street."

Mitch wrote something on his notepad. "That tells us that this woman has to either know your sister quite well or has done some serious research."

"Or she could *be* my sister," Drake shot back.

Mitch remained silent, but his silence spoke volumes. He obviously had serious doubts.

Drake had no idea what to think. "Why show me her face for a short period only to disappear again? Is she trying to lure me to D.C. and, if so, for what reason?" He took another large mouthful of his drink. What the hell was going on, and why now after all these years? His gut tightened as his instincts told him the truth, a truth he didn't want to hear. "Fuck. You're right. It's a setup but, my God, Mitch, it looked like her, right down to her mannerisms." He ran a hand through his hair. "I want to take the jet to D.C. right now and find her."

"I know, but you can't do that. We need more information so we can determine the level of danger before you go anywhere."

"I understand. It's the only reason I'm still sitting here." He ran his hands over his face and then sat back in his chair. "I get your point. It's a setup, an obvious one too, and if I wasn't so damned desperate to find my sister, I would have spotted it a mile off. It was a clumsy and stupid attempt to trick me into thinking she really was my sister."

He set his drink down and propped his elbows on the desk. He rubbed his face with both hands again. "Get your people together and start working on this. It's top priority. I'll pay whatever is necessary. I want to find my sister. I may not have a clue as to what the situation is at this moment, but I'm sure as hell going to figure it out. I've waited sixteen long years to see my sister, and I'm done waiting."

CHAPTER THREE

Drake paced in his home office. He had given up trying to function at his conglomerate headquarters in midtown. For the first time in years, he had no desire to work. Mitch had summed up the situation perfectly with the warning he had issued before leaving Drake's office: *Don't let your heart overrule your head on this one.*

His sharp bark of laughter broke the silence in the paneled room. He wasn't known for letting his heart play a factor in anything. He was a complete hard-ass, or asshole, as he'd been called too many times to count. But being an asshole was how he got to the top. Still, Mitch was right. His heart wanted him on the corporate jet on its way to D.C., but his head was telling him seeing his sister was too good to be true.

He leaned his elbows on the desk that faced the floor-to-ceiling windows and stared out at the view of Manhattan below. What was going on? Why would someone want to pretend to be Kathleen? Had he hurt someone so badly that they wanted to inflict as much pain as possible on him? He sighed. Revenge was a distinct possibility. He'd run over a lot of people on his way to the top.

He glanced over at his small conference table as his business phone rang. He wasn't picking up. They could hold the meeting without him. The eight empty chairs with the plush leather one at the head of the table, were just a reminder of all the work he was missing. The phone stopped ringing.

He spun his desk chair toward the windows and rubbed his eyes. The ticking of the art-deco clock on the shelves should have soothed him, but it failed this time. He would do anything to bring his sister back. Give up everything he had ever worked for in a heartbeat if Kathleen could be back in his life again. Did someone know this? Were they trying to use it against him? His cell phone rang, breaking the heavy almost-silence and startling him.

"Drake," he barked into the phone.

"Drake, it's Mitch. We've got something you should see. Can—?"

"Get here ASAP."

"We already are. Release the elevator," Mitch said and hung up.

He hurried into his living room and punched in a code on the discreet wall panel. He heard the elevator power up and the sound faded as the car descended. Would all three brothers come for this? Probably. He would expect nothing less than the best, and the three of them together were outstanding.

Having Callahan Security as part of his team meant he slept easy at night, at least in terms of his security. Now he doubted he would sleep well again until he had his sister back or, at the very least, knew what happened to her.

The elevator dinged, and the doors opened. Mitch and his brother Gage stepped out, followed by a short, rather stout, older woman carrying what looked like a medical bag.

Drake cocked an eyebrow. "Where's Logan, and who is this?"

"Logan's back at the office, making calls. We're trying to obtain the CCTV footage from near your hotel, but there's a lot of red tape. It's Washington D.C. Nobody wants to give up video of anything without asking a battery of questions. Logan's the man to deal with the red tape."

Drake nodded. "Good."

"This"—Mitch gestured toward the woman—"is Nurse Linda. You had an appointment with her at your office today to receive shots for your upcoming trip to Morocco."

He sighed. He had totally forgotten his appointment with Nurse Linda like so many other things these days. "Yes, well, I doubt I'll be going to Morocco any time soon. Sorry you came for no reason."

Nurse Linda smiled. "The vaccinations will last for at least a year, if not more. Might as well do it now so they are out of the way." The look she gave him brooked no argument. She was like a Catholic school nun without the habit. She had short salt and pepper hair and wore a crucifix around her neck. She also had a ton of bangles on her right wrist. They jangled when she moved.

"Fine. Let's go to my office." The two men and Nurse Linda followed him down the hallway. "Can I offer any of you something to drink?" He walked over to the bar.

"No, thanks," Gage answered for both he and Mitch.

"No, thank you," Nurse Linda said. "Why don't you sit here on this chair while I ready everything." She moved the chair out from the long table and stood between the two. Drake walked over and took a seat then rolled up the sleeve of his white button-down shirt.

"Actually, if you could take off your shirt, that would be helpful. I'm sure you don't want all the shots in one area," Nurse Linda said.

He dutifully took off his shirt and laid it over the back of his chair while Nurse Linda got everything ready. She wiped a small area on both upper arms and shoulder areas. “Now I’m just going to check your vitals to make sure everything is okay before I administer the shots.”

He glanced at Mitch and frowned. Mitch seemed to be enjoying this immensely since he was grinning. "Better you than me. I hate getting shots."

Nurse Linda took out a blood pressure cuff and fastened it to his upper arm and then pumped away like she was trying to inflate a tire.

“Is all this really necessary?” His patience was shot.

“Just going to take your pulse now. I must say your blood pressure is a little high. You should exercise more and maybe try and relax a bit.’

Is that what the answer was, exercise and relaxation? He wanted to strangle Nurse Linda but he bit his tongue instead. She was only doing her job. He was the one being an ass.

She reached down and grabbed his wrist. After thirty seconds, she tried to remove her hand and failed. "Oh, I’m so sorry. I got one of my bangles stuck on your watch."

Drake cursed silently. He reached over with his other hand to help her untangle herself. The watch was the last gift he’d ever gotten from Kathleen. It meant more to him than anything else he owned.

Gage came across the room. "Don't move. I’ve got it." He removed the watch from Drake’s wrist and the bangle from Nurse Linda and went back to the desk to sort them out.

Mitch was outright laughing now. “You’re having a fantastic day. I can just tell.”

Two minutes later, Nurse Linda was done. "Sorry again about your watch. Your arms and shoulders might be sore for a couple of days."

Gage handed her back her bangle, and Drake put his watch back on his wrist.

"Thank you for coming," he said, and Gage walked her back to the elevator.

"What do you want me to see?" Drake buttoned up his shirt again.

Mitch walked over to the table and popped open his laptop. "I brought my own. This is not connected to anything, so no one can hack it to find out what we're doing." He pulled out a USB stick and inserted it in the side of the laptop.

"We analyzed the video you gave us and came up with this." He hit play, and Drake watched the video. The woman went up in the elevator, only this time when the doors opened on the sixth floor, she didn't disappear. "They looped the video in the hallway but not in the elevator. We viewed the video from the elevator camera, and you can see her until the doors close."

Drake leaned closer to the screen. The woman walked down the hallway at a fast pace. She didn't pause or stop anywhere. She continued toward the other end of the hallway until the elevator doors closed and they couldn't see her any longer. The video showed the empty interior of the elevator again. "So, what happened? Where did she go?"

Mitch continued. "We think she turned the corner at the end of the hallway and took the stairs down. We're guessing to the basement since she doesn't appear again in any other hallway video footage or on any other elevator.

"Whoever hacked the original video could have done it again to block her exit, but we don't think so. The fact that they missed the elevator footage leads us to believe they are more of an amateur than a professional. Plus, we can find no other footage of her outside of the hotel. She had to have left by the back. You have cameras in the front.

Gage took over. "Our guess is she changed in the stairwell into some sort of staff uniform, and when she left the stairwell in the basement, she blended in with the other staff and walked out of the hotel."

Drake glanced at both men. They were telling him something important, but he was missing the message. He was off-kilter, and his brain wasn't firing on all cylinders. *Focus.* He reviewed what they just told him, but it was no use. "I'm not following," he growled.

"Drake," Mitch said in a quiet voice, "you have cameras all over your hotels, even in the staff areas. If this was your sister, even if she changed her appearance, the software would've caught her and sent out another notification when the program picked her up again outside of the stairwell. You said you received a notice of a sixty percent match. That's not great odds, but if the software didn't ding her on the way out—"

"Then it isn't my sister," he finished for Mitch.

He stared out at the view of the city as the last flicker of hope died in his chest. He had been so sure. So willing to believe the picture was her after all these years. He wanted her back so badly that he had fooled himself into believing it was true. Even when Mitch pointed out earlier that it wasn't likely to be Kathleen, he'd kept that small spark of possibility alive.

Idiot. Rookie mistake. What was wrong with him? He closed his eyes and let out a long breath, and then forced his eyes open again. He went back over to the bar. He poured himself a healthy shot of scotch and took a big gulp.

Gage said, "What concerns us is someone wants you to believe this woman is your sister. They want you in D.C., and we need to understand why."

He nodded, but he was still stuck on what they'd just said. How could he have been so stupid to have missed it?

Because he wanted it to be Kathleen so badly, he'd fooled himself into believing it was possible.

"Fuck!" he roared as he threw the glass across the room. It hit the wall and shattered into a million tiny pieces. In his desperation to find Kathleen, he'd lost sight of reality. He needed to do better. *Be* better.

"Look," Mitch said in a quiet voice, "you want to find your sister, and someone is taking advantage of that. Direct your anger at them." He closed the laptop.

Drake took a deep breath and sat down hard behind his desk. "What are you thinking?"

Gage sat down opposite Drake. "Who knows about your missing sister?"

Mitch came over and dropped into the matching chair next to his brother's. "And did you do anything lately that would piss someone off enough to make them want to lure you to D.C.?"

Drake let out a bark of laughter. "I piss people off every day. It goes with the territory. But I don't think I've done anything lately that would push someone over the top. The last big mess was the thing with the Triads in Macao. We got that all sorted. The Triads aren't pleased with me, but they've enough on their plate with the government clamping down on the people of Hong Kong. My understanding is a lot of the members involved were arrested, and a significant portion of the remainder were killed in some sort of turf war."

"What about your sister? Who knows of her disappearance?" Gage asked again.

He shrugged. "Not many." Drake tipped his chair back and steepled his fingers under his chin. "All told, there's maybe a half dozen people."

Gage picked up a rubber band from Drake's desk. "That you've told this year?"

"That I told—ever."

Gage glanced at Mitch, who gave a small shrug.

"You're surprised," Drake said. "You shouldn't be. You're aware I don't like my business to be out in the world. I never saw fit to tell many people about Kathleen's disappearance. Once the police stopped investigating, I made the decision I would find her myself. There didn't seem to be a point in talking about the situation until I had the means to begin the search."

Gage and Mitch exchanged another look. Drake sighed inwardly. People who had close family never understood his obsessive need for privacy. After having hordes of police officers crash around in his life, investigating him and his family when Kathleen disappeared, he swore he would find a way to be as private as possible. His business was his own. He knew the brothers were all involved in each other's lives, and that worked for them, but it didn't work for him.

"If you don't have family who you can trust, then how do you choose who you confide in? I've told a handful of people, people I thought I could trust. I was right for the most part. These people will help me if they can. There was no need to randomly share the fact." Drake didn't mention that the pitying looks people had given him at the time of his sister's disappearance and then a year later after his grandmother died had almost driven him over the edge.

"Well, we know someone, who is aware Kathleen is missing, is out there using that knowledge to draw you to D.C. We need to figure out why."

Drake froze for a second. He blinked once and tilted his head. "There's something else."

Mitch cocked an eyebrow. "What's that?"

"We know that whoever that woman is, she knows, or at least knew, my sister."

Gage frowned. "Why do you say that?"

"The whole reason I thought it was my sister was because she had the identical mannerisms. She walked like my sister, tilted her head the same way. Held her bag the exact same way. This woman had to have access to my sister or access to video of her. Remember, she disappeared sixteen years ago. I don't have any old video around. My grandmother died just a year after my sister disappeared, and she didn't leave any video behind either. This woman has to be connected to my sister."

Gage played with the rubber band. "Do you think this woman could be an old friend of your sister's?"

Drake thought for a second and then shook his head. "No. I didn't remember those mannerisms until I saw this woman doing them. I can't imagine a friend from sixteen years ago would remember how my sister walked or held her purse."

"He's right," Mitch agreed. "No one remembers that type of thing after all that time unless they see it. So, where does that leave us?"

"I need to go to D.C." Drake rose from his chair.

Gage stuck out a hand and motioned for Drake to sit back down. "Hold on a second. I know you are anxious to find your sister and to follow this up, but running off before we have a better handle on what's going on is foolhardy and dangerous. We need to think this through."

Drake let out a harsh breath and sat back down. "I am confident Callahan Security can keep me safe. What's to discuss?"

"I am grateful for your confidence in us," Mitch said, "but I agree with my brother. We need to make a plan before we run off half-cocked."

Drake curled his hands into fists. This was not what he wanted to hear.

Mitch got up and went over to the bar. He poured

another scotch for Drake and grabbed a beer for himself and his brother. He put the drink in front of Drake and handed a bottle to Gage. "Now, let's start at the beginning and hammer out some details."

"Right." Gage took a swig of his beer. "You'll want to stay at your hotel presumably, but I'm not sure that's a great idea. If they can fool with the cameras, then they can probably access the whole security system. We need to be able to keep your living area airtight. By the way, Dani is running all the protocols for the security at all your hotels. It will take a few days, but we want to find out if it's just the D.C. hotel they breached. So far so good. She did say she thinks it was an inside job."

"Wonderful. More good news." Drake took a small sip of scotch.

"Don't you have an apartment in D.C.?" Mitch inquired.

Drake nodded. "I do, but I leave it closed up. I haven't stayed in D.C. for any amount of time in a few years. I usually just stay at the hotel when I'm there."

"I'll have our guys open the apartment up and secure it." Mitch got up out of the chair and walked away to make the necessary calls.

"What else?" Drake asked.

"Well, we still need to put feelers out to try to identify who's behind this." Gage set his beer on the desk. "How are your acting skills?"

Drake cocked an eyebrow. "What are you thinking?"

"Once you're in D.C., probably in a day or two, I want you to pretend you absolutely believe this is your sister in that security footage, at least in the beginning. We need to find out who the inside person is at your hotel, and there could be more than one. We want them to believe you are convinced. It might make them sloppy. Hopefully, it will make whoever is behind all this reveal the next step in their plan.

"Also, we will assign extra security. Some with you and even more hidden behind the scenes." Gage paused again. "You need to understand that no matter what rabbit hole this takes us down, your security and safety will be paramount."

Mitch walked back into the room and tucked his cell into his pocket. "That means you must listen to us even if what we tell you goes against your instincts."

Drake looked back and forth at both men. They were deadly serious. They were telling him he had to do what they say. He hated being forced to listen to others. He did not do well with authority figures. Never had. "What you're telling me is my ability to make rational decisions around this is probably compromised and I have to trust your judgment over my own."

There was a pause, and then both men nodded. He took a gulp of scotch. Could he do this? Could he put his entire fate in someone else's hands? No way in hell.

He shrugged slightly. "So be it." He was going to find out what was going on, and if it meant he had to lie to two of the men he trusted most in the world, he was okay with that.

Anything to find his sister.

CHAPTER FOUR

"Who's the inside man?" Drake demanded as the limo rolled down the tree-lined street. The combination of the gray sky and fine mist in the air made the city seem dreary, but the blooming cherry blossom trees announced that spring had sprung in D.C.

"Looks like someone by the name of Nigel Follows," Gage stated. "Mitch sent you the file."

The phone cut out, and Drake missed the next sentence. "Can you repeat that?"

"I said, he received a wire transfer of five thousand dollars to his bank last week and another five thousand the day after the woman appeared in the hotel. He works in security, and he was clocked in on the day of the incident."

"I want to speak with him."

"Yes. Jake and Dragan will arrange it. Follows is working this afternoon and tomorrow so you can go to your apartment and settle in. We'll set something up for tomorrow."

"I'll go to the hotel first." He pulled the phone away and looked over at Jake. "Tell Yazley to be prepared." Jake nodded and pulled out his phone. Drake put his own phone back to his ear.

"Drake"—Gage's voice came down the phoneline—"Mitch won't be there until late tonight. We would prefer you wait for him."

"I understand," he responded and then clicked off. He had no intention of waiting. He already delayed getting here by two days so the apartment could be secured properly. Logically, he understood Gage's concerns, but emotionally, this was the closest he'd come to finding Kathleen in sixteen years. Waiting was not an option. He may not specialize in security, but he understood how things worked. He knew how to elicit information from someone. How did they think he'd survived in the hotel trade all these years? Some little shit had breached his security. He wanted details, and he wanted them now.

"The hotel please," he called to the driver. He glanced at Jake and Dragan. Neither man said a word. Either Gage told them to go along with him or they both realized arguing was futile. He settled against the seat and grabbed his phone. He scanned the file Mitch sent on Fellows and then caught up on his emails and read the headlines of the day as the limo whisked him through the damp streets to his hotel.

They pulled into the circular drive, and the limo stopped in front of the main doors. Jake and Dragan got out before Drake had even undone his seat belt. The door opened, and he climbed out. Flanked by the two men, he entered the lobby. The Jasmine Door in Washington D.C. was one of the jewels in his holdings. The hotel was gorgeous. The opulent lobby of white marble and deep wood tones created an inviting atmosphere for his guests. He hadn't taken two steps into the lobby when his head of security, Mr. Yazley, approached him.

"Mr. Drake. Good to see you. I do hope you had a good flight."

Drake wanted to scream at the man that he didn't have time for pleasantries, but he didn't. Instead, he pasted on a small smile. "Yazley. Good to see you as well. My flight was fine. Where are we going?"

"I have Nigel waiting for us in a room in the back." He indicated the way and fell into step with Drake. "I have to say I'm quite surprised. Nigel is an exemplary employee. He came to us from the Jasmine Door in London. I think there's been some sort of mistake."

Drake didn't bother to respond as he walked across the lobby. His people didn't make mistakes. Well, maybe they had in hiring this Nigel character. He strode down one of the long galleries that ran along the outside of the hotel. The glass outer wall of this gallery offered a view of a garden. The inside wall was done in rich cream and gold wallpaper. Pictures of different landscapes from the local area were hung every ten feet or so. There were overstuffed leather chairs and small tables all the way down the long hallway.

Drake stopped about halfway and turned. A doorway that blended so well it was almost hidden provided the entrance to the business side of the hotel. A control panel tucked behind a rather lush potted bush provided the only indicator of the entrance. Mr. Yazley tapped in a code, and the door clicked open. The men entered, and Mr. Yazley closed the door after them.

They walked through the rabbit warren of hallways until they came to a small room next door to the security hub. There was a man standing outside in a hotel security uniform. Mr. Yazley nodded at the man, and he opened the door. Jake walked in, took a look, and then nodded to Drake, indicating it was safe. Drake entered the room.

Nigel Follows was little more than a boy. Lank hair

flopped over his eyes and he bit his lip. The way he slouched in his chair reminded Drake of a child waiting outside the principal's office.

Nigel's parents lived back in England. His dad drove a city bus and his mom worked as a nurse. He was twenty-five according to the file Mitch had sent. The picture in the file didn't do the kid justice. He was even skinnier than the camera indicated. He straightened up in his chair and tried to look calm. Mr. Yazley started to speak, but Jake put a hand on the man's arm and shook his head.

"I will proceed from here alone, Mr. Yazley, and will let you know if I need anything else," Drake said.

Yazley opened his mouth but closed it again. Dragan came inside the room and switched places with Jake. Jake guided Yazley back to the hallway and closed the door behind them. Drake knew from experience that Jake would stand guard in the hallway until he emerged. He appreciated the show of force. Dragan was the more intimidating of the two men since he was well over six feet and all muscle. The suit he wore emphasized, rather than hid that fact.

Drake pulled out a chair and sat down directly opposite Follows. Dragan casually leaned against the wall near the corner.

"Mr. Follows. Can you please tell me who hired you to put the video cameras in a loop this past Friday?"

Follows swallowed. "I have no idea what you are referring to Mr. Drake. Sir." His interlaced fingers rested on the table. He attempted to appear relaxed, but his white knuckles and his jackhammer knee lightly tapping the table leg were dead giveaways.

Drake threw a still photograph of the mystery woman on the table. "Nigel, I don't have a lot of time to waste on this so let me be clear. You are going to tell me what is going on and who hired you, and you are going to do so quickly. There is no 'or else' in that sentence because that would imply you have a choice of some kind. You do not. Start talking, and all of this will be over quickly. Waste my time, and this will be excruciating for both of us."

"Really, sir, I don't—"

Drake let his features fall into what his adversaries in business dealings called his death glare. "Nigel, I am aware that ten thousand dollars was wired to your account here in D.C. in two payments, one before Friday and one after. You worked on Friday, and you were the only one in the security area at the time this woman entered the hotel." Drake tapped the picture.

"You helped the woman. There is no question. Please explain to me in detail how your involvement in this event occurred. Your cooperation will be duly noted if it is given quickly. If you do not cooperate, your parents…well, let's just say they will not be...happy in the near future."

He was bluffing. He had no intention of hurting the boy's family nor would he hurt the boy. He would, however, make sure Follows could not obtain a job at any hotel. He would also make sure Follows's parents knew what he had been up to at work. The file had also indicated Follows had a girlfriend. If he had to, Drake would threaten her next.

Follows looked at Drake and then at Dragan, who took the opportunity to stand up straight and unbutton his suit jacket, which fell open to reveal his gun.

Beads of sweat popped out on the young man's forehead. "I didn't do anything."

Drake kept his face neutral. "Nigel. This is your last chance. Speak, or your life will change. Forever."

Nigel glanced back and forth between Drake and Dragan. His lip started to tremble. "Fine. She paid me, okay?"

The refined accent disappeared. In its place, the sound of

a street kid. "I really needed the money. My girlfriend fell pregnant, and baby stuff is bloody expensive. Like crazy expensive. It seemed harmless enough. She didn't do anythin' while she were here. I kept an eye to it. No one got hurt. Nothin' got nicked. She just wanted to walk through the hotel. Where's the harm in that?"

Drake leaned forward. "How did she find you?"

I was gettin' coffee one day, see, and she come up to me like and asked me if I would like to make a few quid. I was like 'piss off,' but she said, 'I know you need money for your baby.' And I was like, 'How'd you know about that? I ain't even told me mum yet.' She just smiled and said, 'That's okay, it can be our little secret.' Then she said I needed to record a loop of an empty hallway at the hotel, just like a minute or so of it, so she could use it. I thought she was a nutter, but then she said she'd pay me five thousand quid! For taping an empty hallway? Who could turn that down? So I said yeah."

"What happened next?" He couldn't blame the kid. If someone had offered him five grand when he was broke to record an empty hallway, he would have done what she asked, too.

"Well, I had to record it, didn't I? It was hard. People are always walkin' up and down the hallways. The cleanin' people roamin' 'round. I don't work nights, so people are always comin' and goin' durin' the day. And I had to wait 'til nobody was around, see. It took me a bloody week to get a clean stretch of hallway for two minutes. She kept callin' me, too. Askin' about like it was no big deal. I told her, if it was no big deal, she could bloody well do it herself.

"Anyway, I got it done and called her. Said I had it for her. She met me at the coffee shop again. She said now I had to stick it in the system, so she could walk through the hotel without bein' seen. I told her no, no way. It took too long to get the clip. How was I goin'ta get it back in the system? She offered me another five thousand quid. So I said I'd try. She'd said I'd better do a damn sight more than try. She got right up in my face, she did."

"So how did you pick the day and time to do this?" Drake asked.

Nigel shrugged. "She did. She told me when and what time. I can tell you it wasn't easy. Damn Hurly, one of the other guards, picks that day not to go out for a chat to his girl on his break. They'd had a fight, see, and he didn't want to talk to her. I practically had to drag him out. I told him to go get us snacks, and I would pay. He's a big guy, eats a ton. Cost me thirty dollars to get him his snacks. Anyway, he took so long draggin' his damn heels that I was a bit late doin' it. I was supposed to turn off the elevator camera and run the loop in the hallway so when the doors opened, the elevator wouldn't catch her walkin' down the hall. They'd be off, but I stuffed it up and forgot the elevator cam. Stupid Hurly messed up everythin'."

"How did she get out?"

"She went down the stairwell, and then she went out through the loadin' dock in the back of the hotel. She changed in the stairwell, so she were wearin' a hotel uniform like, and then she just walked out. The camera don't work in that stairwell. Hasn't in forever. No one wants to get it fixed cause that's where everyone takes a smoke break if it's rainin'."

"Did anyone see her in the stairwell?"

Nigel shrugged. "I don't know, do I? I wasn't gonna ask anybody about no bird walkin' through, was I? It'd blow me cover, and I didn't want to get caught or anythin'." He shook his head like Drake was stupid for asking the question.

"Do you still have her number?"

" I deleted it, didn't I? I didn't want it in my phone in

case anyone asked me questions, like you lot. Then you wouldn't know I talked to her."

In spite of himself, Drake liked the kid. Nigel might not have been the sharpest tool in the shed, but he didn't want to hurt anyone. "Do you remember the number?"

Nigel shook his head. "No. No way. No idea."

"Nigel, I'll tell your mother your girlfriend is pregnant. I have no doubt she'll be on the next flight over. Do you want your mother to move in with you?"

Nigel went pale. He spit the numbers out so fast Drake missed a couple of them.

"Again, slower please."

Nigel complied, and Drake memorized them. He had no illusions that it would lead anywhere, but he would kick himself if he didn't follow up every lead.

"So, what's goin' to happen to me?" Nigel asked.

"You know what, Nigel? I'm going to move you to a different job. You're going to do security at one of my parking garages. You don't steal cars, do you, son?"

"I never stole anything in my life."

Drake raised one brow.

"Well, 'cept Mrs. Wilson's knickers, but it were a joke. They were huge, and she had them out on a line. I took 'em and used 'em as a rag to clean my bike. Worked good, too. Cleanest my bike ever was."

Drake fought to keep a smile off his face. It sounded like something he would have done in his youth. "Okay. I'll leave the details with Mr. Yazley. You will report there for work tomorrow morning." Drake got up. "By the way, if I find out you lied to me, I will hunt you down and make your life miserable. Your mother and I will become close."

"I understand. I'm tellin' the truth. Honest." The kid dragged his finger across his heart.

Drake nodded and walked out of the room.

CHAPTER FIVE

Spencer leaned against the wall and made like she was looking at her phone as she watched Drake exit his hotel. The first part of her plan had worked. Drake was finally in D.C. Now what? How was she going to see him without alerting the world?

Time was running out. He'd taken forever getting to the city. She'd watched him for days in New York. His security team was thorough. They were going to be a problem. She'd hoped he would be on a plane right away, but it had taken him a week to show up. Did he realize she wasn't his sister on the video? Or had his security team held him back? She was guessing it was the latter but at this point anything was possible and the whole thing was just as likely to come back and bite her in the ass.

The shiny black limo drove off, and Spencer walked over to her own rental parked at the curb. She didn't need to rush. They were going to his apartment. She'd bet on it. She drove, worming her way through traffic.

What had happened at the hotel? Did they find out about Nigel? Guilt plagued her for using him, but he'd been such an easy target. Maybe she should send him more money.

She needed a face-to-face meeting with Drake, and he needed to be alone. How could she make that happen? Was this whole thing doomed from the start? An operation like this needed months of planning, not a few days. She needed a team, not just one woman. She chewed on the inside of her cheek.

Spencer lacked the resources and the time for a complicated plan. Her friend was in trouble, and she needed to do all she could to bail her out. Kathleen Drake had helped her back when she needed a friend. Coming to Kathleen's aid now was the least she could do in return. Really, saving Connor was the most important thing. Kathleen made Spencer swear she would do just that. Save Connor. Spencer had known Connor since birth, and she couldn't let anything happen to him.

The limo pulled up in front of his building. Spencer pulled into the opening of a service alley, and parked. Drake's security men got out, and then the man himself emerged from the car. They all went into the building. Spencer stayed parked at the curb. She needed to figure out a way in. The building had tight security, and she would bet Drake's apartment had an extra layer or two. She mulled everything over as she monitored the people moving up and down the street. Maybe there was another way. What if she could get Drake out of the building?

Okay, Drake outside the building was a much better idea she needed him and in an environment she could control. But where? A couple of spots came to mind, but she quickly dismissed them. Then she cocked her head and smiled. She knew just the place. Now, how to get him there was the real question.

"Nigel," she called to him as he started to walk out of the coffee shop.

He turned. "No," he said and shook his head for emphasis. He pushed open the door and hit the sidewalk at a quick pace.

Spencer almost had to break into a run to catch up with him. She grabbed his arm. "Nigel."

"No way. I lost me job 'cos of you. We're done." Nigel turned and started walking again.

"Drake knows about the video?" She wasn't surprised and, as a matter of fact, was counting on it now.

Nigel rolled his eyes. "Why do you think I lost me job!"

"Nigel, I'll give you another five thousand. I need you to make a phone call."

When he stopped abruptly, Spencer almost walked right into him. "Drake was at the hotel yesterday. What happened?"

"I just told you, I lost me job, that's what happened. He fired me, didn't he? He knew I helped you and how much you paid me. Even that you put the money directly into my account. Now I gotta work at his parkin' garage. Me girlfriend is pissed."

"So he demoted you to the parking garage. At least you still have a job. Buy something nice for your girlfriend out of the next five thousand, and she'll forget all about your demotion."

"I don't want the money. If Drake fires me, I have to go home. I'm not goin' back to me mum and dad's."

"Tell Drake I'm paying you to talk to him."

"What?"

"That is who I want you to call. I need you to call him and tell him to meet me at the Vietnam Veterans Memorial tonight at ten. Also tell him to come without his security. If I see one hint of his people, I'll leave."

"He'll fire me or kill me—"

"He'll say thank you for telling him. Five thousand bucks. Make the call right now." She offered Nigel her burner phone. She'd grabbed a new one that morning just for this purpose.

Nigel stared at the phone in his hand.

"Hit the button, Nigel. The number is already programmed in. Tell Drake that I tracked you down again and asked you to call him. Be totally above board."

He looked up at her and back at the phone, indecision written all over his face. Finally, he hit the button and raised the phone to his ear. Spencer took out her other phone and immediately transferred another five thousand dollars into Nigel's account.

"Mr. Drake, sir, it's Nigel Follows. That woman, the one from the video, is here with me right now. She wants me to give you a message. Meet her at the Vietnam Veterans Memorial at ten p.m. tonight. Come alone. None of your security blokes, yeah?"

Nigel glanced at her. "I could try, but I don't think the phone has a camera and it wouldn't matter much anyway. She's got a huge round black hat on and is wearing big sunglasses. You can't see none of her face. She's gotta scarf over her lips like, too. She's wearing a long coat. Yeah, black. Black boots, too." There was a pause. "She's wearing gloves."

Fingerprints. Drake was trying hard; she'd give him that. And she was sure his people would work on pulling the CCTV footage, too, but the red tape would be tough to break through on this one. She allowed herself a small smile. Working at Homeland Security did have its benefits.

"Sir, she's paying me another five thousand quid for this call. Crazy. Yup. I'll be on time to work." Nigel hung up and handed the phone back to Spencer. "He said he'll be there. Alone."

"Thanks, Nigel. You take care of yourself and that baby." Spencer turned on her heel and walked away quickly. She went down two blocks and over two more. She entered the parking garage and took the stairs. The cameras in this particular garage weren't working as of this morning. The repair people couldn't come until next week. *Shame.* She grinned. Stripping off her disguise in the stairwell, she wrapped her clothing up and bunched it in the plastic bag she'd had stuffed in the coat pocket. She came out of the stair well on the third floor dressed in a pair of jeans, a white blouse, and a navy blazer and headed directly to the rental car. She threw the bag in the passenger seat and climbed in.

Then she waited. She checked her email, both work and personal, and did a bit of online shopping. An hour and fifteen minutes later, she pulled out of the garage. There'd been three women parked on this floor that left before she did, and there had to be more parked on the other floors that had left as well.

Drake's people wouldn't be able to identify her in the disguise, even with the software that the hacker built for Drake. She'd covered up all identifying features and changed her walk. If they did manage to track her to this garage, letting other women leave first muddied the waters.

At some point in the future, everything would come to light, and all her actions would be examined under a microscope. She would be lucky if she was just fired. More than likely, she would end up in jail. But all of that was down the road. First things first.

She needed to kidnap Jameson Drake.

Spencer arrived back at her apartment after driving around aimlessly for another hour. She rode the elevator up from the garage and, when the doors opened on her floor, she swore. She hit the close door button, but she was too late. Brian Fielding, her partner at Homeland, had already seen her. Might as well face the music.

"Where've you been?" he demanded as she exited the elevator and walked down the hallway toward him.

"Out." She dug in her jeans pocket and pulled out her keys. "What do you want, Brian?"

"Why aren't you at work?"

Spencer opened the door to her apartment and walked in. "I told you, I'm taking a leave of absence." She dropped her keys on the small table in the hallway and walked over and put her purse on the kitchen island.

Brian followed her in. "That doesn't tell me anything. You're sabotaging your career. You need to be at work."

She'd been ducking Brian since she announced the L.O.A. to him last week. She had no intention of having this conversation with him. Sadly, there was nowhere to hide in her apartment since it was essentially one large room. There was a separate bedroom and bathroom, but she wasn't going into either of those rooms. Brian had been actively pursuing her for months.

She took off the blazer and slung it over one of her kitchen stools she had by the island. "Brian, I'm taking some time off. The rest is none of your business. Now, please leave."

He walked over until he was standing directly in front of her. "You are a star at work. Everyone knows you're going straight to the top. This leave of absence is going to slow you down. The brass don't want to deal with people having issues. This could be the kiss of death for your career."

Spencer gritted her teeth. How had she ever considered

dating this asshole? The one-night thing they'd had after breaking a big case had been a huge mistake, and she'd known it immediately. Why hadn't he? His blond-haired, blue-eyed good looks disguised a very domineering personality. Controlling was another word for him. No thanks. Not interested. She'd already been down that road once and had been lucky to escape with her life.

She folded her arms across her chest. "Brian, please leave."

He reached out and grabbed her upper arms. "I don't understand why you are shutting me out. What about us?"

"There is no us. It was a one-time thing fueled by cracking a case, too much booze, and lack of sleep. We are not together. Now leave."

He squeezed her arms. "This is about that woman, isn't it? The client you had when you were with the Marshals working in Witness Protection. The chick you're friends with."

In a weak moment, she'd mentioned that her friend Kathleen might be in trouble. *Fuck.* Brian was a lot of things, but stupid wasn't one of them.

"Brian, this is about me. I want a break."

"So take a vacation."

She tried not to overreact to Brian's grip, but it triggered her, and panic clawed its way out of her chest into her throat. *Fuck you, buddy.* No man was ever going to stop her voice again. "Brian, let go of me and leave," she demanded through clenched teeth.

"No. You need to forget about that friend and whatever shit she's involved in. That's the Marshals' job. Your career is here in D.C. now, and you need to get back to it before it's too late. Tell Kindler that you made a mistake and you don't want a leave of absence. You're ready to be back at work."

Spencer wrenched her arms out of Brian's grasp and took

a step back. Her heart thudded in her chest at the thought of being overpowered. Not. Ever. Again. "You are upset because you want to ride my coattails to the top. You know I make you look good, and you don't want to put the time in."

All the color left Brian's face but then raced back until his cheeks were bright red. "That's not true!"

"It is true, Brian. You know it. I know it. Hell, even Kindler knows it. He offered me a new partner if I wanted. He's worried that you are the reason I'm taking a break. And you know what? I told him I'd think about it. We're done, Brian. You and me as partners, as friends, as anything. Get the fuck out of my apartment! Now!"

"You, bitch! I'm good at my job, and everyone knows it." He stuck a finger in her face and started shaking it. "Don't say I didn't warn you. Your career will be over after this little leave thing you got going. I'll see to it. I'll make sure everyone knows you're having issues. We all know what that means. You're done at Homeland!" he roared. He whirled on his heel and stormed out of her apartment, slamming the door behind him. Spencer raced to the door and slid the security chain into place. Her shoulders drooped as she walked back over and collapsed onto the stool nearest to her.

The last thing she needed in her life was to have that argument. She hadn't wanted to say those things, even though they were true. She just wanted Brian to leave her alone. Why couldn't he have seen that? The doors to the life she'd led for the last seven years seemed to be closing much faster than she could process.

She had known when she walked into Kindler's office and asked for a leave of absence that she was probably damaging her career. Until then, she'd been on the fast-track. Another couple years, and she would have had Kindler's job, and they both knew it. Kindler was fine with it since he was being groomed for bigger and better things as well.

He'd tried to talk her out of taking a leave of absence, but she'd been steadfast. The truth, the one she didn't even like to admit to herself, was that she was unhappy. She didn't like her job, and she hated most of the people in the department. It wasn't them. It was her. She needed something more. Not going into work this past week or so had been nothing but a relief. The thought of never seeing Brian again made her stomach settle. She was making the right decision. Kathleen was just the excuse.

When Kathleen had called in a panic, Spencer had come alive again. She missed field work. She missed planning operations. She craved the hands-on nature of her work at WitSec. Pushing papers and doing computer work in D.C. was just not the same. She was damn good at it, but it didn't have the same allure. She used to jump out of bed every morning, and now she got up like she had weights on her feet.

She stood up and grabbed her kettle. She filled it then plunked it on the burner. She turned on the gas and leaned on the counter to wait for the kettle to boil. The career thing didn't matter much anymore. It was dead, or would be as soon as she grabbed Drake. She needed his help to keep Kathleen and Connor safe, and she wasn't sure he would come willingly.

CHAPTER SIX

Drake stood in the window and looked out at his back garden. He had a flowering cherry tree in his yard, and the branches were in full bloom. He used to love to come to D.C. He had been dating an interesting woman at the time, Deandra. She worked as a lawyer by trade but, really, she was a behind-the-scenes force in many of the policy decisions that went on in government on both sides of the aisle.

He had met big-name politicians and lobbyists when they were dating. He also met a large part of the intelligence community. He had been tempted at the time to ask them to help with finding Kathleen, but Deandra had persuaded him not to.

Looking back, her lack of support had been the beginning of the end for them. She thought he would be an asset to her, and he was, but once he had something he wanted in return, she'd decided her interest in him did not outweigh the risk to her career. He couldn't blame her. He wanted help to find a sister that everyone had written off as dead years ago.

The police said his sister had committed suicide by jumping off the Poughkeepsie side of the Walkway Over the Hudson, in the state historic park. Today they would have investigated more, but sixteen years ago, they saw Kathleen as just another girl who was unhappy with life and chose to end it.

Deandra said dredging up what happened wouldn't change the outcome. People would think he couldn't accept the loss and take him less seriously. She had a point. Deandra was smart and always had her finger on the pulse of government and business in D.C. Still, he often wondered if things would be different if he had asked the then Secretary of Homeland Security for help.

He looked down as his phone vibrated in his hand. Gage. He answered the call. "What's going on?"

"Good news. There are no system intrusions in any of your other hotels. It only happened the one time with this Follows character. We set up surveillance at the hotel in case the woman returns. Logan is still working on getting the CCTV footage from the surrounding area, but he's hitting walls at every turn. He says it isn't the normal runaround. He thinks there could be more to this. Did you piss off anyone in D.C. lately or...ever?"

Drake frowned. "I'm sure I have, but no one comes to mind. Does he think he can acquire the footage?"

"Eventually, probably. But it won't be anytime soon."

Not that it mattered. He was meeting with the woman tonight.

"Drake?"

Gage's voice cut into Drake's thoughts. "Sorry, just thinking about who could be blocking things. What were you saying?"

"I asked if there was anything new on your end."

He didn't hesitate. "No, not a thing. We spoke to

Follows yesterday, but he's a dead end. The cell number he gave us is to a burner cell that's been turned off. He can't give us a description of her, and I believe you guys are working on tracing the money she wired."

"Right, we are but, again, we're hitting roadblocks. Whoever she is, she knows what she's doing."

"Agreed. Keep me informed if anything changes."

"Will do," Gage replied. "And tell us if things happen on your end."

He hung up and put his phone down on the coffee table. A small niggle of doubt entered his mind. He should have told Gage about the meeting set for tonight. When Follows called earlier, he'd told Drake to come alone. If he showed up with backup of any kind, the woman would disappear. He couldn't let that happen. This was as close as he'd gotten to his sister in sixteen years.

Right after his grandmother's car accident, she had begged him to keep looking for his sister. *"She's out there, Jamie. I know she is. Promise me you won't stop looking."*

He'd promised, and his grandmother had died ten minutes later. His mother had bipolar disorder and had run off years ago. He and Kathleen had never known their father. No one would speak about him. Drake knew, in that moment, he wouldn't let his grandmother down. He needed to find his sister no matter the cost. She was the only family he had. Now, how was he going to slip away from his security team?

Twenty minutes later, Drake and his bodyguards were in the car, heading to the hotel. He had called Mr. Mayfield, his hotel manager, and asked if he would like to meet for dinner in the hotel restaurant. He also had invited Yazley. With plenty of actual work to do, he did need to meet with the two men. He decided to hold the meeting over dinner and use them as a cover to escape.

The driver pulled the car up in front of the hotel, and the four-man security team went through the usual drill. Mayfield and Yazley met him in the lobby, and they walked directly over to the restaurant.

He spent the better part of the next two hours quizzing the other men about the hotel and their thoughts on how things were going. Small improvements were necessary on the security front, obviously, although Drake had been quick to reassure both men that people were bribed the world over. There was no real way to counteract that other than paying well and hoping for loyalty.

As the men sipped their after-dinner coffee, he brought up the fact that the high-end suites weren't as in demand as they used to be. "What are some of the factors, do you think, Edgar?"

Mayfield swallowed. "May I be candid?"

"Please," Drake said.

"When you bought the hotel about ten years ago, the main guest rooms had all just been refurbished. They are well-maintained and are standing up to the wear and tear. All the amenities are on point and, for the most part, the rooms are exactly what our clients expect and enjoy.

“We did a major redesign of the main common spaces, this restaurant, the bar area, and the spa. These spaces are holding up beautifully. They are still fresh and display the appropriate amount of opulence and taste. At that time, we discussed redoing the upper tier suites but decided to hold off. They had been done recently, and we gave them a light touchup. Now, however, they are starting to look a little worn around the edges."

Drake took a sip of his coffee. "You think now is the time for some renovation?"

"I do," Edgar said. "As you are aware, D.C. has a great

many hotels to choose from, and to be competitive, our high-end suites need to be at the top of our game."

Drake glanced at his watch. "Do you think we could go up and look at the Presidential Suite? I understand it's free this evening. I would like to see for myself. Redoing the suites would cost a fair amount, not to mention be quite disruptive to the guests and hotel staff."

"Of course," Mayfield said, "we can go inspect the room. Are you gentlemen through with your coffee?"

Both men nodded, and all three stood. Yazley cleared his throat. "Mr. Drake, if you don't mind, I will be heading home."

Drake proffered his hand, and the two men shook. "Thank you so much for staying late. I think we've covered a lot of ground this evening. Send me an email regarding those changes you want to implement."

Yazley gave a quick nod. "Thank you. Have a good evening." He strode out of the dining room.

Mayfield commented, "Yazley is so damned relieved, you can see it all over his face. He seemed terrified you were going to fire him."

Drake shrugged. "Edgar, the whole incident wasn't his fault. As much as I want to blame him, there's not much he can do if people agree to a bribe. If he makes the changes to the security setup, circumventing the system should be much harder to accomplish."

The two men started out of the dining room. Dragan and Jake flanked them with one hotel security person ahead and one behind as they walked down the hallway to the elevators. Drake turned to Jake. "We're going to see the Presidential Suite and discuss changes to be made. It might be a long night, gentleman."

"No problem, sir," Jake responded. They knew the drill. They had been with him long enough.

"Still," Mayfield continued, "you could have fired him, and I appreciate that you didn't. Yazley is a bit of a limp fish in some ways, but he's solid. I can depend on him to back me up with the staff and the guests. He's excellent at his job as well. His only weakness is he likes to help some of the young ones a bit too much. He can be a bit too forgiving."

"You don't have to sell me on him," he said as they all stepped into the elevator.

Mayfield used his master key to unlock the button to the Presidential Suite.

Drake had the urge to lean against the wall. He hadn't slept well since the video "match" of his sister came up on his phone. He was exhausted. "If Yazley's only fault is forgiveness, then he's a better man than I."

"Than us both," Mayfield conceded.

The doors opened, and the men walked down the hall to the suite. Mayfield opened the door, and Jake went in to clear the suite. When he returned, he took up his post outside the door along with Dragan and the other two men.

Drake and Mayfield entered the suite, and Drake took in the decor. The room was decorated in varying shades of creams and browns. The thick carpet was slightly worn in spots. They walked into the living area where they would have been greeted by a view of the mall through large windows if not for the rain and fog. The furniture ranged in shades of beige and brown as well. "I'm seeing what you mean. You're right. Updating is necessary. Tell me your thoughts."

Mayfield smiled. "New furniture, new paint, new carpet and window treatments in a more current design. I would also like to buy better televisions. One for here, one for each of the bedrooms, and I thought possibly one for the dining area." He pointed around the corner. "It's too hard to angle the table so someone can eat and view TV if they want. I think if we put in something discrete, maybe something that can 'disappear' into the surroundings somehow, that would work."

Drake didn't move, but he nodded. "I'll leave everything up to you, Edgar. I trust your judgment on this as I do on most things." He cocked his head. "How long have we been acquainted, Edgar?"

"I think it's about twelve years. We met back when you bought the Rancott Hotel in Chicago. I was the manager."

"Right." He nodded. He and Mayfield had a friendly relationship, more so than he did with the majority of his managers, but he was uncomfortable with what he was about to do. It went against his style, not only as a boss, but as a person. He hated asking for favors. Owing a favor put him at a disadvantage, and he hated being in the negative column for anything. "Edgar, I need a personal favor. It's a big one. You can say 'no,' and it won't affect our working relationship."

"I was wondering when you'd get around to what you really wanted."

Drake frowned.

Edgar smiled. "In all the years I've known you, you never eat in your own hotels with your staff. You like to take them outside so they can speak freely. I know this because it's what you've always done with me, and I've adopted the same policy because it works so well. You calling me up and suggesting dinner at the hotel is out of character."

"Shit." He ran his hands through his hair. He'd hoped he wasn't doing anything to tip off his security detail or anyone else on what he was planning. He wasn't as good at this subterfuge thing as he thought.

He looked over at Mayfield. "Edgar, I need to ditch my security detail. I—"

"Say no more. I don't need details. You know the back

way out of the suite. There aren't any cameras in this back stairwell, as you know, so you won't be seen until you cross the delivery area to exit by the loading dock."

He offered Mayfield his hand. "I can't thank you enough."

"Think nothing of it. I'll stay here and work on plans for the suite refurbishment. Is there a time I should expect you?"

He paused. "I'm not sure."

"Okay. What time should I raise the alarm?" Mayfield asked as he glanced at his watch.

"I don't follow you."

Mayfield frowned. He opened his mouth but then hesitated. "Jameson, I'm feeling very much like the reason you're leaving your security behind might require you to be in a dangerous, or perhaps compromising, position. Should that happen, you may need some help. You can, of course, call me if you don't want your people to know. I'm suggesting however, as a backup plan, that if you haven't returned by a certain time, I tell your security so they can come find you and perhaps lend you a hand."

"Jesus, Edgar, maybe I should get you to manage this situation. I appear to be in way over my head."

"I'd be happy—"

Drake waved him off. "No. No. I'm just exhausted and not thinking clearly. I've gotten soft. Obviously, I need to adjust my strategy." He glanced at his watch again. "Let's say one a.m. If I'm not back by one, open the door and tell Jake or Dragan. They'll take it from there." He offered his hand to Mayfield once more. "I can't thank you enough, Edgar."

Mayfield shook his head. "It's my pleasure, Jameson. You took a chance on me all those years ago, and it changed my life. This is a very small thing."

Relieved Drake headed to the kitchenette area. The secret panel across from a closet blended in with the rest of the wall, making it difficult to see. He pushed on it and heard a soft click. The small door sprang open just a crack. Drake opened it to reveal a pin pad. He typed in a code, and the whole wall panel next to him slid open silently. It revealed a stairwell. He looked back and gave a wave to Edgar, then he started down the stairs. The door would close automatically in thirty seconds.

He gave a small prayer of thanks that his hotel only had eight floors. He could not imagine walking down from the thirty-fifth floor. Of course, the stairwell probably wouldn't exist if the hotel had been a high-rise. The stairwell was part of the original structure built back in the late eighteen hundreds. The hotel had been redone many times but the stairwell was always kept a secret.

A couple of minutes later, Drake hit the ground floor. He put his hand on the doorknob to open the fire door and took a deep breath. He had no idea what was waiting for him if he met with this woman. Was she going to kidnap him and ransom him off, or would she kill him? The smart thing would be to get his security team to check everything out. But then the whole thing might blow up and screw up any chance of finding out if this woman knew his sister. She said for him to come alone.

He exhaled and opened the door. He walked across the loading dock like he owned the place—because he did. His employees wouldn't say a word. What did they care where he entered and left the building? He could not miss this meeting. Not a chance. He needed to find his sister even if it killed him.

CHAPTER SEVEN

Spencer eased back behind the tree. Drake hadn't arrived yet, but it was still a few minutes to ten. Who was she kidding? It wasn't like she was going anywhere. She had one shot at this. If he didn't bite, then a more direct approach in the form of a gun would have to be used and that could go all kinds of wrong.

She clenched her hands into fists. No matter how many times she went back over the events in her head, Spencer still couldn't place the mole, but she knew for a fact that he or she existed. How else had Giuseppe Caridi Jr., abuser, mobster, and convicted felon, found out about his son? Not to mention where Connor and Kathleen lived.

The all-out panic in Kathleen's voice when she called that day three months ago still sent shivers across Spencer's skin. She was beside herself. Joe, as he liked to be called, was at her front door. If Kathleen's phone hadn't alerted her to someone being on her front step, she and Connor would have been home. Instead, she got the message as they were walking through her back gate, coming from her neighbor Kyla's backyard.

The chime on Kathleen's phone had saved her life and saved Connor from a life of crime with his father. Now Spencer needed to figure out how to keep them safe permanently. But how could she hide them from the mob when Joe and his people seemed to always be one step ahead? The fucker. All those years in prison hadn't changed him at all. He was still a piece of shit.

Spencer kept an eye on the monument, but the walkway in front remained empty, not surprising on this cold, dark, and rainy spring night. Who would volunteer to be out in this?

Spencer glanced toward the Lincoln Memorial. Not a soul in sight, thank God. Fewer witnesses if she ended up needing to do something desperate. Fingers crossed, it wouldn't come to that. Scanning the tree line, she didn't see anyone lurking, but CCTV cameras covered the entire park. There was nothing to be done about that.

Chances were good that no one would look at the cameras. There needed to be a compelling reason for someone to sit down and go through all the video. If they did watch the video, her career would be over. Who was she kidding? Her career would be over anyway after all this, no matter what strings her parents would try to pull. It was more likely they might *not* try to help, which was just fine by her.

She'd taken the job at Homeland as a last-ditch effort to get closer to her parents. To be a real family. But the joke was on her. Kathleen and Connor were more of a family to her than her parents ever were. Kathleen was the sister she never had and the person who'd helped her through the loss of her child at the hands of her abusive husband. That wasn't something she would ever forget. There was no way she would let anything happen to her or Connor. She owed Kathleen that much if not more.

Spencer wiped moisture off her face. The combination of the hat and the trees kept the rain from hitting her directly, but her cheeks were wet, and the dampness had started leaching into her bones.

She glanced at her watch again. Drake should be here any minute now. If she handled this right, he should want to come with her. He should want to be with his sister again after all these years, shouldn't he? Spencer sighed. She had no clue how he would react. Time did strange things, and she could never be sure what people would do in difficult situations.

A man appeared on the walkway along the wall. It was hard to get a clear view, but he appeared tall and thin. He wore a trench coat and carried an umbrella. She couldn't tell at this distance if the man was Drake. She needed a closer look but, surely, Drake would be the only one to stop on a night like this. The man continued along the path, coming toward her. Burrowed among the trees, Spencer wasn't afraid of being seen.

She squinted to focus through the falling rain. A sound hit her ears. The man was talking on a cell phone. He did not stop by the wall but kept going. He continued along the path until he walked past her. She remained hidden. He kept walking until he took the fork in the path that led to Lincoln Memorial Drive.

False alarm. Just some suit out walking in the rain. Her heart thumped in her chest as adrenaline raced through her veins. How many men in suits were out walking at this hour? Could the man be a lookout or a plant of some kind? Would he try to come around from behind and sneak up on her?

Spencer shifted her position slightly, moving a few trees over. She had a better view from her new spot in case anyone was trying to come up behind her. *Ridiculous.* She should have realized her vulnerability earlier. She'd never make it as a spy. Being an analyst made her lose sleep at night already. Sometimes ignorance really was bliss.

She waited for another five minutes with the rain hitting the leaves on the trees all around her. It was good the trees were in bloom. If it had been winter, there would have been less cover. A motion in the corner of her eye made her turn back to the monument.

Another man walked along the path. He too was tall but not as thin. He filled out his clothing better. He wore a suit jacket but carried no umbrella or overcoat. Water ran down his face. He stopped in front of the monument and looked around.

Drake? Her heartbeat ticked up. She'd been staring at him through her scope for days, but at this distance with the rain, it was hard to be sure. The man was built like Drake. Wide shoulders tapered to narrow hips. Drake certainly took care of himself, which shouldn't surprise her. He spent time at the gym and ate healthy from what she'd observed. He had a reputation as a hard-ass that expected perfection. He would expect the same of himself.

Spencer waited until the man turned away and then slid slowly out from the tree line. She quickly moved to the path and put up her black umbrella. Her heart hammered in her chest, and a cold sweat broke out across her back, causing her to shiver.

She kept her head down as she approached the man. She didn't want him to be able to identify her if something went wrong. Her long black trench coat and wide-brimmed black hat kept her covered. She was a walking cliché, but reality was, the outfit did disguise her identity. Just another executive hurrying across town on a wet night. That was what she wanted to project.

She came level with Drake and glanced up. Their eyes

met, and she stumbled. Shock ricocheted through her system. *Drake was Connor in man form.*

He reached out and steadied her. "Are you alright?"

His voice was different than she imagined. Deeper. Sexier somehow. "Um, yes. Thank you. I didn't see you there. I guess I should pay more attention." She gave him a quick smile and started walking again.

Blood rushed loudly in her ears as she pulled in oxygen. Her palms were slick on the stem of the umbrella. She walked past the end of the monument and kept going down the path.

She didn't want to approach Drake until she was sure he was alone. And had herself back under control. Jesus, seeing him through a scope was totally different than face-to-face. They weren't joking about his charisma. It hit her like a sucker punch to the gut. No wonder this guy never lacked for female companionship. He was charm, grace, style, and sexiness all rolled into one man with those amazing green eyes. Oh, boy.

She took a deep breath and exhaled. It didn't matter what he was like in person. He was still the target, and she had one chance to get him out of here. She had done her research on the meeting spot and had arrived early to make sure they would be alone.

She glanced around the park one final time and tried to discern if anyone was hiding farther away. The falling rain created too much of a curtain to see clearly. She grimaced, and her teeth chattered. Being wet for hours had left her chilled.

At least if she couldn't see anyone, they probably couldn't identify her either. She did a small circle and came back along the path. She moved swiftly but silently until she was only a few feet from Drake.

He turned and looked at her again. She studied him from under her umbrella. He probably couldn't see much of her face, but she took in all of his. He was much better looking in person. His...presence was overwhelming, and she had no doubt he knew it. He was a man used to wielding his authority and not being questioned. There was no mistaking he was Kathleen's brother and Connor's uncle. She uttered a silent prayer and then cleared her throat. "Mr. Drake, your sister needs your help."

Drake blinked as if trying to absorb the news. Then his gaze did a quick sweep of her and the surrounding area. "Who are you?" he asked.

"A friend of your sister's. She's in trouble and needs your help."

Drake's eyes narrowed. "Where is she?" He glanced around again.

"Not here. I can't tell you where, but I can take you." Spencer tried to keep her face neutral. Her breathing was loud in her ears. This is where everything could all go south. *Please believe me.*

"How do I know you're telling the truth and my sister is alive? It's been sixteen years with no contact. How can I be sure this is real?"

The pain in this man's words hit her hard in her chest. She understood that kind of pain. The pain of loss. She reached into her pocket and pulled out an envelope. She handed it to Drake.

He took it and immediately ripped it open. Pulling out the picture, he examined it in the ambient light. She tilted her umbrella slightly so the rain wouldn't fall on the picture. She freed a small flashlight from her pocket and turned on the beam so he could check the picture more thoroughly. She felt rather than heard his breath catch.

"My sister kept this in her wallet." Drake glanced at her and then back at the picture.

Spencer nodded.

"This doesn't prove anything. You could've gotten this from someone. The news might have mentioned the picture. This means nothing."

She was prepared for this. "Turn the picture over." She hoped the message would be enough to convince Drake to come with her but, if not, she felt the weight of the gun in her pocket. There were always other ways to get what she wanted. She preferred the simplest method, however. Shooting Drake and having to drag him to her car was last on the list, but she would do whatever it took to save Kathleen and Connor.

Drake flipped the picture over and saw writing on the back. She had no idea what the note said. She asked Kathleen to write a message with something that only she and Drake would know. Drake's hand started to shake. The muscles in his jaw were tight.

"Does that convince you?" she asked.

He turned the picture back over and stared. "Where is she?" He looked up at Spencer, and she had to stop herself from taking a step backward. She had dealt with all kinds of assholes in her life, but rage on Drake's face was beyond anything she had ever seen. His green eyes were chips of ice. Hatred oozed from every pore and hit her like a rogue wave in the ocean.

The knots in her belly wound tighter. She put the flashlight back in her pocket and curled her fingers around the butt of the gun. "She's safe. For now. She needs your help. I'm trying to help her but...I don't have your resources."

"My resources. Is that what you want from me? Money for my sister?" Drake grabbed her umbrella, lifted it over their heads, and leaned in closer. "Because I'm telling you right now, I will kill you if you don't tell me where she is." His eyes burned into her.

She pulled her gun out of her pocket and aimed it at Drake's belly. This was not going the way she'd hoped. "Step back." Her tone said she was not afraid even though her insides roiled. She ground her teeth. "I don't want your money. I need you to come with me. I won't risk calling her. I will take you to her."

"And I should just go with you because you produced some picture? How stupid do you think I am?"

"The note—"

"You could have found out about that. You've had sixteen long years to figure something out. Why would I risk my life over some note?"

"Because if you don't, Kathleen will die." There, she'd said it out loud. The thing that had been haunting her for months now. Not saying it was her way of keeping reality at bay, but she couldn't protect Kathleen indefinitely. Eventually Joe would catch up to her. Spencer was good at her job, but she was only one person. This situation required a lot more help. Drake had the resources necessary for keeping Kathleen and Connor safe indefinitely, and she thought she might be able to trust him.

"Look, I know this isn't ideal—"

"Ideal?" Drake roared. "This is fucking madness! Where is my sister?"

She took a deep breath. "Calm down. I do not want to shoot you, but I will if I have to. I can't tell you where she is because it would put her life in danger, but I can take you to her. I know you want to see her, but you must trust me. I promise you I have your sister's best interests at heart."

Drake stared at her, his jaw pulsing. "Why now? Why after all these years?"

She sighed. She'd known question was going to come up. "Kathleen always wanted to contact you, but any breach of protocol put her life at risk. At the time, we thought she would be safer without contact but...things have changed. She needs you now."

Drake looked around as the rain streamed down his face. He turned back to Spencer and gave her a once-over. "If I don't come, will you shoot me?"

She hesitated and then nodded. "I need you to come no matter what. It would be better for everyone if you came willingly." She had no idea how she would make that happen —it would be damn near impossible—but she would find a way if it meant she had to drag his body across the park to her car. Drake studied her closely. She didn't blame him for being overly cautious. She'd have turned tail and run by now.

He glared at her as if willing her to say more or, better yet, produce his sister on the spot. "Is she close by?"

She shook her head. "No. She's in another state. To be clear, I'm not asking you to come with me for an hour or two. You're going to be gone for a week, probably more. Your sister's problems are not...insignificant. It will take some doing to solve them."

She really didn't want to say more until she knew what his choice was going to be. Everything would be so much easier if he agreed with her plan. Kathleen hadn't seen him in years, and he had a fierce reputation. This was not a man to be trifled with. Instinctively though, she wanted to trust Drake.

Being Kathleen's brother had much to do with it since Kathleen was her best friend, more like a sister, but the memory of how his hand shook when he saw the note on the back of the picture... This man loved his sister. He'd had software developed just to find her, or so the rumor said. She wanted to believe in that. On the other hand, he wanted to kill Spencer a few minutes ago, so who knew how this would all turn out.

He tilted his head. "What do you want me to do?"

"For a start, you need to come with me now. We'll be leaving town, but you cannot contact anyone and tell them. You need to leave your cell phone here and anything else that can be tracked. You will be out of touch with your security and your work, basically your entire world, for the next while. Your only point of contact with anyone will be me. Your sister's safety depends on it."

Drake's jaw muscle jumped, and she would later swear that his eyes pierced her to her very core. He then gave a small shrug and nodded. "Let's do this."

“Okay, then,” she said and all the tension left her body. Her knees got weak in relief. She didn't have to beat him over the head and throw him in her trunk. *Thank you, God.* "Okay. Come on. Let's go." She gestured for him to start walking ahead of her toward the Lincoln Memorial where she parked her car.

She put her gun back in her coat pocket but stayed a couple steps behind in case he had a sudden change of heart. They would drive straight to the airfield after leaving here. No stopping or passing go. She tapped his arm and pointed to her car.

Drake nodded. "Is she okay? Kathleen?"

Spencer kept her face neutral. "She is for the moment. Hopefully with your help, we can make that permanent." She swept the parking lot and environs for any sign of trouble, but it all looked good. "Give me your phone."

Drake handed it over with no hesitation. A good sign. She unlocked the car, went over and opened the passenger door, then threw her umbrella in the backseat. "Get in," she said and waited until he moved around to the driver's side and slipped behind the wheel before she climbed into the car.

"Where are we going?"

She gave him directions but didn't mention the location. He would find out soon enough. She reached back to the floor behind Drake's seat and brought out a towel. She handed it to him. "Here. Dry yourself off." He took the towel and wiped his face and hair as best he could as he drove.

She had him follow the route she knew so well and, within minutes, they were on the highway. She put down her window and threw Drake's cell out onto the road. She glanced at him, but the tightening of his lips was the only sign of displeasure. He was pissed to be sure, but he was going along with her for the moment. How long would that last? Unease settled in her belly.

She had him take the next exit and then get back on the highway in the opposite direction. "How much time do we have before your people start looking for you?" she asked. "Assuming they aren't already following us."

She knew he was not fully supportive of the plan, and she didn't blame him one bit. It almost seemed too easy, but she wouldn't look a gift horse in the mouth. She knew that she could lose his people during the next leg of their journey if they were being followed.

"One a.m."

She glanced at him. It gave them some time. She sincerely hoped it was true because they would be long gone by then.

CHAPTER EIGHT

Drake leaned back in the driver's seat. He tried to at least appear physically relaxed even though he was anything but. That photograph had done him in. His sister had always carried it in her wallet.

The two of them on Christmas Day, taken when he was maybe three or four, so she would have been nine or ten. He'd followed her everywhere. She was his best friend. It had always been that way. Right up until she went away to university. It had been tough at first, but he'd adjusted. Kathleen stayed in touch with him the whole time she'd been away.

When he went off to university and she had a job, she'd still made a special effort to be there for him. She'd called him at least once a week when he was at school. But his last year of university, she'd become more distant, calling less and less frequently. At first, she had seemed genuinely busier, but then her demeanor changed. Looking back now, it was easy to see she'd gotten into some kind of trouble, but he'd been so caught up in his own world, he didn't notice. Then just after graduation, she disappeared. Well, the cops said she committed suicide, but he could never accept that. In his mind, she disappeared.

Following the woman's directions, he steered into a small airfield. They were flying somewhere. She'd said as much earlier. Still reeling from the note on the back of the picture, he'd lost his focus. Not a new experience these days.

Jamie, I'm in trouble and I need your help. I'm sorry I disappeared. I will explain everything. I love you, Snuggles. Kathleen xoxo

No one knew she called him Snuggles. Not even their grandmother. When he was little, he could crawl into her bed when he had a nightmare. She was his big sister, and he thought she would protect him from the world.

"You ready?"

He blinked. The woman's words had jerked him out of his reverie. "Yes." He put his hand on the door handle but stopped. "What's your name, or what should I call you?"

"Spencer. You can call me Spencer." With that, she opened the door and got out of the car. She went around to the trunk and grabbed a large duffel bag. Drake had nothing, so he waited and then followed her to the hangar.

Spencer punched in a code which opened the small door. They entered the hangar, and she went over to another panel in the wall and hit the code to open the main bay door. She turned around and walked over to the parked jet.

He'd been in a lot of jets over the years, but nothing this small.

"It's like a minivan with wings."

Drake blinked. "What?"

She nodded toward the plane. "It's like a minivan with wings, but it will get us to where we need to be quick-time." She glanced at him and narrowed her eyes. "Stand over there against the wall."

He hesitated but then did what he was told.

"Turn around and put your hands behind your head."

Drake froze. "Excuse me?"

"You heard me." She pulled the gun out of her pocket again.

Until this moment, he'd never hit a woman, but Spencer was tempting him mightily. If this all turned out to be some sort of con, he would take great pleasure in snapping her neck. He turned slowly and faced the wall.

She gave him a very thorough pat down and then stepped back. "You can turn around and bring your hands down."

Drake turned to face her. "Satisfied?"

"If you fuck with me when we are in the air, we will crash. Just a reminder."

"Understood," he ground out. He stared at the tiny jet with its jaunty red stripes. It looked like a children's toy. He was fine with flying, but the tiny jet made him uncomfortable. Could he even fit in the seat? His legs were long. Was he going to eat his knees the whole flight? Hopefully it wasn't a long one.

He leaned against the wall as he watched the woman run through some kind of checklist around the outside of the plane. The rain streamed through the open door, and the wind bit into his skin. Being wet did not help things. What he wouldn't give for a hot shower, dry clothes, and a large scotch.

The woman nodded to herself and then went around and opened the door of the airplane. She walked to the nose of the plane and gestured for him to join her. "Okay, time to go."

He came around to her side of the plane and watched as she opened the storage compartment and put her bag inside. Then she went up the steps and entered the aircraft. He climbed the stairs after her.

She took off her coat, throwing it across one of the passenger seats in the back of the plane. He noticed that she'd moved her gun to a shoulder holster under her left arm. She was wearing a pair of dark jeans and a black cashmere sweater.

She backed up so she was in the passenger area and pointed him to the co-pilot seat. "Why don't you sit there?"

He dutifully moved in that direction, but she touched his arm. "You may want to take off your suit jacket first. Throw it on this seat." She tapped one of the passenger seats.

He nodded and took off his jacket. He was bent over so he didn't hit his head. It took him a minute to get his jacket off. When he threw it on the seat, Spencer picked it up and immediately wrapped it over the back of the seat. She did the same with hers. "They'll dry better this way." She gestured to the co-pilot seat and then closed the door.

"Wait" he said as he sat down, "you're flying the plane?" He had no idea why that didn't register earlier. Jesus, he was slipping. His concentration and ability to focus were obviously non-existent at the moment.

Spencer glanced at him as she sat down in the pilot's seat. "Yes." She started hitting buttons and turning knobs. The engine roared to life. Within a minute, they were rolling out to the tarmac, and a few minutes after that, they were airborne.

"Don't worry. I have a lot of experience flying. I've been doing it since I was sixteen. This airplane also has a lot of safety features." She turned to him. "If I get disabled for some reason, hit this button." She pointed to a large red button. "The airplane will land itself at the nearest airport. It will also automatically send out a message to all the closest airfields to let them know it's an emergency situation, so they can handle clearing any air traffic and notify emergency personnel, like fire and police."

She reached up and pulled back a flap on the ceiling that revealed a handle. "This is a parachute. Should we get into a situation where there is a major mechanical issue with the airplane and I can't land it safely, I'll pull this, and we will float to the ground." She put the flap back in place and checked her gauges. "Feel better?" she asked with a smirk.

He did actually, but he wasn't about to admit it. "You know you basically told me I could kill you and still land safely."

"Yes," Spencer agreed, "but then you would never see your sister again, and I'm banking on you wanting to see her more than you want me dead." She leaned over and hit another button. "Before I said anything, your hands were folded in your lap so you wouldn't touch anything, and your knuckles were white. The flight is a couple of hours, and I didn't want you to sit there tense the entire time. It's very draining to be around someone like that." She glanced pointedly at his hands, which were now loosely resting in his lap.

Son of a bitch. She'd known about his discomfort and tried to fix it. Who the fuck was this woman, and what did she have to do with his sister?

"I bet you've never even given plane safety a thought before now, even though you fly around in private jets all the time. You trusted your pilots instinctively. Now you're all nervous. Is it because I'm a woman?"

He looked at her. "No. It's because I had to meet you in a park in the rain and have no idea who the fuck you are and what you want."

Spencer laughed. "Fair enough," she said as she took off her hat.

Her long blond hair fell down around her shoulders. When she turned to look at him, he realized her eyes were hazel and she was younger than he'd thought. Maybe in her mid-thirties. Much better looking, too. She had high cheekbones and full lips. In another setting she would have definitely caught his eye.

He nodded. "Thank you. Now where are we going?"

She smiled. "For this leg of the journey, Dallas/Fort Worth. It's going to take a few hours. There's no bathroom on this jet, so if you have to go, there's a bottle in the back." She pointed over her shoulder. "If you reach behind your chair, there's a thermos full of hot coffee. I don't know about you, but I sure could use a cup of something warm."

"Sounds like heaven right about now." He reached behind his seat and found the thermos. There were a couple of disposable hot liquid cups with it. He unscrewed the top of the thermos and poured the first cup. The coffee smelled damn good. He started to hand it to Spencer but pulled it back. "Wait, can you fly with coffee in your hand?"

She laughed. She had a nice laugh, throaty and sexy. She reached for the cup. "The plane is on autopilot. I can keep an eye on the gauges and drink coffee at the same time. We're above the clouds, so it should be smooth going all the way to Dallas/Fort Worth."

Drake poured himself a cup of coffee, too. Spencer reached for his cup, and when he frowned, she pointed to the thermos. "You need to put the lid back on that."

"Oh, right." He was all discombobulated, which was driving him nuts. He prided himself on being on his game at all times. Something about this woman, her mastery of the situation, had him off kilter. He sighed as he recapped the thermos and put it back behind his seat. He reached out, and she handed him the coffee.

"Not sure if you drink it black, but I don't have much in the way of options. No fridge or anything on board."

"Black is fine." He took a sip and sighed. It felt beyond good to have something warm in his gut. He was chilled to the bone. Spencer reached over and made an adjustment.

Suddenly, heat came out of a vent by his feet. "Thanks. I was colder than I realized."

She nodded. "Me, too." She burrowed deeper into the pilot's chair. "If you want to sleep, feel free."

"I'm good," Drake said as he shifted, getting more comfortable in the seat. Sleep would be damn near impossible for him. He'd put his life in this woman's hands, a woman who held him at gunpoint little more than an hour ago but was now making sure his feet were warm. The whole situation was bizarre.

He took another sip of coffee and looked out the window. The clouds broke suddenly, and he could see the ground below. Clusters of lights showed up along their path. Nameless cities and towns disappeared behind them.

He glanced at his watch. Another hour or so, and Mayfield would be telling Jake and Dragan that he'd left and did not come back. Then all hell would break loose. Would they find him? It wasn't a matter of if, but when. The Callahan brothers were too good at their jobs. Would he have enough time to help his sister before they showed up? Or would they mess everything up? It was a risk.

He glanced over at Spencer. "My security detail will report back in a little less than an hour. Then the shit will hit the fan. I can't guarantee they won't find us quickly. Maybe I should call them and tell them not to worry."

She glanced at him but went back to her gauges. "No, I don't think so. You and I both know they won't listen to you. You could fire them at this point, and they'd still come looking for you. I know of their reputation and yours. They won't quit until they see you physically, and that just can't happen at this point. It would put your sister in danger."

"Then maybe you can tell me about what's going on, and we can be better prepared."

Spencer frowned. "I think it's better if Kathleen talks to

you about it. There's...so much, and I think a lot of it will be hard for you to hear." She shot him a quick glance. "I know that's not what you want, but it's the way it has to be. What I *can* tell you is your sister loves you very much, and she is beyond sorry for everything that's happened."

He curled his hands into fists. This needed to be over. Logically, he knew if he'd waited this long, a few more hours wouldn't matter, but it seemed interminable. "Can you at least tell me why my security detail would endanger my sister?"

She sighed and looked out the side window. He couldn't see her face at all. She turned back to check the gauges. "It's all so difficult to explain." She pushed her hair back from her face and took a sip of coffee. "There is a group of people out there that want to hurt your sister. They have friends in high places. It's better for everyone involved if we keep this as low-key as possible until we really understand what we're dealing with."

He let out the breath he'd been holding. He was no closer to understanding what was going on, but at least he had some vague idea of the scope. Power and influence were things he understood. Friends in high places—that's how things were done in Washington, New York, and just about every large city or small town across the world. It was something he was familiar with. Something he could hold on to. Something he was very good at.

"So you know, you and I are on the same side." Spencer touched his arm. "I want to protect your family. I'm sorry if the subterfuge has been off-putting or extreme. I just won't take any unnecessary chances."

"I...appreciate that." And he did—if she was telling the truth. If she was lying, he'd see her dead. He'd been through too much in the last year to take anything at face value. He'd made a great many enemies, and even more with the whole

Triad situation in Asia. Honestly, he had no clue if he was flying to see his sister or careening toward his own death. Or maybe both.

He put his cup in the little garbage bag behind his seat and then leaned back and closed his eyes. He wasn't going to get any more out of Spencer about the situation. He might as well try to clear out his mind. Who knew what the hell would happen next?

CHAPTER NINE

Spencer eased down the landing gear. They'd made good time, and the tower had cleared her for final approach. She spoke quietly to the tower and prepared to land. Drake slept in the seat next to her.

She admired that he could catch some shut-eye at a time like this. On the other hand, she was so damn tired she could probably sleep standing up in a corner. She reviewed the checklist for landing one more time and then brought the plane down gently.

Drake sat up and looked around startled.

"Sorry. I tried to make the landing as smooth as possible."

He blinked. "No. It's fine. I guess I fell asleep."

She nodded as she taxied down the runway and then turned onto another taxiway. It took a few minutes, but finally she came to a stop just outside a hangar. She went through her usual landing routine and turned to Drake. "Grab your coat. Time to go."

"After you," he said and gestured for her to lead the way.

Spencer got up and grabbed her coat. She opened the

door and went down the stairs of the airplane. Charlie, one of the maintenance guys, stood at the bottom, holding her duffel bag. She started walking with him across the tarmac.

She glanced back and signaled to Drake that he needed to catch up. She chatted a little bit with Charlie, but it was hard with all of the noise from different planes taking off and landing. They continued along the tarmac to the next hangar over.

"You have a great flight, Ms. Gordon. We'll take care of your plane for you."

She nodded. "Thanks Charlie. See you soon."

He handed her the bag and then peeled off and went into the left side of the hangar. She glanced back at Drake and again gestured for him to catch up. She picked up her pace and walked around the corner to a different hangar. A sleek new Gulfstream was parked inside. It was white with the logo for John Lewiston's company on the tail.

"Where are we going?" Drake asked, but she didn't acknowledge him. Instead, she squinted at the car approaching on the tarmac and immediately recognized the driver. "Shit." She grabbed his sleeve and pulled him over to the side of the hangar and maneuvered him behind a rolling staircase. When she stepped in behind it as well, there wasn't much room between the staircase and the wall, so they were forced to be close together.

She hadn't realized just how large Drake was until that moment. Being a little over five-seven, most men were not that much taller, but Drake was over six feet to be sure.

His eyes were a deeper green than they appeared before. The rifle scope had made him look different somehow than he did up close and personal. His scent, a citrusy aroma mixed with some sort of spicy maleness, swirled around her.

She blinked and breathed deeply, relishing their close proximity. Not smart since his scent lingered around her, making her hyperaware. Her chest was almost pressed up against his. All kinds of crazy, inappropriate thoughts immediately ran through her head.

She quickly turned and looked around the edge of the stairs. Giving herself a mental shake, she refocused. She needed all her wits about her. It was fucking the middle-of-the-night o'clock, and Amber Wright had shown up. The desire to scream was epic. She had timed everything specifically so Amber would be home sleeping. Instead, the pain in the ass was currently pulling up next to the jet. The woman made Spencer grind her teeth. As John Lewiston's admin, Amber had more power than most, and she loved to wield it.

"What's going on?" Drake demanded.

"Nothing." She tossed the word over her shoulder.

"Nothing. I see, so that's why we're hiding behind some equipment in an airport hangar? Because we're having fun? Does this have to do with Kathleen?"

She turned back toward Drake and stumbled slightly. He reached out and steadied her. Crap, that was the second time tonight. What was wrong with her? The heat from his hands seared through her coat to her skin. The thunderous look appeared again on his face. If he made a scene now, they would be in serious trouble.

"Look, this doesn't directly involve Kathleen."

His eyes narrowed. "You need to be more specific."

"This is about me. That woman who just arrived? She is the head admin for the owner of this airplane, and she's a nosy pain in the ass. She must've found out about the flight. I was keeping it a secret." She turned around again, breaking contact with Drake, and peeked around the edge of the portable staircase. The aircraft door was on the other side of the airplane, so she couldn't tell what was happening. "Fuck," she mumbled again.

"Why don't you want the assistant here? Were you going to steal this airplane?"

"What?" She whirled around. "No, I'm not stealing it! I didn't want her to know because she would tell...people where I can be found, and it's much better if they don't know."

People, namely her parents. Amber was a raging bitch, and she snitched on Spencer every chance she got. They'd hated each other from the moment they met. The women were about the same age, but Amber had a superiority complex, and if she could make Spencer's life difficult, she would. In this case, it could put Kathleen and Connor in jeopardy.

The Lewistons and her family had been friends for years. John offered them the use of his jets all the time. She'd called the pilot directly to arrange the flight. She rarely used the airplanes, but every once in a long while she would, and Amber would immediately call Spencer's parents and tell them.

She went back to watching the airplane. Amber's feet and legs appeared as she walked back over to her car and drove away. Spencer stayed hidden. Should she chance the flight now? What had Captain Monroe told Amber? Would her parents, and by extension the world, know where she was?

"Are we going, or do we need to make other arrangements?"

Spencer bit her lip. "I'm not sure." If she took the chance, and Amber told her parents where she was going, they were bound to turn up and make a big deal out of her taking a leave of absence. With her mother being a former ambassador, and her father, a current senator, people would notice if they showed up. Their presence could endanger Kathleen, not to mention the screaming matches that would ensue between them.

If she and Drake tried to find other transportation to get to Kathleen, then there would be a paper trail to follow. So, a chance her parents would show versus a paper trail directly to Kathleen—there was no contest.

"Okay, we're going over now." The crew for this plane was a lovely bunch that she'd flown with before and she would just have to trust them. She came out from behind the steps, and Drake followed. His impatience with her leaked from his pores. Well, tough shit. He was just going to have to deal with her issues. If he really became a problem, she would shoot him. She rounded the plane and started up the steps. She walked through the door and smiled at the crew standing just outside the cockpit. "Hi, Captain Monroe. How are you?"

"Great, thanks Spencer. How are you?" He offered his hand.

"I'm good thanks." She shook his hand and moved out of the doorway so Drake could enter.

The captain indicated to the first officer and said, "This is Jim Acosta."

The two shook. She nodded toward Drake and said, "This is my friend, Bob Grey."

Drake blinked but didn't say a word. He offered his hand to each man in turn.

"Great to have you two on board. The flight should be a nice, smooth one tonight. Why don't you go back and get comfortable? Janine is back there, and she'll find you some snacks and drinks. We should be underway in about fifteen minutes or so."

"Captain Monroe," Spencer started, "I saw Amber leaving. Did she...? That is, did you say anything to her about me or us?" She indicated Drake. She wanted to kick herself for sounding so stupid. She was a strong woman, but somehow Amber got under her skin.

"Ms. Wright is...very efficient. She dropped by to find out where we are going. I suspect she has a...friend here at the airport who reports all of our comings and goings. Mr. Lewiston is charitable with his fleet, and Ms. Wright feels the need to know every detail."

"I see." Spencer stifled a groan.

"So, I told her the truth, we're taking the airplane back to the east coast for service." The Captain smiled. "I didn't see the point in mentioning our detour to drop you off."

She grinned. "I owe you one."

"Not at all. People need their privacy, and Ms. Wright needs to get a life." He winked as he touched her shoulder. "But you didn't hear that from me." He turned and entered the cockpit, immediately settling in the captain's seat.

Spencer moved to the back of the plane and stuffed her duffel, her coat, and hat in a cupboard, straightened her black sweater and then found a seat. She hadn't flown in this jet before. The interior was done in creams and beiges with touches of silver here and there. The seats were a sumptuous cream-colored leather and very soft.

There were six seats at the front, three facing forward and three facing backward. There was also a deeper brown sofa farther back in the cabin on the right side, and across from it was a built-in set of drawers with a table on top. Rumor had it that the sofa could be made into a bed, but she didn't ask.

She was willing to bet the bathroom on this jet was amazing. *Someday*, she promised herself, she would have an airplane with an actual bathroom. She sighed. If she ever managed to have a job again after this.

Drake sat down across the aisle from her. "Where—?"

"Hi Janine," Spencer said cutting him off. She didn't want to explain things to Drake yet. If he reacted in any way, Janine was there as a witness. The fewer people who paid them any attention, the better.

"Hey, Spencer, how are you?" Janine asked. She was a short, bleached blonde with a big white smile.

Drake smiled at her and extended his hand. "Bob Grey."

"Nice to meet you, Mr. Grey. Can I get either of you something to drink?"

Spencer smiled. "I'd love a glass of white wine." Or the bottle. Exhaustion was her constant companion these days, and she was on edge. She needed a serious amount of sleep.

"Coming right up. We have your favorite on board." Janine smiled at Drake. "And for you?"

"I'll have...a glass of the same."

"Wonderful. After we're airborne, I'll bring you a menu, and we'll see if we can't get you fed." Janine offered a big smile and went to the galley to pour the drinks.

True to his word, the captain had them off the ground in fifteen minutes. Spencer sipped her wine. It was all surreal. The fact that they had made it this far gave her reason to hope.

Drake leaned slightly toward her. "Can you tell me where we're going now?"

"What? You don't like surprises?" She cocked an eyebrow at him.

"I hate surprises." His eyes clouded over. He was dead serious.

"Here we are," Janine said as she handed them each a menu. "It's a long flight, so if you want to pick a few things to nosh on that might be good."

Spencer nodded her thanks and buried her nose in her menu. She was aware of Drake still staring at her. He no doubt wanted to curse up a storm and shake the answers out of her, but he was just going to have to wait.

"So, what is it your family does that they are so friendly with John Lewiston?"

She gave him a tight smile. "My dad is in politics, and my mother is one of his top advisors."

"I see. And you? What is it exactly that you do?"

She turned and looked directly into his eyes. "I work for Homeland Security." *Take that!* A feeling of satisfaction stole over her when Drake's eyes widened. Maybe that would keep him from asking too many questions.

"What does Homeland have to do with my sister?"

Or maybe not. She sighed. "Not a thing."

"I don't understand." He was frowning, and his hands were clenched on the arm rests.

"Look, Drake"—Spencer lowered her voice—"everything will be explained to you when you see your sister." She glanced at where Janine was preparing their meals. "I'd rather not talk about everything now. I need you to sit back and relax for the rest of the flight. I know it's hard, but you've waited this long. A few more hours won't kill you." She smiled. "At least, I hope not."

"Funny." He wasn't finding any of this humorous. He glanced out the window into the darkness. It had been a long time since humor had been a part of his life. He hated surprises and not being in control. It drove him crazy. He was having a hard time not throttling Spencer. His life was always organized perfectly. This was so far out of his comfort zone he might as well be on the moon.

He felt a hand on his arm and turned to find Spencer leaning over. "By now your people are looking for you. When we land, we're going to have to move quickly to get to safety. We need to remain as anonymous as possible. I have a friend picking up some clothing for you."

Drake grunted. The idea of his lack of clothing hadn't

occurred to him, but now that she mentioned it, he would love to get into some clean, dry clothes. Even after five hours, his pants still felt a bit damp.

"Don't worry, I'm pretty good at shopping for clothes." She smiled again.

He had to admit, he liked her smile. It made her eyes light up.

"Here's the thing," she continued in a quiet voice, "I am aware Callahan Security is good at what they do, and I don't doubt their loyalty, but you have to let me know if you see any of them or anything that would lead you to believe they've found you. If, at any time, you see something, you need to tell me immediately. The reason your sister is in trouble is because there is a rat in the organization. If the Callahan people can find you, then others will find you. If it were me, I would follow them to you, so it's of vital importance you speak up if, and most likely when, you see them. All of our lives depend on it."

"I will but"—he peered over at Janine who was still in the galley area—"I think they could be helpful, and I obviously trust them with my life."

Spencer sighed. "I understand that, but right now I don't want to add any other people to the equation. I need to find the leak first and then go from there. If your people even spoke to the wrong person, it could set off a catastrophic chain reaction. I've been working to avoid that. As it is, I'm worried. The more people who know the secret, the less chance it stays a secret."

Janine came down the aisle toward them. Spencer removed her hand and sat back in her seat. He felt the loss immediately. He liked being close to Spencer, as long as she didn't have a gun in her hand. He noticed when she took off her coat that the gun and holster had disappeared.

She smelled faintly of lavender. Her presence was...reassuring in an odd way. It was nice to finally know he wasn't crazy. His sister was alive, and this woman knew it, too. It was as if someone had lifted a thousand-pound weight off his shoulders.

Granted, he was on a plane with what could turn out to be a crazy woman with no idea of where he was going and no idea what was going on. Still, somehow the knots in his gut had started to unfurl and his shoulders were lighter than they'd been in sixteen years. Maybe, just maybe, this would all work out and he would get his sister back.

"There you go, Bob," Janine said as she pulled out a side table from the wall of the aircraft. He blinked. He'd momentarily forgotten he was supposed to be some guy named Bob.

Janine continued setting things up with a tablecloth and cutlery. She soon brought over his food and offered him some more wine. He accepted everything with a smile and tucked into his steak. Maybe he was stress eating or maybe he was actually hungry, or being on the verge of possibly finding his sister made everything seem better, but the food was quite good. He cleaned his plate.

He glanced over, and Spencer had cleaned hers as well. She'd also ordered the steak, which he admired. He hated women who constantly ordered salad. There were few things in life that were as uncomplicated as enjoying a good meal. Why wreck it with only eating leaves?

"Would you like some dessert?" Janine asked.

He normally didn't indulge in dessert. He didn't have much of a sweet tooth, but Spencer gave a hearty "sure," so he did the same. Minutes later, after clearing their place settings, Janine returned with warm chocolate-chunk cookies. He took one and smiled. It had been a long time since he'd had a cookie. It tasted as good as it smelled.

"Good, aren't they?" Spencer said.

"Very tasty. Where did she get them?"

"The food is always the best on John's airplanes. I have no idea where he gets it, but it always makes the flight that much better."

Drake glanced out his window. As good as the food was, he sincerely hoped he hadn't just consumed his last meal.

CHAPTER TEN

Turning off the Liliuokalani Freeway, Drake's palms broke out in a sweat as his heart rate went stratospheric. He was minutes away from seeing his sister in Oahu of all places. How was she dealing with the sun? Her skin was so fair. Shit, what a stupid thought. His brain was all over the place. His lungs hurt as he was having trouble regulating his breathing.

Actually seeing his sister after sixteen long years. A sister that the police said had died. It was unbelievable. He glanced at Spencer. Should he trust her? Maybe she was taking him to his death, and he was a willing participant. Honestly, he didn't care. If it meant he got to see his sister again even for a few short moments, then he was willing to take the risk.

His grandmother's face rose in his memory. She had made Drake promise to find Kathleen. Like him, the old woman never believed Kathleen killed herself. Not for an instant. He knew Kathleen had something going on in her life, and maybe he should've said something sooner, but he never thought Kathleen would choose death over life. She would never give up. There were too many things she wanted to see and do. Too much living to be done. She had been the most upbeat person he knew.

He wiped his palms on his pants. It felt extraordinarily weird to be nervous. Jameson Drake never allowed himself to be anything but confident. Nausea rolled through his gut as they came to a stop in the driveway. Spencer parked the car and turned to him. "Are you ready?"

He didn't trust himself to speak. He gave her a curt nod. Reaching for the door handle, he took a deep breath. He had never let himself truly relax since the day Kathleen disappeared. His body felt ancient as he got out of the car, as though he was moving in slow motion or through water.

The small, neat, one-and-a-half story mid-century modern house had a tidy yard and a beautiful garden filled with a riot of color. All the tropical plants moved in the breeze. Kathleen had loved gardening. She used to work alongside his grandmother. He'd forgotten that. So many memories crowded in. Memories he purposely had forgotten or pushed away.

As they approached the door, Spencer stopped. She cocked her head and placed a hand on her gun underneath her coat. Drake froze. He didn't think his heart could beat any faster, but it double-timed in his chest. This couldn't be happening. Nothing could be wrong. He needed to see his sister. Now.

He started to brush by Spencer, but she grabbed him and held him back. She shook her head but remained silent. She approached the door carefully. When she pushed on the wood, it swung open slowly. She took out her gun and stepped inside with Drake right at her heels.

"Kathleen?" she called quietly.

The room was one big open space. There was an overfilled sofa littered with papers. Glassware and cups were all over the coffee table in front of it, along with plates and other debris. There was a TV against the windows which would be odd under normal circumstances, but Drake understood immediately they wanted to block the windows so people couldn't see in. What exactly was his sister into?

The living area opened up to the kitchen in the back of the house. The island had three bar stools tucked underneath the overhanging counter. There was a thump and the clanging of pots. Someone was in the kitchen, searching for something.

Spencer crept forward silently, both hands on her gun. She went wide until she was level with the island. Drake was only steps behind her.

"Put your hands where I can see them and stand up slowly."

A scream sounded and more crashing. Suddenly Kathleen's face appeared over the top of the island. "Jesus, Mary and Joseph! Spencer, you scared the hell out of me!"

"Me!" Spencer yelled back. "What about you? This place looks like a bomb went off, and the front door wasn't latched."

"Connor! I'll throttle that kid when he gets home from school. He's—"

Drake must've made a sound because his sister suddenly swung in his direction and stopped talking. He had forgotten the sound of her voice and how she always exuded energy.

Her red hair was now black, but her blue eyes still sparkled. His gaze locked with hers, and he froze once again. He wanted to run across the room and hug her, but he couldn't move. Was this real? Was Kathleen right there in front of him? This had been a dream for so long. And now that he was here, he couldn't bring himself to believe it. His sister Kathleen was not only alive but standing ten feet from him.

"Jamie," she breathed.

His body shook. Adrenaline shot through his limbs. The whole world slowed down until nothing moved, and yet he observed every detail. He saw every color and every shape.

Kathleen straightened up and moved out from behind the counter. She was just as tall as he remembered but slightly rounder. Well, sixteen years did that to everyone. She walked right over and stood in front of him.

He looked into her face and saw his grandmother staring back at him. The tears from all the years he had missed her started pouring down his face. He couldn't stop them any more than he could utter a sound. He stood there dumbfounded.

Kathleen stepped up, put her arms around him, and hugged him tight. His arms automatically encircled her, and he took a deep breath. She smelled like roses. Still, after all these years—roses. The tears came faster, and he didn't try to stop them. He hugged his sister, burying his face in her neck and let it all happen. He needed this to be real. To last forever. To never stop.

"Jamie, love. I'm so sorry. I missed you so very much. Every damn day."

"Kathleen," he croaked, but he couldn't say anything else. His throat closed over again, and he swallowed hard.

"Hush, Snuggles."

He choked out a laugh. If people ever found out his nickname was Snuggles, he would never live it down. His hard-won reputation for being a tough, aggressive, ambitious son of a bitch would die a quick death. Snuggles hadn't existed anymore. Until now.

"Kathleen, I've missed you more than you can imagine." He started to pull away so he could see her face, but she stopped him and kissed his cheek.

She let go of his shoulders but held him at arm's length. "You've turned into quite a man," she said, giving him the once over. "You look like granddad but with a bit of great Uncle Seamus thrown in."

He grinned. "You look like Gran except for the hair. I assume that's a dye job?"

She nodded. "Horrible, isn't it? I'm not suited for black hair at all."

He nodded. "It's so good to see you. I never gave up trying to find you. I never gave up hope."

Kathleen's eyes misted over. "I know, Jamie. I know. I'm so sorry to put you and Gran through it. I...was stupid and thought I would be able to handle everything better than I did. It's all my fault. Will you ever forgive me?"

"Always. Kathleen, having you back in my life is a miracle. I don't care what you did. It's over, and you can come home. We can be a family again."

"Ah, Jamie, I wish the situation was that simple." Tears ran down Kathleen's face. "There is so much to tell. So much to deal with. I don't know where to start."

Spencer cleared her throat. "How about I make some tea? Why don't you two go into the backyard and chat. I'll bring you both out some when it's ready."

Kathleen nodded. She took Drake's hand and led him out to the backyard. They sat down, side by side on a porch swing. "You look good, Jamie."

"So do you." He couldn't stop smiling. Sitting next to Kathleen again after sixteen long years of being on his own, he was completely overwhelmed. "I love your garden." It seemed a silly thing to say, but it popped out.

Kathleen smiled. "Thanks. I work hard on it. Working with plants always reminds me of Gran. I talk to her while I'm gardening, and I feel closer to her and to you."

"Does she ever answer back?"

Kathleen laughed. "You know Gran with her thick Irish accent. I can hear her in my head. 'Now Kathleen, what would you be doing that for? That plant needs sunshine not shade. You know better."

He laughed. "Yes, that's her all right." He squeezed his sister's hand. "I miss her."

"Me, too. I'm so sorry you had to deal with her death all on your own, Jamie. I...wanted to come back and help you, take care of you, but...it just wasn't possible."

"Neither of us believed you committed suicide. She made me promise before she died that I would find you again." When he took a deep breath, it somehow felt like he hadn't breathed in years. His chest expanded well beyond its normal state. He felt so light and free. Like someone had finally cut the belt that had been tied so tightly around him.

Kathleen bit her lip. "I'm so sorry."

"Stop apologizing. We're together now. That's what matters. We need to make up for lost time. You need to come back to New York with me. And we need to throw a party and invite the world. I—"

"Jamie, we can't."

"Yes, we can. I'll take care of the planning. Well, I'll get my people to take care of the details. We can do it in any city you want. I own hotels in most countries. I own a few hotel chains. High-end hotels. Classy. Ones you and Gran always wanted to stay at, but we could never afford to. I own them. The largest chain is the Jasmine Door, five-star chain all around the world, so we can throw the party anywhere you want." He sounded like a kid again. His sister must think him a right idiot.

She put her hand on his leg and smiled. "I'm so proud of you, Jamie. You have done so well. I know Gran would be proud. But we can't throw a party. At least not...now. The reason I disappeared... It's complicated, and the problem hasn't gone away. If I go to New York, they'll try to kill me and take Connor. I just can't risk it, Jamie."

"My people can protect you, Kathleen. They're excellent. They saved my ass a couple of times and saved my businesses, too. They can protect you. I promise." He took a beat. "Wait. Who's Connor?"

Kathleen smiled, but her eyes were sad. "How about I start at the beginning? I'll explain everything."

Spencer came out and set down the tea on the outdoor side table next to the swing. She brought over a mug to Kathleen. "How do you take yours, Drake?"

"Just a bit of milk, please." Tea was the last thing he wanted at the moment, but it reminded him of his grandmother. She always said everything goes down better with a cup of tea. He accepted his mug and took a sip.

Spencer sat down on a nearby chair. "Drake, what you're about to hear is classified. No one else is supposed to be read in but, at this point, it has become such a mess, I'm not even sure what's going on or who I can trust, so we're winging it."

She smiled at Kathleen. "Your sister asked if we could bring you in, and I agreed. Only someone with your resources can help." The smile slid off her face, and her eyes went cold. "But if you tell anyone or make any moves without consulting me first, I will do whatever I have to to protect Kathleen and Connor. Are we clear?"

He studied her for a second and then nodded. She was serious. The message was clear. If he fucked this up in any way, she would kill him. Good to know. The feeling was mutual. What the fuck was Kathleen involved in? He took a sip of tea and turned to his sister.

She gave him a small smile and squeezed the hand she'd been holding all this time. She then let go. "Jamie, I made a huge mistake. I did a bad thing." She took a deep breath. "Do you remember when you went back to school in September the year I went off to work in the city?"

He nodded.

"Well, I got this job as an accountant for a large tile and flooring company. Gran was so proud. It was a good job that paid well. A good stepping-stone on the way up the corporate ladder. If you remember, I didn't want to start at the bottom in some big corporation. I thought I already had enough experience working for Mr. Lawrence in town, and I had the degree. The woman who hired me agreed. They gave me a lot of responsibility right from the beginning. I looked after the books for all three of their New York stores.

"It was great. I loved my job, and I knew how to do it well. I made some changes that saved them lots of money. They were happy with my work, and I was over the moon working there.

"And then I met Giuseppe, who everyone called Joe, the owner's younger son. The owner and his wife divided their time between Staten Island and Italy and rarely came to the store. They decided to make Joe their New York manager. It was love at first sight." She took a sip of tea.

"Joe and I started dating immediately. I remember that I didn't tell Gran right away because Joe was a bit older than me and more worldly. I didn't think she would like him. Or, at least, that is what I told myself. The truth is, now that I look back, I think I knew from the beginning something was wrong. Joe used to get all these secret phone calls and leave in the middle of the night." She shook her head. "I'm getting ahead of myself."

All the joy Drake had experienced seeing his sister drained from his body. His shoulders knotted up just like they did when a deal started to go south. He always knew when bad things were going to happen because his body told him. His early warning system. This was going to be ugly. Did he want to hear it? Maybe he should just stop her now. As if he had a choice. He took a sip of tea to water his dry mouth, but scotch would have been better.

Kathleen sighed. "Joe started asking me about the books, and did I know of anything we could do to hide a bit of money? Nothing major. He won big at the casino and didn't want to pay tax on the money."

She frowned and looked down at her lap. "I was so stupid." Kathleen closed her eyes and opened them again. "I wanted to show off. There's no other word for it. I wanted Joe to think I was as wonderful as I thought he was. I wanted him to be proud of me. So I said sure, and I hid the money. Soon, he came with more. I hid that as well. Then hiding money became a regular thing, and I hid it all without asking questions.

"Jamie, you need to understand"—she touched his arm —"I didn't just hide the cash. I buried it. I was always so good with numbers, and I understood the banking laws. I'd been trying to convince Mr. Lawrence for years that we could put money offshore and save a bundle. But he would never go for it. I did the research anyway, and everything I had learned, I put to use. Jamie, I laundered more money than you can imagine and did it really, really well."

"Money laundering. You cleaned money for these people." He attempted to keep his voice neutral, but it was damn hard. How could she be so fucking stupid?

"I know, Jamie. I was an idiot. It… I…" Kathleen sighed. "I get how ridiculous it sounds, but it seemed like a game. Like it wasn't real. Joe and his father were thrilled. They kept saying how wonderful I was, and I know Gran loved us, but with mom disappearing and never knowing who our father was, it just…well, it was so good to hear that someone else thought I was smart and amazing."

He took a deep breath. "Believe it or not Kathleen, I understand what you mean, and if circumstances had been different, I might have ended up…well, on the wrong side of the law, or more likely dead." He gave his sister a sad little smile. “We all did the best we could with what we had, including Gran.”

Kathleen nodded. "The thing is, in the end, you made better choices, and now I’m still in a horrible situation because of mine. I was so naive. It never occurred to me the money came from drugs until the amounts started growing and were too difficult to hide. I went to Joe and told him we needed to stop or, at the very least, slow down or we’d start attracting attention. Jamie, these people were part of the mob."

And there it was, the other shoe. The thing that his body knew was coming even before she said it. His sweet, amazing, older sister laundered money for the mob, and she was on the run. Fucking son of a bitch. This wasn’t just bad; it was the worst case scenario. It was beyond anything he’d ever imagined.

Kathleen swallowed, and her hands began to shake. "Joe lost his mind when I told him we had to stop. I'll never forget the look on his face. Never. He hit me for the first time that night. He told me I had to find a way to hide the money. Laundering the cash was my job, and if I didn't do my job well, he would kill me."

Drake put on his blank face, the one he used in business so his opponent wouldn't know the storm that was raging inside of him. Killing Joe with his bare hands wouldn’t even satisfy his bloodlust at this moment. He wanted to smash the man into the ground. His sister had gone through hell while he partied away his last year at university. It made his gut churn, and bile rose in his throat.

"I didn't know what to do. I wanted to tell Gran and you, to have you protect me, but I was ashamed of my stupidity for getting involved in the first place. I'd been so naive. So stupid." She shook her head.

Drake didn't trust himself to speak. He gripped his cup

so hard it made a cracking sound. He leaned over and put it down on the table. He attempted to rein in the rage coursing through his veins.

"It gets worse, Jamie." Kathleen stood up and started pacing in the yard.

How could anything be worse than laundering money for the mob? He was afraid to ask. He didn't think he could deal with anything else. This was beyond his wildest nightmares. "What else?" was all he managed to croak out before his throat closed over.

Roberto, Joe's brother, came to town, and we all went out to celebrate our engagement. He was kind to me, and I thought maybe, just maybe, if I told him what was going on, he might help me. When we left the restaurant, Joe said he had to take care of something, so we drove over to Redhook. The area was deserted back then and a not-so-great neighborhood.

"Joe got out of the car and walked over to speak to this group of men. Roberto stayed with me. I thought this was my chance to tell him. Roberto spoke about their family home in Italy and how much I would love it.

"I was about to tell him when I heard the shot. I jumped and looked over at Joe. He held a gun, and one of the men in the group was on the ground. Joe kicked him and said something to the men. He turned and came back to the car." Kathleen's knuckles were white on her fists. "Roberto didn't even stop talking the entire time. As if Joe killing some guy was just business as usual."

"So you turned witness against Joe for the murder and the money laundering." It was the only thing that made any sense. Drake had a hard time even looking at his sister. This should have been the best day of his life. Instead, the nightmare was just getting worse.

Kathleen bit her lip. "I also found out I was pregnant so I

didn't have much choice. I wasn't going to bring a baby into that world, and I certainly didn't want to end up in jail while being pregnant."

His heart squeezed in his chest. "Connor?" The word escaped as a whisper.

Kathleen nodded and smiled. "Knowing he was growing inside me gave me the strength to do what had to be done. I contacted the FBI. I told them that I had information on the activities of the Caridi family. You would've thought Christmas came early, they were so happy. Joe's uncle was the consigliere to the boss of the Lucchese crime family. Anyway, they promised me immunity and a new identity if I had proof, and I testified at Joe's trial."

Kathleen's eyes filled with tears. "I was so torn. I didn't want to go away and not tell you or Gran, but if I did, then there would be no deal and I would go to jail. Connor would be born in jail. No"—she shook her head—"I would've been killed, and Connor wouldn't have been born at all. I couldn't kill my baby, and I couldn't raise him with Joe as a father. I wouldn't introduce him to that life. So I took the deal, and I testified. Joe went to jail for twelve years."

She tilted her head. "I had Connor, and they gave me a new name and a new life." Tears ran down her cheeks. "I wanted to tell you, Jamie. Leaving you behind just about did me in, but I was afraid for you and Gran.

"If they thought for one minute I had talked to you, you would all be dead, too. When Gran died in that accident, I was terrified." She gestured toward Spencer. "I made them investigate, but they assured me that the Caridi family had nothing to do with the accident. Just a dark, rainy night where a deer ran onto the road. They said they found the deer in the ditch on the opposite side of the road."

Drake swallowed hard and nodded. He was unable to do or say anything else. His muscles wouldn't move. All these years, she'd lived her life, never once reaching out. It must have been hell for her. It certainly had been hell for him.

The rage had been replaced by a crushing weight on his shoulders. He closed his eyes. It all could have been avoided if she had just reached out. They would have gone into hiding together. All of them. He would've found a way to make it work. He shook his head. *Hindsight is twenty-twenty,* as his grandmother used to say. Kathleen made choices all of them had to live with, and at some point, he would have to deal with his anger about that, but now he had to come up with a plan to rescue his sister and his nephew from a life in hiding. He drew in a deep breath and got to his feet.

He walked to his sister. "It's over and done, Kathleen. We're together now, and I have a nephew to meet. Where is he?"

CHAPTER ELEVEN

Kathleen moved out of the hug. "Connor is at school at the moment. He is having a tough time. He was born after I went into protective custody. When we had to run, he was torn from the only life he had ever known. He's angry with me, and I don't blame him. I thought being in school would give him some structure at least. It's risky, but being home all day made him miserable."

Spencer glanced at her watch. Connor should have been home thirty minutes ago according to his school schedule. She didn't want to panic Kathleen, but fear lurked in the pit of her stomach. "I have someone watching him all day at school, so he's safe. He doesn't love it, but he understands, and Will is a good guy. They seem to get along."

She'd texted Will a few minutes ago, but her phone screen remained blank. No new texts. Sound the alarm now or give them a few more minutes? It was a tough call. Kathleen had been through so much. On the other hand, the more time that elapsed since school got out could mean something bad was going down, and the bigger the lead Joe and his people would have *if* they had him at all.

The siblings sat back down on the swing. Drake cleared his throat. "Spencer, maybe you can fill me in on the missing details, like why is my sister still in trouble? And why is Homeland Security involved?"

"Homeland is not involved, although maybe it should be." She frowned. She didn't trust the people over at the U.S. Marshals office anymore. She pushed some loose hair behind her ear. "Kathleen had been in custody for about five years when I was assigned to be her contact."

"I thought she wasn't involved with Homeland," Drake commented.

"She isn't. I was with the U.S. Marshals Service then. We became instant friends. We're not supposed to get close to the people we're assigned to protect, but Kathleen and I clicked. We became close. Like sisters."

Kathleen smiled and nodded her agreement. "I don't know if I would have made it through some of those dark days if it hadn't been for Spencer."

Spencer shook her head. "It was you who helped me through dark times, and I will never forget it." She owed Kathleen so much. Kathleen had been the one who made Spencer realize life would go on even after losing her baby at the hands of her abusive now ex-husband. She wasn't going to share that with Drake, but she would be forever grateful to Kathleen for her support and friendship. Turning back to Drake, she continued, "I worked with them for eight years. I went to Homeland about two years ago, but we stayed in touch. Maintaining our friendship went against the rules, but we were careful, and we needed each other's support."

Kathleen nodded again. "Absolutely."

Spencer said, "Kathleen, do you want to tell the next part?"

Kathleen sighed. "We were living in Arizona. I was working as a middle school secretary."

"Seriously?" Drake started to laugh.

Kathleen rolled her eyes. "I know, it's hard to picture, me with all those kids. I hated babysitting, and I always said I never wanted to work with kids when we were growing up. Desperate times, I guess. I actually ended up enjoying it.

"Anyway I was at a neighbor's place about three months ago. I was coming home through the back fence with Connor when I got a notification someone was at my front door. I had one of those doorbell camera things. I looked at my phone to see who it was, and it was Joe. I couldn't believe he was standing there on my front porch."

Spencer glanced at her still blank screen. "Joe had gotten out of jail three weeks prior. The Marshals knew about Joe getting out, and someone was supposed to be keeping tabs on him but, apparently, he slipped out without them noticing and showed up on her doorstep.

"Anyway, we'd trained for this so Kathleen borrowed her neighbor's car and got her and Connor out of there. She went to the bus depot and picked up their go bags and money. She called me and her current contact at the Marshals. She met them at the safe house."

"I checked in with the friends at the Marshals, and everyone appeared to be on it. They were investigating how Joe found her, but she and Connor were safe. New identities were being established and a new life was being set up for them in a new state.

"Two days later, Joe and his men showed up at the safe house. Kathleen and Connor barely got out in time. One of the Marshals guarding them was not so lucky. He got shot in the chest. He's still recovering. I was on the scene by then, and I got them settled in a new safe house that I had arranged without telling the U.S. Marshals Service.

"A week or so later, I finally agreed to put Kathleen and Connor back under protective custody with a good friend of mine that I trusted, but when we showed up at the meet, my friend was already dead, and Joe was hunting for us.

"We ran, and I got Kathleen and Connor out of Arizona and over here. They've been set up for a few months now. I haven't told the U.S. Marshals Service or anyone else where they are. I don't trust anyone except Will. I knew him out of the Arizona office. He flew out here to help me keep an eye on them. I took a leave from work to bring you here."

"How does Joe keep finding them?"

"That's the question, isn't it? I have no answer for it. Yet. But I have some ideas. It's one of the areas I need to pursue." She stood up. "I need to check on something. I'll just be in the house if you need me." She smiled at Kathleen and nodded to Drake.

Spencer went into the house and called Will. His phone went straight to voicemail. The ball of fear in her stomach grew. Where could they be? Did they go for ice cream? She called Will again, but he still didn't pick up.

She tapped her fingers on the kitchen counter. Where the fuck could they be? She called the school and spoke to the secretary, but she said he left at the normal time and, yes, he'd been with Will. So where did that leave them? Had Joe and his men jumped them along the way home?

"Only you and Connor would think of a food at a time like this," Kathleen said with a laugh as she and Drake entered the kitchen. "Well, Connor wants to eat all the time regardless of what's going on. Teenage boys are like that."

"I can't wait to meet him," Drake responded. He glanced over at Spencer and cocked an eyebrow.

She shook her head. What the hell was she going to say? "I lost your nephew before you even got to meet him?" That wouldn't be helpful. She hit the tracking app on her phone but it couldn't locate Connor's phone. The last known location was his school.

A few minutes later, Kathleen said, “I hope you really are hungry.” She came around the counter with a tray full of sandwiches. She put it on the table. "I had some leftover roast beef, Jamie. Your favorite."

Drake smiled. "Sounds good."

Spencer sat down and took a bite of her sandwich. Kathleen was an excellent cook, and the sandwiches were probably tasty, but her worry about Connor had her struggling to chew and swallow.

She sat back in her seat and stared at her phone while the siblings chatted about random things as they ate their lunch. The only thing she could do was call the cops and report Connor missing. Under normal circumstances, being fifty minutes late for a teenage boy wouldn’t be seen as a big deal, but with Joe out there hunting them, and with a potential mole in the Marshals Service, fifty minutes was a lot. She would have to tell them the whole story, but they would take her seriously. Should she do it? Should she pull the trigger and make the call?

"So, how about a shower and a change of clothes?" Kathleen looked at her brother. “I'd be willing to bet you could use both right now. Travel is always exhausting."

"Yes. I could use a shower for sure. I didn't have an opportunity to grab clothes before I left, so I guess I'll have to do some shopping."

Spencer leaned forward. "As I think I mentioned earlier, I went ahead and got some clothes for you. You'll find them upstairs in the front bedroom."

"Okay then. I guess I'll grab a shower." He stood up, and Kathleen stood with him. They hugged. "It’s so very good to see you again, sis. I can't tell you exactly how much." When they parted, his eyes were bright. He turned and walked up the stairs. Kathleen sat back down at the table.

"I still feel so guilty for leaving."

Spencer sighed. "You did what you had to for you and your son. It was the right decision. Sometimes, the right decisions aren't the easiest to live with"—wasn't that the truth—"but one look at Connor, and you know you did the right thing."

Kathleen nodded. "I did do the right thing, but I don't think the guilt will ever go away. Jamie was in college, a twenty-three-year-old kid when I left. He was still trying to figure out what he wanted to do for a living. He'd spent an extra couple of years at university because he kept switching his major. I regret not being there to help him sort it all out."

"Well, he's a man now and he obviously has it figured out."

She grinned. "Yes, he certainly is and much better looking, too." She looked at Spencer. "You could do worse."

Spencer choked on her cold tea. "Seriously. He's here to help. I'm not interested in getting involved with your brother. He's got a reputation for being an arrogant asshole. I don't need any more of those in my life."

Kathleen cocked her head. "We'll see."

Spencer put her tea down and glanced at her phone. Still nothing. Maybe Connor was just rebelling, and Will didn't want to alarm Kathleen. "What else is going on? How is Connor adjusting?"

"He's not so happy these days. He hasn't forgiven me for not telling him about his dad."

Spencer frowned. "It's not something you can tell a kid. He will understand that when he's older. He's in those cranky teen years when everything is a slight against him, and no matter what you do, he would be mad at you."

Kathleen nodded. "I know, but he has a point. I ripped him from his whole life, everything he's ever known. Now he's hiding out and attending school under a false name. It's awful for him. I can totally understand why he's so mad, but his anger is hard to live with." She fidgeted with the napkin in her lap. "The thing is, I'm angry, too. I'm mad I made those mistakes all those years ago. I'm full of rage that Joe would kill that man and try to kill me. The fact that he wants to kill me is bad enough, but the thought of him taking Connor... I am almost paralyzed with fear over it."

"I understand, but we're not going to let that happen. Your brother is here now, and he's going to help. At least that's a plus, right? And he'll give Connor a male role model to look up to. He's very successful, so maybe Connor will be inspired."

Kathleen rolled her eyes. "The only thing Connor is inspired by these days is video games and girls."

"Well, Drake can help with that score, I'm sure. He's got quite the reputation as a lady's man. He can give Connor some pointers."

Kathleen threw her napkin at Spencer. "I do not want my brother to give my son pointers about girls. Dear God. That would be awful, for sure. Jamie never dated a girl longer than three months when he was in college, and I'm not sure he's changed that much. So what about you? What about that partner of yours?" Kathleen asked as she grabbed a second sandwich and took a bite.

Spencer sighed silently. She didn't feel like discussing her love life, or lack thereof, but it made Kathleen relax and gave her some semblance of a normal conversation. She didn't want to destroy that unless she had to. "I told him off just before we left. He's an asshat, no question.

Kathleen laughed. "Asshat, I like that term, but sorry he turned out to be a jerk."

"Look Kathleen..." Spencer hated to do this, but she didn't feel she had a choice. "I'm slightly concerned. I can't seem to locate Connor and Will. They should have been home a while ago."

Kathleen's face clouded over, and then suddenly she smiled. "Connor has his first surfing lesson today. I totally forgot to mention it the last time we spoke. Oh my God, you've been trying to find them this whole time, haven't you? I'm so sorry." She reached out and squeezed Spencer's arm.

"But I can't track Connor's phone, and Will's phone goes straight to voicemail. They should be reachable at all times."

"Cal, the surf coach, said reception at the beach where they teach the kids is horrible. I wasn't sure if we should do it, but Will said it would be fine. Cal gave me a number to call." She got up and dug out a piece of paper from her purse and then handed it to Spencer. "This is it."

Spencer took the slip of paper and made the call. Twenty seconds later, she was speaking with Will. "Thank God, I was starting to worry."

"Sorry, Spencer, I didn't realize you were going to be in town, or I would've told you. Connor is just finishing up with his lesson. We'll be there shortly."

"Okay, thanks, Will." Spencer clicked off the call.

"I'm so sorry for worrying you. I just didn't think. Seeing Jamie again chased everything out of my brain."

"I get it, and it's not a problem. Just tell me of any schedule changes in the future whether I'm here or not." She gave Kathleen a tight smile. Her phone rang again, but she didn't recognize the number. Probably some telemarketer. The area code was Arizona, though, which made her slightly uneasy. Someone from the Marshals Service? How would they have this number? This was a burner phone so they wouldn't. She ignored the call and gave herself a mental shake.

The call did remind her that she should call Eddie at some point. He'd be relentless at tracking her down if she didn't call, and she needed the Marshals to think she was on Cape Cod taking some downtime.

Kathleen grabbed her arm. "Let's go get you settled as well. I put you in the back bedroom across from mine. Why don't you grab a shower and freshen up? Connor will be thrilled to see you when he gets home. "

"Sounds like a plan." Spencer followed Kathleen up the stairs. The knots in her stomach were slowly unfurling. The crisis was averted, at least for now, but who knew what was coming? It was just too easy for things to go wrong. Hopefully, Drake could be of some help, but the more she interacted with him, the less she was sure his involvement was a good idea. He wasn't exactly known for his flexibility and laid-back style. They were going to butt heads for sure. She just had to make sure she held her ground. It would be so much easier if he weren't so damn sexy and smart.

CHAPTER TWELVE

Drake let the heat from the shower warm his bones. His heart had gone cold the moment he came upstairs. Everything hit him like a sucker punch to the gut. His sister was alive but in serious trouble. Big-ass, deep shit kind of trouble. The kind that got people killed. He put his hands against the back wall of the shower and let the water hit him between his shoulder blades. What the fuck was he going to do? How was he going to fix this mess?

Drake had worked his ass off after he got lucky all those years ago. He had taken a huge risk, and it paid off for him. He'd won a small group of old broken-down hotels in a poker game, three in a tiny beach town in the Caribbean. The next month, the Ritz Carleton announced they were building a new hotel and residence right down the street.

The gods had smiled on him, and he'd known it. He had been fortunate enough to meet the right people at the right time and acquire the guidance and knowledge he needed to become a huge success. His sister had not been so fortunate. It so easily could have been him in her place. He'd been on a dark path back then. If lady luck hadn't smiled on him during that poker game, chances were good he'd be dead by now.

Kathleen could've reached out for help, but to whom? He wanted to think he would've helped but, honestly, what could a twenty-three-year-old have done to fix her situation? Would he have confronted Joe and his family? Probably. He'd been such a dumbass back then. All balls and no brains. It had taken getting his ass handed to him a few times before he'd learned that brains were mightier than brawn, and the combination of both was deadly.

He'd had no money and no skills back then, and Grandmother wouldn't have known what to do either, other than tell Kathleen to go to the police.

Maybe they all would've ended up in Witness Protection, but more likely they would be dead. Guilt washed over him just like the shower spray. He'd been lucky and his sister had not. That is what it all came down to.

Drake washed his hair and his body, then turned off the spray and toweled off. He was mad at his sister. Livid in fact. Laundering money? What the fuck was she thinking? Stupid didn't cover it.

But deep down he knew why she'd done it. For the same reason he'd worked so hard at school to get that scholarship. Because no matter how much their grandmother loved them, she resented having to raise them.

Her daughter, their mother, had mental issues and ran off somewhere, leaving Gran with two small children to raise by herself. Granddad had died the year before. Drake and Kathleen had both done their best, but neither one had measured up to what Gran thought they should do. After all, if she was making all this effort, why weren't they?

He wrapped a towel around his waist and opened the

bathroom door, coming face to face with Spencer. She had a towel in one hand and a makeup bag in the other.

"Oh, sorry." She took a step back. "I didn't realize you were still in there."

"Yes, well, I thought a long shower might help me recover after all the travel."

He smiled down at her. The light from the window in the hallway caught the golden flecks in her hazel eyes. The deepening shadows under them only emphasized their size. Spencer Gordon was quite stunning up close.

He glanced down at her full lips and wondered what kissing her would be like. A small frisson of electricity passed between them. Twelve hours ago, she held a gun on him, and now he wanted to kiss her. How times had changed.

"Um, would you mind moving?" she asked. Her voice sounded low and husky.

Drake caught her checking out his chest, and he smiled again. "Of course. My apologies." He moved out of the doorway and brushed by her.

She must feel the chemistry, too. The timing couldn't be worse at the moment, but maybe someday when this situation with his sister ended, he would ask her out on a real date.

He went on a lot of what he thought of as "fake dates" with the "see and be seen" group of women. The flavor of the month. The "It" girl of the moment. He made sure to be very clear and up front with these young women about what he wanted from their acquaintance. He was equally clear he would not change or be changed, so they needed to be realistic. Most were.

He only had a few minor brushes with those who couldn't grasp that he didn't love them, or even like some of them.

Mitch had asked once why Drake bothered with the

charade, and Drake explained that, oddly enough, in the boardroom it mattered who occupied his bedroom. As long as he appeared to be single, he had to put up a smoke screen of young, lovely ladies or others would start to be curious about his life. This way no one took any great notice, and his private life remained just that, private.

Spencer cleared her throat. "Thanks." She went into the bathroom and started to close the door.

"Spencer, earlier you seemed distracted when you were talking about Joe always knowing where Kathleen and Connor were. There's more to that story, isn't there?"

She looked around him down the hallway and then stepped back out of the bathroom. "Look, the story that went around the U.S. Marshals Service was that they were hacked and that's how they found Kathleen's location but..."

"You don't buy it?"

She shook her head. "No. I don't think there is a hacker."

He frowned. "I don't follow. You think they made up the story?"

"Oh, I think it *looked* like there was a hacker, but my gut tells me there is more to it. It's damn near impossible to hack the list, and for good reason."

"So you think it was an inside job?" He lost any benefit from the hot shower as his shoulders tensed. An inside person at the U.S. Marshals Service working against them just lowered their odds of survival.

"Possibly. Either way, it still leaves us unable to trust anyone at the Marshals Service. I made sure that no one knows Kathleen's location. They've asked me a million times, and I keep telling them that she's gone underground like we taught her and she doesn't trust the service after everything that happened."

"But they think she contacted you. After all, you said you were close."

"Yes, but I told them that, given a choice between her son and our friendship, she would not pick our friendship. There are fifty states she can travel around without having to show any paperwork. She could be anywhere."

He crossed his arms over his chest. "Do they believe you?"

"Probably not. I've been behaving as if it's business as usual until now. I told my boss that my leave of absence was to figure out what I want to do in terms of my career, and I left word that I would be at my friend's beach house up in Cape Cod. I even have someone staying there that sort of looks like me, so it should be fine for a while anyway. Not that I expect anyone to come looking."

He leaned on the wall. "What about the flights? I thought you said it was your plane. The first one, I mean."

"It is, but I bought it under a company name, and I listed others as the owners and officers. Also, no one knows I have my pilot's license. I got it quietly a few years back as a surprise for my dad. He likes to fly." Her brows lowered into a frown.

Drake cocked an eyebrow. Something wasn't right. "But you never told him?"

Her lips drew into a thin line. "Never got around to it."

He shrugged mentally. Her family drama wasn't his concern. "So we're good here for a while. The pilot and your family friend won't say anything?"

She shook her head. "No one will say a word, but we need to find a more permanent solution."

"Let me bring my people in on this. I know we can make some headway." He was going to need all the help he could get. This was outside of his purview. He had no more clue now what to do than he would've sixteen years ago.

"No. Not until I have a better idea of what's going on."

"Then why bring me in if not for my contacts?"

"Because it's not a matter of *if* Kathleen and Connor are found; it's a matter of *when*. Joe is not going to stop looking. I've done my best to cover their tracks and mine, but you know as well as I do that there is always an outside chance of someone saying something or seeing something, and if Joe wants to find them as badly as I think he does, then he won't stop until he finds that person and makes them talk."

Fuck! "You don't want to come up with a solution. You want me to hide them. To keep them moving and keep them hidden."

She nodded. "There is no solution to Joe, at least not at the moment. I can only do so much, and I can only do it here in the U.S. You can do it across the world." She leaned toward him. "That's the other thing I didn't tell Kathleen. Joe has resources now that he's out."

"What do you mean?"

"Roberto, Joe's brother, did well for the family. He still runs the legitimate businesses in Italy, but he's also become a much bigger part of the mob. He's one of their chosen men, which means Joe's got more friends now and access to money. Plus, he blames Kathleen for everything."

Drake's gut churned. "Money and drive means a formidable enemy." He pushed off the wall. "Enjoy your shower."

He went down the hall to his bedroom where he examined the clothing Spencer had purchased for him. She bought him the kind of underwear he wore and several of the clothing brands he had in his closet. She'd done her research on him. How she had found out what he wore was beyond him. Maybe Homeland Security had a file on him. Did they go into that level of detail?

His heart tripped in his chest. He never stopped to think about the government keeping track of him before, but it made sense. He traveled the world, moving from one country to the next constantly. He did business with friends, as well as enemies, of the U.S. He had another hotel opening in China next month.

He reached down to grab a shirt off the bed and froze. Work. They must be going apeshit with him missing. He couldn't believe business had just crossed his mind now. He always had work on his mind, but since he'd met Spencer, he hadn't thought about work once. Well, work would have to manage without him for a bit. Or they wouldn't manage, and he would come back to a massive mess. Either way, there wasn't much he could do about it now.

He pulled the navy T-shirt over his head and slid into a pair of faded jeans. They fit him like a glove. He was impressed all over again with Spencer's attention to detail. When this was over, if she needed a job, he would be happy to hire her, although working alongside her every day would be a form of torture. Concentrating would be tough. Dating her would be much better than working with her. Oh, the things they could do and the places they could go. He smiled.

There was a commotion downstairs and he surmised that his nephew had arrived home from school. He had a nephew. Jesus. It was so surreal. Yesterday, he couldn't even be sure he had a sister, yet today he had Kathleen back and her son. He closed his eyes and said a silent prayer of thanks. Now he had to figure out how to keep them both safe.

He left his room and went quickly down the stairs. His nephew stood in front of the island, facing his mother and Spencer, who stood in the kitchen area. The kid was tall and thin and built more like Drake than his mother. His hair was a slightly deeper brown than Drake's, but he kept it longer.

What should he say to the kid? How would he like having an uncle? What will it be like having a nephew?

Surreal didn't cover it. A touch of nervousness ran through his gut.

Spencer's gaze connected with his. She must have taken a two-minute shower. Her hair was still wet, but she'd pulled it up into some kind of bun thing. She wore jeans and a dark green T-shirt. He couldn't help but notice the color made her eyes look more green than hazel.

Connor sighed. "School's school. You know how it is. The kids are nice, but they've known each other forever, and I'm the new kid." He shrugged. "How come you're here, Spencer? You said you wouldn't be back for a while. Is something wrong? Are we going to move again?"

Spencer leaned against the kitchen counter. "I don't know."

Connor snorted. "What a surprise? You don't seem to know much these days."

"I'm trying to be honest with you, Connor. There's a lot going on, and we're trying to get everything sorted. It might take a while."

"Whatever." Attitude rolled off his nephew in waves. Drake remembered being that age. Attitude was like breathing. It happened naturally without any effort.

"Connor," Kathleen said, "don't be flippant with your Aunt Spencer. She's trying to help us."

"She's not my aunt," Connor snarled.

"You might want to dial back the attitude a bit," Drake commented. "The lady is trying to help you."

Connor whirled around, and Drake froze. Holy shit! It was like a time warp and looking in the mirror at himself at fifteen. His eyes were staring back at him. Weird didn't quite cover it.

Connor's eyes widened, and his mouth popped open. "Who the hell are you?"

"I'm your uncle, Jamie." He offered his hand to Connor, who ignored it and glared at Drake.

"I don't have any uncles."

"Yes, you do," Kathleen said gently.

Connor turned to face her. "Jesus, you lied about that, too? How do I even know you're telling me the truth now?"

Drake had the urge to reach out and smack the back of the kid's head. Is this what his grandmother had felt like? If so, then he suddenly had more sympathy for the lady. "Because you look exactly the same as I did at your age. The family resemblance is uncanny, actually."

Connor turned back to face Drake. "What are you doing here?"

"Spencer asked for my help, so I came." Now that the shock had started to wear off, he took in the details of Connor's face. It was a slightly different shape, and his skin tone was a bit more olive than Kathleen's, but the eyes, nose, and lips were all Drake, and so was the attitude.

"So, now you've come to help. Why didn't you come help before?" He looked back and forth between Drake and Kathleen. "Why am I just now finding out about an uncle? Is there anything else you haven't told me? Do I have any half brothers or sisters you've forgotten to mention?"

"Connor!" Kathleen gasped and put a hand to her chest.

Connor bolted up the stairs two at a time and then, a second later, a door slammed.

Kathleen dropped her head to the kitchen counter. "He's so angry. It's all my fault. I should've told him the truth, but I wanted him to grow up as normally as possible. I wanted him to have a happy childhood."

Spencer caught Drake's gaze and gave him a look. Apparently, he was supposed to reassure his sister but, at the moment, he kind of agreed with Connor. Kathleen should've been honest with him, or at least more honest. He didn't blame the kid for being pissed off. He was pissed off, too. Keeping secrets like this was never going to help Connor. Not long-term.

If Kathleen had reached out sooner—ten, or even five, years ago—maybe he could've done something. With Joe in jail, things would've been easier. Now it was a hell of a mess with no easy way out. If Kathleen hadn't been such an idiot all those years ago, none of them would be in the current situation.

What's done is done. His grandmother's voice rang in his ears. He sighed. "Let me go up and talk to him."

He turned and took the stairs two at a time just like his nephew had before him. He knocked on Connor's door, but he got no response. "Connor?" Crickets. "Connor, I want to talk to you." Still, nothing.

He tried the doorknob, but discovered it was locked. He looked at the lock and then went in search of a bobby pin. Two minutes later, he came back, and fifteen seconds after that, he opened his nephew's door.

"Connor?"

The kid sat at his desk with his laptop in front of him and his back to the door. He wore headphones. Well, that explained the lack of response. Dangerous for the kid not to hear someone coming up behind him in light of the current situation, though. He'd have to speak to Connor about that, but maybe later after he got the kid calmed down.

The room was a decent size but plain. The walls were white, and there were beige blinds over the windows. The generic furniture and neutral grayish-beige comforter made the room feel like a poorly done, three-star hotel room, not the room of a teenager. Drake went up and tapped the boy on the shoulder.

Connor jumped. "How the hell did you get in here?"

Drake smiled. "I picked the lock. I can teach you if you want."

"You're going to teach me to break into places? Are you a criminal like my mom and dad?"

Drake ground his teeth. Harsh. "Your mother is not a criminal. She made some bad choices, but she made up for her mistakes." He sat down on the edge of the bed and faced his nephew. "Look, Connor, I know this is all a bit...overwhelming."

"Oh, yeah, you know, do you? Did you grow up and learn your whole life was a lie?"

"No, but—"

"Then you've no idea." He turned back to face his screen and started to put his headphones on. Drake leaned over and snatched them off Connor's head.

"Hey, asshole, give them back!"

He leaned forward so he was eye to eye with his nephew. "I'm going to let you get away with that just this once. Be disrespectful again, and you won't like the consequences."

Connor opened his mouth and closed it again.

"Now, I was going to say I know this is overwhelming because I'm feeling the same way."

Connor snorted and rolled his eyes.

"Last week, I mostly believed your mother to be dead, and I had no clue you even existed. Today, I saw her for the first time in sixteen years, and she tells me I have a nephew, so yeah, I understand being overwhelmed."

"What do you mean, 'mostly believed'?"

"I never gave up hope that your mom was still alive. The story the police gave at the time didn't make sense. I've been looking for her ever since."

"So she lied to you, too? Why aren't you angry at her?" Connor asked. The hurt was written all over the kid's face.

Drake sighed. He wasn't going to lie to the kid. Too

many people had done that already. "I am angry with her. As a matter of fact, I'm livid. I would love to go down there and scream at her for putting me through the agony of not knowing for sure what had happened to her. I would love to rake her over the coals for being so stupid and not trusting me enough to tell me what was going on. I want to yell at her for getting mixed up with that asshole in the first place." He swore. He just insulted the kid's father. "Er, I mean..."

Connor shrugged. "It's okay. I know what you mean. So why don't you tell her off?"

"Because she's my sister and, more than all that, I love her. I'm so glad to have her back in my life, to have you both back with me that, in the end, it doesn't matter."

Drake frowned. "Connor, yelling and screaming about things doesn't change them. And even though you think yelling will make you feel better, chances are good it won't because you will hurt someone's feelings, and that never makes anyone feel good."

Connor looked down at his hands.

Drake paused, thinking of the best way to say what he wanted to tell Connor. "I own a business. I learned that if I take that anger and turn it into something productive, I can usually achieve my goals. Sometimes that is buying a new property. Other times, it's destroying the person who aggravated me."

Connor looked up. "Can you teach me how to do that?"

Drake blinked. Shit. He hadn't thought that one through before he said it. This dealing with kids thing was harder than it looked. Like walking through a mine field. *Gran, I take back all the mean things I thought about you.* He might not be cut out for this uncle thing.

"Connor, I just mean you need to learn to channel your anger to get the outcome you want. One of the things I had to learn as an adult is sometimes 'what I want to do' and 'what I need to do' are two different things.

"You're still a kid, but your situation, through no fault of your own, requires you to behave like an adult. That sucks, but you still have to do it. You can be angry at your mom, but you still need to help her and work with her and Spencer and me to get the two of you out of this mess."

Connor's eyes were bright with unshed tears. "I want to go back to what it was like before. I want to hang out with my friends and not worry about someone coming to kill my mom."

Drake nodded. "That seems pretty reasonable to me. Believe it or not, I would like the exact same thing." His heart went out to the kid. How fucked up was it that he was worried someone was coming to kill him instead of worrying about making a sports team or if the person that he has a crush on likes him back?

"What are you talking about? No one is after you, are they?" Connor frowned.

It was Drake's frown, and it threw him off seeing it on this kid's face. "Um, I'm here to help you and your mom. That's not going to make me popular with your dad and his people."

"So you're on the run now, too?"

He paused for a second as he thought about his security people and his staff who were all probably panicking because they couldn't find him. "Yes, I'm on the run now, too."

"So how are you going to be able to help us then?"

"That's a damn fine question. Why don't you come back downstairs so we can all talk about everything?"

Connor hung his head again. "Mom and Spencer don't want me involved. They won't talk about anything in front of me."

"Connor, do you want to be involved in figuring this out?"

The boy nodded.

Drake stood up and clapped Connor on the back. "Come on, we'll go downstairs and start figuring everything out. Don't worry, I'll handle your mother and Spencer."

Connor stood as well, and they started out of the room. "Uncle Jamie, do you like playing video games?"

Drake smiled. "As a matter of fact, I do. I actually own a partial stake in Ocean Games."

"No, shit? That's awesome!" Connor said as they came down the steps. "I love their game, *Dark Knight Overlord.*"

"Me, too. It's one of the reasons I invested in their company. My accountant thought I was crazy, but now I'm laughing all the way to the bank." He grinned at his nephew. Then he turned to his sister and Spencer who were still sitting on the couch in the living room. "Let's go over to the table and start assessing the situation." He put his hand on his nephew's shoulder. "Connor needs to be a part of this. It affects him, and he should have a say."

When Connor shot a glance at his mom, his shoulder tensed under Drake's hand.

Kathleen stood up, frowning. She looked back and forth between the two and then sighed. "Fair enough. But does anyone mind if I cook while we talk? I need to keep busy."

Connor smiled. "Works for me. I'm starving."

Kathleen smiled. "Of course, you are. You're always hungry." The two walked over to the kitchen area.

Spencer came to stand next to Drake at the bottom of the stairs. "You've known your nephew for all of two seconds. What makes you think he's ready to hear all of this? What makes you think he's ready to cope?"

"I've known *me* my whole life, and he's just like I was. Kathleen has already pulled the rug out from under his world once. She needs to give him the tools to deal if it happens again. Knowing the situation is the best way for him to start to process everything. Knowledge gives him the idea he has some control over the situation."

"But he doesn't have any control. None of us do. We're working against unknowns. There's very little we can control."

Drake smiled. "Yes, but sometimes the illusion of control is all you need."

CHAPTER THIRTEEN

Spencer glanced at her phone and then went over and opened the door. "Hey, Will."

"Hi, Spencer," Will said as he walked in carrying a few grocery bags. "Nice to see you. Sorry again about the mix-up earlier."

She smiled at her friend. "I should have given you a heads-up I was in town." It was hard to be mad at Will. Not only was he a nice guy, but he sort of resembled Santa Claus. He had white hair and twinkling blue eyes. He also had a large round belly. He retired from the Arizona office of the U.S. Marshals Service a couple of years ago due to some slight health issues, but he was always picking up a few side jobs to makes some extra cash, and as he liked to say, "Keep his hand in."

Will walked over to the kitchen area and put the bags on the floor. "Hey, Kathleen. I got everything on your list."

"I can't thank you enough, Will. You're such a godsend."

Will smiled. "My pleasure. I don't mind grocery shopping. I do it for my family all the time."

"Your wife must appreciate that," Kathleen said as she started digging in the bags and putting away the groceries.

Will laughed. "Not always. I get too many treats." He waved at Connor. "I got you some of your favorite doughnuts." He winked. "See you bright and early for school tomorrow."

"Sure thing, Will." Connor grinned. "And thanks."

He turned, nodded at Drake, and then headed for the door. "See you, Spencer."

"Thanks, Will. See you soon." She closed the door behind him. That was the other thing she loved about Will; he never asked questions. He assumed if Spencer wanted him to know who Drake was, she'd tell him. Will was one of the good guys. She'd learned a lot from him when she worked at the Marshals Service.

Spencer turned back and was about to suggest they all sit down to talk about the future when she stopped short. Drake was sitting on a stool in front of the kitchen island chatting with his nephew and Kathleen was busy cooking.

The scene stole her breath. Kathleen was smiling and laughing. Connor was grinning, too. They were being a family. Her heart lurched against her ribcage. Family like this was something she'd always wanted and could never seem to manage to create.

She quietly moved past them out to the backyard. It was small and didn't require much checking, but the Drake family deserved some privacy, and she needed to escape. The scene was breaking her heart.

She walked the fence line and checked to see if there were any loose boards or anything. The six-foot privacy fence was one of the reasons she chose this house for Kathleen and Connor. Also because Ewa Beach was a nice family community. The school was close, and people were friendly.

Someone would notice if a group of men showed up and started hanging out.

The ache in her chest dulled as she surveyed the yard one more time. Kathleen and Connor were the ones that had to live in the crosshairs, but she'd blown up her life for them. Her career at Homeland had probably stalled out, and she didn't even want to go back. She didn't want to go back to the Marshals either.

It was distinctly possible that someone over there had gone rogue, and she doubted she'd be able to trust any of them again after this, even if they found out who it was. It left a bad taste in her mouth.

So, where did that leave her? She had no idea. The only thing she did know was that she needed to keep Kathleen and Connor safe.

Kathleen had literally saved her life by showing her how to live through the toughest of times and do it with grace. She would do the same for her friend. And once they were sorted, she'd figure something out. A way forward where she might be able to have her own family.

The sound of Drake's laughter coming through the open window sent a slight shiver across her skin. He was so damn frustrating. What the hell did he know about keeping Kathleen and Connor safe? He was as insufferable as he was sexy. She'd love to punch him in the nose. The memory of him standing in the hallway in nothing but a towel popped into her mind, followed by all kind of images of other things she'd like to do to him.

As much as she hated to agree with Drake, he wasn't wrong. Kathleen and Connor deserved a better life than they were getting. And he was their real family so he should have a say in that. Damn. She hated that he was right. He was right a lot, no doubt, and probably knew it. It went along with his insufferableness, and it made him even more attractive. She always found intelligence in a man to be sexy as hell.

"Dinner's ready," Kathleen called through the window.

Spencer took a last look around and then headed inside. The food smelled good, and Kathleen had outdone herself with the pineapple chicken, but Spencer wasn't particularly hungry. She let the conversation flow around her and kept mostly to herself. They needed this time together. Who knew how long they would get to stay together this way?

After dinner, Connor got his stuff from his room and started doing his homework on the dining table and Kathleen went back to the kitchen to clean up. Drake offered to help, but Spencer beat him to it. There wasn't enough room for everyone to be in the kitchen.

Drake leaned against the island. "Are we going to talk about the future after Connor is finished with his homework?"

Spencer shook her head. "I think we're all pretty tired. It's been a bit of a roller-coaster day for everyone. Why don't we pick it up tomorrow?"

Kathleen smiled. "I think that's a great idea."

"Well, then…" Drake covered his mouth with his hand and yawned. "I am tired, so I think I will go up and see if I can sleep." He went over to his sister and gave her a big hug. "I'm so glad you're okay. Don't worry, we'll figure something out. I'm not losing you again."

Kathleen hugged him back for a long minute and then let go. Drake walked over to the table next to Connor and hit him on the arm. "We'll play *Dark Night Overlord* tomorrow, okay?"

"You're on," he said with a smile. Drake smiled back. He turned to Spencer and gave her a nod. "Let me know if you need help with...anything."

Spencer sighed to herself. She would keep the place

secure. She didn't need his help, but she humored him with a nod. This was her job, her responsibility, and she was the best at it. She didn't need amateurs messing it up, but she understood why he wanted to volunteer to help.

Five hours later she was still staring at the ceiling. Jet lag was always a problem for her. It took days for her to get back into a regular sleep cycle. One sheep, two sheep... She giggled. As if that had ever worked.

She glanced at her watch. One a.m. and not a creature was stirring. The house was silent. The palm trees outside moved in the breeze. Hawaii was one of her favorite places on earth. She loved the people and the weather. And surfing. Catching a wave was like flying. There was no greater freedom. Connor taking surfing lessons was a brilliant idea. He would love it.

She closed her eyes and worked on relaxing her muscles. Was Drake sleeping? She couldn't hear him moving about so she assumed so. He was going to be more of a pain in the ass than she thought. She'd been hopeful he would just fund everything and leave her to organize, but she should have known better. He was a very successful businessman, used to getting his own way. He wasn't going to just blindly listen to her. He probably didn't listen to anyone.

It didn't help matters that he was so damned good-looking. The memory of him standing in the bathroom doorway wearing nothing but a towel rose unbidden from her memory yet again. Hot didn't go far enough. The man was positively on fire. His defined chest led the way to his ripped abs, and they were the gateway to what was beneath the towel. Drake took her breath away.

It had taken her a moment to be able to speak after he opened the door and scared her. The chemistry between them was palpable. Under different circumstances, she'd take him to bed in a heartbeat. Knowing that he usually dated young hot things didn't matter. She didn't want to date him, just spend the weekend in bed with him, and she was damn sure he'd say yes, too. She put an arm across her forehead. But now wasn't the time for that.

The whole situation was frustrating and agonizing in equal parts. That pretty much summed up Jameson Drake, too. With a dollop of hotness that he, of course, knew he possessed.

Really, he was the quintessential player. Rich, gorgeous, successful. In her parents' eyes; the perfect man. The exact type they tried to push her way. Oh, he lacked political ambition, but as career politicians both of them, they would soon convince him he should run for some office. Politics was their life. The one they'd chosen for themselves and for their daughter.

Why was she even thinking of Drake as husband material? There was no way she'd ever marry him. He would be too controlling. Too concerned with always being in charge. That was the last thing she needed in her life. No. She wanted an equal partner who listened and supported her. Drake might be sexy as hell, but he was a bad boy, and she'd dated enough of those to last her a lifetime.

She rolled over. Her parents were going to freak out when they found out she'd taken a leave from Homeland. They'd been super pissed when she joined the Marshals instead of going to law school. When she'd pointed out she could have gone into military service, they announced that would have been better career-wise. Right. Who cares if your child dies overseas fighting a war? As long as they do it as a hero, it's all good.

She rolled onto her back again and went back to examining the ceiling. *Brain, shut down.* Wouldn't it be fabulous if there was a switch to flip to get into sleep mode? Just awake and then asleep. How amazing would that be? She rubbed her eyes.

Then…the sound was subtle at first. A small scratching noise. Like mice running in the walls, except there weren't any mice, at least not that she'd ever heard before. She sat up and listened in the darkness.

The sound stopped, and then there was a small *clink,* like the sound of glass hitting something. She reached under her pillow, grabbed her gun, and slid out of bed. Entering the hallway, movement on her left made her drop into a crouch position and swing around. Drake was standing just outside his door. She noted he was wearing jeans and nothing else.

She nodded at him and then pointed to the other two bedrooms. Drake nodded back. He moved over to Connor's door and opened it slowly. He disappeared for a second and then came back out with some sort of long tube in his hand. She wasn't sure what it was, but he must have felt it was a weapon of some sort.

Fair enough. She didn't have another gun to offer him, and she had no clue what self-defense skills he possessed. She'd just have to remember to announce herself when she came back upstairs.

There was another sound downstairs. Footfalls. Possibly more than one person. Spencer slowly made her way down the stairwell one step at a time. There was no wall on one side from about halfway down, which made her a target. She kept low with her back to the inside wall and had her gun out in front of her. She came to the landing and stayed there in a squat. She cocked her head but didn't hear anything.

Where the hell could they be? The house was tiny. If they'd come in the back door, then they could only be in the back room or the bathroom, otherwise she'd see them.

Unless...one of them was crouched down behind the sofa. The other one was probably in the bathroom. If she went all the way down the stairs, they would take her out immediately .

It was a standoff. She waited another thirty seconds. The sound of her heart pumping hard in her chest filled her ears. What was the best course of action?

She took in a long, slow breath and let it out again. All of her senses were hyperaware. She swore she could hear the guy breathing behind the sofa.

Could she turn the tables on them? If she went down the stairs and then immediately to her left, she might have an angle on both of them. There was no cover, though, and she would be backlit by the windows.

It wasn't much of a plan, but it was the only one she had. Her legs were starting to cramp. She'd lose her ability to move with any agility shortly. She needed to do something, and going back upstairs wasn't an option. That would draw them up, and if she missed killing them in the stairwell, then she and Drake, Connor and Kathleen, would have to jump out of the second story windows. What was the chance they could do that without getting hurt or captured? There were more men outside; she'd bet her life on it.

She was a damn good shot. Each bullet just had to count, but she wanted to face them down here. Drake would figure out a way to help Connor and Kathleen upstairs if she didn't make it, and Kathleen knew the basics of how to stay off the grid if it came to that.

The plan sucked, but nothing better was going to come along. Calling nine-one-one only meant more attention, which is what they desperately needed to avoid.

She shifted her weight slowly and went down the last few steps and then immediately went left. Keeping low, she stopped in front of the TV. It blocked the light.

She swept her gun back and forth between the sofa and the door to the downstairs bathroom. When the first man popped up from behind the sofa, she swung her gun in his direction. He took a quick shot at her, but missed and hit the TV behind her. He had a silencer on his gun but the *pffftt* of the shot seemed abnormally loud to her. She fired back and nailed him dead center of his chest. He went down with a grunt.

The second guy came out of the bathroom, and there was a loud bang. She swung around, but he was already falling. She turned toward the stairs and saw Drake standing there with the tube in his hands.

She advanced and doublechecked that both men were down. Neither was moving, but there was movement out of the corner of her eye. "No! Don't hit the lights yet."

Drake froze.

She moved back over to the window and searched the street. An SUV parked down the block suddenly shot out of its parking spot and sped by the house. It had to be the getaway vehicle. It looked like a BMW, probably an X7 by the shape of it. But what had spooked them? She continued to monitor the street but didn't see anything else that triggered an alarm.

She grimaced. She hated that she'd missed the opportunity to question any of them. It would be nice to be ahead of them for once. At this point, she'd settle for not being behind. They were out-manned and out-gunned at every turn, it seemed. She was desperate to find out who the leak was and how they were being tracked.

"Hit the lights," she said.

Drake did as he was told, and the room lit up. A cell rang somewhere in the house. Spencer glanced around and realized it belonged to the guy she'd shot. The ringing stopped. "Probably their ride, checking to see if they were okay. Would be nice to know what made them take off like that."

She turned around and stopped short. Staring at Drake,

she couldn't believe her eyes. "You shot the guy with a potato cannon? Seriously?"

Drake shrugged. "It's all I had. It worked." He gestured to the guy who was still on the floor.

Spencer shook her head and then walked over to check the guy out. She felt for a pulse. There was none. She blinked and tried again but no pulse. "You killed him. With a potato cannon. How is that even possible?"

"I hit him in the head. I'm guessing skull fracture."

"Jesus Christ."

"Jamie?" Kathleen's voice drifted down the stairs.

"Kathleen, Connor, it's safe," Drake called.

"Stay upstairs." Spencer glared at Drake. "They don't need to see this."

Drake glared back. "Yes, they do. They need to see what danger they are in so they understand the decisions they are making. You want Connor to toe the line, you show him reality."

"No fifteen-year-old needs to see this," she hissed.

Drake growled back, "You're wrong. This is exactly what he needs to see. You want him to forgive Kathleen, he needs to see what she's been protecting him from all this time. He needs to understand this isn't a game. The consequences are real."

"He'll have nightmares. He'll probably end up in therapy."

Drake snorted. "He's going to need therapy anyway."

"Fuck!" she snarled. "I have to go secure the rest of the house. Everyone needs to pack a bag. Essentials only. We have to be gone in twenty minutes, tops."

She walked into the back room. She wanted to strangle Drake. There was no question about it. He was quickly becoming her least favorite person. But he was right—again. It was why she hated him so much.

Connor needed to really grasp the gravity of the situation, and seeing two dead guys on his living room floor would do that for sure. It did not help that Drake was sexy as hell in his jeans and nothing else. He was the epitome of sexy hero coming to her rescue, and she hated him even more for it.

She crouched down. There was a hole in the glass beside the door. They had used a glass cutter and then reached in and opened the door. That's the scratching sound she'd heard. They were getting better at this...more sophisticated. Worrisome was an understatement.

She stood up, went outside, and checked out the backyard. No one was there, and it all seemed secure. She went back into the house, walked around the bodies, and took the stairs two at a time. Entering Kathleen's room, she watched as her friend stuffed clothing into a bag.

"I'm packing as quick as I can," Kathleen threw clothing into her suitcase.

Spencer nodded. "Make sure you take what's important. The rest we can replace later."

Kathleen looked up. "I know, Spencer. I remember how to do this. Connor is packing as well. He doesn't have much, so he'll be quick."

"Okay. Let me go check on him." She walked out of the room and started down the hall, only to come face to face with Connor and Drake. "All packed?"

They both nodded. "Set to go," Connor said.

"When there's time, you can explain to me why you had a potato cannon in your room." She glared at Connor. Then she did an about-face and headed to her room to grab her own things. She didn't have to pack because she'd never unpacked.

She changed into street clothes and put her pajamas back in her bag. Grabbing her gun, she threw her bag over her shoulder and met the others at the head of the stairs. She led the way down. When they hit the bottom, she heard Kathleen swear. She turned. Connor had gone pale as a ghost, and Kathleen wasn't much better. She shot an *I told you so* look at Drake.

"Why don't you go to the garage and secure the car?" Drake said as he glared back. Then he turned to his nephew. "I know this is hard, Connor, but this is precisely why your mother hid the truth from you for all these years. You really are in serious danger. We need you to be strong for your mother and yourself. We will find a way to take care of both of you."

Kathleen wrapped an arm around Connor and looked up at her brother. She gave a slight nod, and then the group moved forward and went out the door to the garage.

Spencer checked over the minivan and deemed it safe. She looked through the windows at the top of the garage door, but the neighborhood looked clear. They all climbed in, and Spencer started the vehicle and hit the garage door opener.

Connor asked from the backseat, "Uncle Jamie, do you promise to help us figure this out?"

"Absolutely," Drake said as he turned around in the passenger seat.

Connor nodded. "So, where are we going now?"

Spencer glanced at the anxious faces in the rearview mirror and over at Drake in the passenger seat. That was the question, wasn't it? What the hell were they supposed to do now?

CHAPTER FOURTEEN

"Take the on ramp to the highway and head back into Oahu," Drake instructed.

Spencer shot him a harsh glance but did as she was told. "What are you thinking?"

He looked at Kathleen and Connor in the back seat. The oncoming traffic lights lit their faces. Both were pale. Kathleen's eyes were bright with unshed tears, and Connor's were the size of golf balls. He couldn't stop scanning his surroundings.

The poor kid had been through the wringer in the last few months. He needed comfort, and so did Kathleen. She acted tough, but she was exhausted. She needed to feel safe and be sure her son was safe. All of this was aging her. Probably slowly killing her.

He turned back to look out the windshield. Spencer was going to fight him every step of the way, but he didn't have a choice. His family needed peace of mind, and he could offer that even if it was only a temporary fix.

He leaned forward and turned on the radio. An oldies

station. He turned to Spencer and spoke quietly, "I think we need help."

"No, shit," she murmured back. "What exactly do you have in mind?"

"I'm calling my team in."

"No!" she spoke sharply and then glanced in the rearview mirror. In a quieter voice, she said, " That isn't an option."

Drake had to strain to make out her words. "Yes. I trust these people with my life, and I am willing to trust them with my family's lives."

"I won't—"

"You don't have a choice, and you know it," he growled. "How did they find us, huh? If you were so careful and you trust your friend Will, then how did they track us down?"

She remained silent.

"Look, I understand that you want what's best for them, but so do I and, currently, your way isn't working." He wasn't one to pull any punches, and hurting Spencer made him feel like shit, but she still needed to hear the cold, hard truth.

He took a breath. "You know as well as I do it's only a matter of time before we aren't so lucky as we were tonight. If someone wants you dead badly enough, they will find a way. Let's make getting Kathleen and Connor as difficult as physically possible for them. Joe obviously knows we're here on the island. We can run, but he'll just catch up to us again."

She remained silent, but her frown deepened. The dark circles under her eyes and the tightness around her mouth didn't make her any less attractive. In fact, they made her all the more so. She cared deeply for his family, and for that, he would be eternally grateful. But now it was his turn, and they would have to do it his way.

"Kathleen is trying to be strong, but she's exhausted and

an inch away from breaking. Connor is lost and angry. They both need some time when they can relax. I can give them that. My people can keep them safe. Maybe not forever, but for now, and then we can look at long-term options. If we need to, we can make them disappear again. Promise."

Spencer still stayed silent. Her face was blank, but he knew she was waging some sort of internal war.

"You could use a break, too. You've been responsible for their safety for the last, what? Ten or eleven years? You need a chance to gain your equilibrium back."

"I can handle this. It's my job. I am perfectly capable—"

"You are, but you are also exhausted and stressed. You aren't eating much, and you certainly don't sleep. I heard you tossing and turning all night."

Her knuckles turned white on the wheel. "I told you I don't do well with jet lag."

"Your lack of sleep has nothing to do with jet lag, and you know it." He took a breath. "You can't function at your best if you're too tired to think. At least with my people here, we can take a few days or a few weeks to regroup and figure something out. With the extra resources, maybe we can discover who the leak is and why they're involved."

Spencer shot him a glance. "What do you mean why? Money would seem like the most obvious choice."

"Money could be the motive, but I can tell you from experience, money may be the reason people say they do things, but it is rarely the only reason. There's usually some sense of betrayal or a feeling of being wronged involved." His thoughts flicked to his past, and his gut churned. He trusted so few people, and yet he'd still been betrayed. He learned a valuable lesson from that experience. Just because he thought he was doing the right thing did not mean that was how his actions would be interpreted.

"You think whoever the leak is has skin in the game and wants to hurt one of us? Some sort of revenge?"

"Could be, or maybe they want to strike back at the department or their boss." He swallowed hard. His former assistant's betrayal still stung. "Or they could be in it for the money. The point is we don't know and we need to find out. Not having to run and hide would make that a lot easier, and so would having my team. Let's just say they have their fingers in many pies. They may be able to dig up information we might not find otherwise."

"So the rumors are true. Callahan Security does operate outside of the law."

He cocked his head. "I wouldn't say outside of the law. More like they dabble at crossing the line on occasion. It has come in handy more times than I can count."

She narrowed her eyes at him and then looked back through the windshield. "Supposing I let you call your people... Where will we stay until they arrive? How will we keep Kathleen and Connor safe for the next twenty-four to forty-eight hours?"

He smiled. "I know just the place. I'm not without resources on the island."

Her frown deepened, creating a V between her eyes.

"Trust me, Spencer."

She shot him a look and then glanced at the rearview mirror. She gave a small nod.

His gut unwound just a fraction. Now all he had to do was get them to safety. "Take the next exit." He turned and looked at his sister. Her eyes were closed, but she opened them and gave him a small smile. She still had her arm around Connor, and he was leaning against her, but his shoulders were stiff and his eyes watchful.

"Now what?" Spencer asked as they came to the bottom of the ramp.

He gave her the full directions to their destination.

"We're going to do a few circles to make sure we're not being followed." She made a right turn and then a left. They spent the next half hour going in circles and winding their way to their destination.

"Where are we going, and are we going to be there soon?" Connor asked. "I need to use the bathroom."

Spencer made the last right turn as instructed by Drake and shot him a look, eyebrows raised.

He allowed himself a small smile. "We're almost there."

They drove down the long palm tree-lined street. One of the crown jewels of his collection was at the end. He let out a breath he didn't realize he'd been holding. He had been outside of his comfort zone since D.C. He wasn't used to taking orders from anyone else or playing by their rules. It had been a long time since he had to do what he was told.

Being back in his own world made him feel much more in control. Nothing had fundamentally changed, but suddenly he felt like he was better equipped to deal with Joe and his people. On solid ground again. They would find an answer to this problem, and if there wasn't one, he would create one. It was as simple as that.

"What are you doing? Why aren't you moving?" Drake demanded as Spencer stayed at the stop light even though the light was green. "The hotel is up ahead."

"I know, but I think we're being followed." She glanced in her side mirror and then into her rearview mirror. "Two cars back. There's not much traffic at this time of night. That SUV turned in behind us a couple of blocks back."

"So why do you think the SUV is following us? It's been two blocks."

"Call it a gut feeling. It looks like the SUV that was out in front of the house."

"BMW SUVs are pretty popular, so it could be anyone." Drake glanced in his own side mirror.

"Yeah, but they slowed down to match our speed." Spencer made a quick left just as the light turned yellow. "Let's see if they follow." Seconds later, the SUV showed up in the mirror. There was no one between them now. She made a right and maintained a slow speed. The SUV did the same. They didn't come any closer, but nor did they drop back.

"I think you're right. They are following us. Do you think they tagged this vehicle?" His gut knotted. All the relief he was experiencing a moment ago was gone.

"No. I think they had people watching the approach to the hotel. The street we took is the only way in. We're going to have to lose them. Kathleen, Connor, make sure you're buckled in. This could get bumpy."

Drake glanced at his side mirror again. "Actually, it's not."

"Going to get bumpy?" Connor's voice rose and cracked.

"The only way in. There's a back way we use for celebrities and deliveries, that type of thing."

Spencer made another right. They were going in a circle. The SUV was starting to pick up speed. "Where is it? These guys are going to make some kind of move very shortly."

"Cross the main drive and keep going. Then take the second left. I'll call ahead and have them open the gates."

Spencer glanced in the mirrors again. "I hope this works because they're moving in." She hit the gas, and the minivan leapt forward. Instead of coming to a stop at the lights, she jammed the gas pedal down. The vehicle roared through the intersection. The driver of the SUV must have been taken by surprise because there was a brief delay before they sped up behind them.

Drake was waiting for the hotel to pick up.

"Good Evening Jas—"

"This is Jameson Drake. Open the back gate! Someone is following me. Have security meet me there! I'm in a blue minivan. Code word, Thor."

"Yes, sir, Mr. Drake!"

He clicked off the call as another SUV that had been approaching turned sideways blocking their route. Spencer swore and drove over the median and took the left down the side street. The SUV that had been behind them followed suit. Suddenly, the back window shattered.

"Get down!" Spencer yelled. She pushed the peddle to the floor, and the minivan leapt forward again, engine whining. Drake's mirror shattered and then so did Spencer's.

"Where's the fucking gate?" she yelled.

"Just around that curve."

Spencer took the curve too fast, and the vehicle started to slide. She managed to right the minivan and aimed for a gate that was just starting to swing open. The sound of more gun shots ripped through the air. Spencer kept her foot down until they crossed through the gate, and then she hit the brakes hard.

"Turn left!" Drake demanded.

The minivan skidded but Spencer managed to keep it from rolling over. They slid to a stop, but the sound of gunfire had her pressing on the gas again.

"Pull up over there!" Drake pointed to a loading dock down the side of the building.

Spencer drove over and stopped the minivan. "Now what?"

The gunfire had stopped, but Drake wasn't taking any chances. He was pulling out his phone when the door next to the loading dock opened, and men dressed in security attire poured out. Guns drawn, they ran for the back gate. One of the men stopped next to Drake's window. Drake opened the window.

"Mr. Drake, come with me," the guard ordered.

The guard moved to the rear of the vehicle and everyone piled out. They went up the stairs and through the door. The security guard, whose name tag read Bill, came through with them. He guided them along the back hallways of the hotel and into the freight elevator. "This will take you up to your floor. Mr. Bauchman, the head of security, will be up shortly."

Drake got everyone on the elevator and turned. "Thanks for your help, Bill."

The man nodded as he stepped back and let the doors close. Spencer turned to Drake. "Do you know him?"

Drake shook his head. "He must be new. I haven't been here in a while." He looked over at Kathleen and Connor. "Are you two okay?"

Both nodded their heads, but they were pale, and Connor looked a bit green. This was a lot for a kid. Hell, this was a lot for him. He hated that this was happening. He was more pissed off that he let things progress this far. He never should've left D.C. without his security. He turned to Spencer. "I'll—"

The elevator was stopping two floors below the penthouse level it was supposed to be on. He tensed.

"What is it?" Spencer asked.

"The elevator is slowing down. This isn't the right floor. This should go all the way to my suite on the top floor."

Spencer raised her gun and stepped to the front of the elevator.

"Surely, it's just cleaning people or the like," Kathleen said.

He shook his head. "Not at this hour." He motioned for Kathleen and Connor to get back to the side of the elevator, and he stood next to Spencer. He could at least block the first shots with his body if it came down to it, but that's all he could do. His heart pounded in his chest, and the blood roared in his ears. He tensed as the doors opened. Spencer raised her gun.

"About time you got here," Mitch said. He was leaning against the wall across from the elevator doors with a gun in each hand. "We've been waiting for over an hour. You took your sweet time coming from the house."

"Who the hell are you?" Spencer demanded, gun trained on Mitch's center mass.

"Allow me to introduce Mitch Callahan, head of my security." Drake grinned and stepped off the elevator. He offered his hand. "I don't think I've ever been so happy to see you."

Mitch laughed as he holstered one of his guns and shook Drake's hand. "I can believe it. Although there was that one time in Europe when you—" He glanced behind Drake and stood up straight. "That's a story for another time." He winked. "Let's go. Follow me." Mitch turned and walked halfway down the hallway. He opened the door to a suite. "We've set up in here." He ushered everyone in.

Spencer shot Drake a hard look and then walked into the room. He waited for everyone to enter before he followed. Gage and Logan were leaning over some paperwork that was spread out on the dining table. They turned around as Drake entered.

"Nice to see you finally decided to join us," Gage said. There was a glint in his eye, and Drake had been around him enough to understand that meant he was pissed. Fair enough.

"I shouldn't have taken off without speaking to you first about it, but"—he glanced at his sister and then Spencer —"there were extenuating circumstances."

Mitch came out of the kitchen with a few bottles of

water in each hand. "Uh huh, we are aware. That's what *we're* for, dealing with your extenuating circumstances."

Logan shook his head at Mitch's offer of water. "If you had let us know what you were planning, we could've made this go much better. We would've had a chance to catch the shooters and find out what's going on."

Drake shook his head at the water as well. "I want something a little stronger." He walked over to the bar that was set up in the far corner of the room. "Anyone else?"

Kathleen cleared her throat. "I'd love a glass of wine, white if you have any."

He nodded and then he looked to everyone else, but they all shook their heads. Spencer just continued to glare at him. What the hell did he do now?

He poured himself a drink and got the wine for his sister, and then he came back to the middle of the room. He handed his sister the wine and took a seat on the couch.

It was sumptuous leather, and it felt damn good to sit and relax after the last few days. He glanced at his sister and marveled all over again how she managed to live like this for sixteen years.

"Mitch, Gage and Logan"—he pointed to each man —"this is my sister Kathleen and my nephew, Connor. That"—he pointed to where Spencer was leaning with her back to the wall with gun still in hand—"is Agent? Officer? Not sure of her exact title, but Spencer Gordon, currently with Homeland Security but formerly with the U.S. Marshals Service. Turns out my sister has been in the Witness Protection program for all these years."

He hadn't *really* realized how angry he was until those words left his mouth. He knew it came out harshly because his sister paled even further, which he didn't think was possible. His nephew swallowed hard.

Drake took a big gulp of his drink. He needed to shut up

and get control again. Being livid at his sister was not helpful at the moment. There would be time later to...process. Wasn't that what everyone called it these days? *Yes, process it later.*

Drake caught a flash of sympathy on Gage's face before it went neutral again. Great. He was being an asshole. He took another gulp of scotch.

Logan stepped forward and broke the awkward silence. "It's nice to meet all of you." He shook everyone's hand and then went back to the table. "I know it's late, but perhaps you could give us the bare bones of what's going on before you all go get some well-deserved rest."

Drake turned to Kathleen. "Why don't you and Connor go on to bed? I'll fill them in, and we can do it in more detail if needed in the morning."

Kathleen nodded and stood. "Come on, Connor." The boy stood up beside her. "Wait, where are we going?"

"That's a good question," Spencer straightened. "I would like to know what security protocols you have in place, and I want to see where Kathleen and Connor are going to sleep. Then I want to review everything you have going on so I can be sure they're secure."

"Of course," Logan said. "We're happy to show you, but I suggest maybe we show you the whole setup in the morning. It's a big hotel, and there's a lot of ground to cover. We can go over the gist of it tonight."

"The whole hotel?" Connor asked. "Do you mean you have guys covering the whole thing? Just for us?" He looked at his mom and then at Drake. "Mom, you can't let him do that. We can't let Uncle Jamie pay for that. It's like waaay expensive."

Drake couldn't help it—he grinned. Then he stood up. "Connor, I appreciate you thinking of the cost. Very practical of you." He caught Mitch exchanging looks with his brothers. What was that about? Then it hit him. "I'm Uncle Jamie to you, but to the rest of the world I'm known by my full name—Jameson, or more commonly, Drake. I own this hotel and a bunch more like it across the entire world."

He didn't think Connor's eyes could be any bigger, but the kid looked like one of those anime cartoons.

"Seriously?" Connor's voice cracked, and Drake's grin grew.

"Yes, seriously."

"You're, like, super rich?"

He nodded. "Yes."

Connor looked at his mom. "Did you know that?"

Kathleen smiled. "Yes, hon, I knew."

"Well, why didn't you tell me? Dude"—he turned to Drake—"you have like a huge number of Christmases and birthdays to make up for. Imma make a list!"

He broke into laughter, and Kathleen joined him. Spencer was the only one who didn't crack at least a smile. Drake gave her a quick frown but turned back to Connor. "How about I buy you a car, and we can call it even?"

"Ooooh, yeah. Like a Porsche or a Ferrari or a Lamborghini. Ooooh, and I want a surfboard, like one of those really good ones. And I—"

"That's enough, you." Kathleen shook her head. "We can discuss it later. Now we need to get you to bed. Where are we sleeping?"

Logan smiled. "We've picked the suite directly across the hall for you two. It has two bedrooms but if you would prefer another room, you can choose from any on this floor."

"The whole floor?" Connor said. "Holy shit, Mom, did you hear that? We have the whole floor!"

"Watch your language!" Kathleen swatted her son on the arm.

Logan gestured for them to walk ahead. "I'll help set you all up. Please let me or one of the men stationed outside of your room know if you need anything. We'll make sure it is brought to you."

"Thank you," Kathleen said. She turned and gave Drake a big smile.

It was so good to see some genuine joy on her face. Drake knew, though, that it was temporary, and if it was ever going to be more than that, he was going to have to find a way to deal with Joe permanently.

CHAPTER FIFTEEN

Spencer cleared her throat. "I want to go over the security plans now."

"Of course." Gage pointed to the table. "We just finished reviewing the whole hotel."

"How long have you guys been here, Mitch?" Drake asked. "And how did you find me?"

Mitch grinned. "You didn't think you outsmarted us, did you? How long have we worked for you?"

"What Mitch means to say is we wanted to err on the side of caution in this situation, owing to the fact you were eager to be with your sister," Logan said as he re-entered the room.

"So he's the diplomatic one," Spencer leaned against the table and crossed her arms over her chest. "Who's in charge?"

"I am," all three brothers replied at once.

She sighed. She was all out of fucks to give at the moment, and the comedy routine was getting old. "Someone needs to tell me what the hell is going on. No one called you, so how are you here?"

Gage pulled out one of the dining table chairs and sat

down. "We assumed that Drake might be out of contact at some point during all of this, whether he planned to be or not, so we installed a tracker."

"A tracker?" Drake frowned. "But I've changed clothes, even shoes. There's nothing I am currently wearing that I had on when I was with you all." He stopped. "Wait, did you have that nurse shoot something into my blood stream?"

Spencer ground her teeth. "There is no tracker that can be deposited in the human body. It would need an energy source to work, and there are no batteries small enough."

"Yet." Mitch smiled.

"Yet," she agreed.

"So perhaps, Mitch, you can tell me exactly how you tracked me?" Drake's eyes narrowed.

Spencer tried not to smile, but she enjoyed the fact that Drake was pissed about this. At least she wasn't the only one annoyed at this point. His annoyance also meant he wasn't aware of being tracked, so he hadn't lied to her about it. That should make her feel better, but it didn't. Jameson Drake made her feel...unsettled, and she didn't like the sensation one bit.

Gage smiled slightly. "If you recall, the nurse got her bracelet caught on your watch. We had her do that on purpose. We put a tracker in with the battery. Don't worry, I know the watch is important to you. We didn't damage it but, it has allowed us to keep track of your whereabouts."

Drake frowned and touched his watch. His eyes narrowed before he shrugged. "Well, I will say I'm damn happy to see you. I didn't expect Joe's people to be waiting by the hotel for us. Stupid when I stop and think now. I guess I should've expected it. Where else would we go?"

"Many places," Spencer said, her voice hard.

"Well, we're here now," Drake growled.

"Perhaps you can fill us in. Who were those men chasing

you? I'm assuming they want your sister?" Gage asked. "And should we also assume they were the same men that were outside the house earlier?"

"You were there?"

"Of course. We kept track of you the whole time, and when we could have people close, we did. Some of our guys spooked the men in the BMW. They followed the men but lost them in some neighborhood."

"The answer to your question is yes. They were the same guys." Drake yawned. "Do you think it's possible we can pick this up in the morning? I need some sleep, and then I need to check in with work."

Gage nodded. "That'll be fine."

"Great. I'll head up to my suite."

Mitch shook his head. "Sorry. You need to use one of the rooms on this floor. No one stays on the top floor."

Drake downed the last swallow of his drink. "Why? Is there a problem?"

Mitch responded, "Security. Being on the top floor leaves us vulnerable to a breach from the roof." He turned to Spencer. "We have men on the roof and the floor above this one. They'll make sure no one gets in from above. We also cleared the floor below, and our men are stationed there as well. The elevators are locked off, and no one can come up the stairwell. It is heavily guarded by human and electronic resources."

Drake yawned again. "Well, it seems you have everything well in hand. I'll take the suite next door." He turned to go and then turned back. "Do I want to know what this is costing me?"

Mitch grinned. "No, you really don't."

"I thought not." He turned and left the room.

"Now, Ms. Gordon, let's go over the security." Logan

smiled as he moved around the table so he could view the schematics as well.

Spencer didn't return the smile but instead spent the next half hour grilling them on their security measures and why they made certain choices over others. In the end, she was satisfied. Damn impressed actually, but she didn't feel the need to share that with anyone, least of all Drake.

"Thank you for going over everything with me. Kathleen and Connor have been my responsibility for a long time. I need to know they're safe."

Gage nodded. "Understood. If you have any questions or suggestions, we're here."

"I appreciate that," she said, and she meant it. She had been in lots of situations where the powers that be didn't bother to take her as seriously as the men on the job, and that lack of respect drove her nuts. "What room should I use?"

Gage smiled. "Any of the ones closer to the center are better. We don't want anyone in the corners if we can avoid it."

"I understand. I'll take the one next to Kathleen and Connor across the hall."

"Which room is she taking?" Mitch asked as he got off his call.

"The one opposite Drake."

Mitch grunted in acknowledgment as he typed away on his phone.

"Good night, gentlemen," Spencer said and left the room. She went down the hall and opened the door on the left. Once inside, she leaned against the back of the door. It had been a long few days, and she was exhausted.

She pulled out her phone and dialed Will's number. It was very late, or very early, but she wanted to let him know

Connor wasn't going to school and, in fact, the job was over. Will could head home to his family. She would send him a bit of extra cash when she paid him. He had done an amazing job.

His phone went to voicemail, which didn't surprise her considering the lateness of the hour. She sent him a text and then made a mental note to follow up with him in the morning, or rather later this morning.

She straightened up and went over to the living room area. It was huge with gorgeous leather sofas and beautiful wooden tables. Koa wood by the looks of things. She loved koa. The whole suite exceeded expectations.

It contained a full kitchen with upscale stainless steel appliances to go with the luxurious living and dining area. A half bath on the left balanced out the bedroom on the right. She walked over and stopped in the doorway.

The bed was king-size and covered in pillows of all shapes and sizes. The comforter was creamy white, and the pillows had colorful tropical flowers. The curtains were all drawn, and she was tempted to pull them back to see the view, but she knew that wasn't a good idea. She would wait until morning.

She walked around the corner to the small hallway that led to the bathroom and stopped. A tub. A huge, beautiful white soaking tub in the middle of the bathroom. She would swear it called her name. Her apartment didn't have a tub. She hadn't had a bath in ages. She looked at her watch and groaned. Four in the morning. Now was not the time to have a bath. She wanted to be up in a few hours.

She sighed then went over to the vanity and ran her tongue over the fuzzy sweaters on her teeth. She needed her toothbrush. Come to think of it, where was her stuff? Her shoulders drooped. Everything was in the minivan. She'd have to go get it. Did she really need clean teeth? Yup. She couldn't sleep without brushing. She went back through the suite and opened the door to the hallway. A Callahan Security guy stood there with bags in his hands.

"Presumably, one of these is yours?" he asked.

"Um, y-yeah," she stammered. The man was drop-dead gorgeous. He was well over six feet with dark hair and ice-blue eyes. Sexy as hell, too. Where did they find *him*? How come all of her partners were aging, slightly overweight, balding men or just plain assholes? There really was no justice in this world.

He stood there staring at her, one eyebrow cocked. "Which one?"

Heat bloomed in Spencer's cheeks. She pointed. "That one?"

The door across the hall opened, and Drake stood there wearing just his jeans. His hair was wet, and his chest glistened as if he had gotten out of the shower a minute ago. He also looked drop-dead gorgeous. Life wasn't fair.

"Dragan, thanks. I was just about to come looking for that."

"No problem, Mr. Drake. Have a good night." Bags delivered, Dragan turned and went back down the hallway.

Spencer watched him go. He was fine coming and going.

"Got everything you need?" Drake asked.

"Um, yeah." When she looked at Drake, she realized he'd been watching her watch Dragan. God, even the name was sexy. Heat rushed up her neck again.

Drake dropped his bag in the room behind him and leaned on the doorframe. "I know you were upset with me when we got here. Why?"

She blinked. She'd been watching the muscles ripple across Drake's chest. It was as distracting as Dragan. Maybe even more so. "I, um, thought you had lied to me. That you knew your people were here, and they'd been here the whole time."

"I don't lie. I hate when people lie to me. I expect complete honesty, and I give it in return. I didn't know they were here, but I'm damn glad they are. I guess I should've known Joe's people would be waiting by the hotel but, honestly, I still think we're better off here than we are running."

She shrugged. "I don't know, but if I'm going to be honest, I will say your people are as impressive as you said. I do think Kathleen and Connor are safe here. At least for now." Her gaze locked with Drake's, and she noticed, not for the first time, that he had sexy green eyes. Bedroom eyes. What the hell was wrong with her? She must be more tired than she thought. "Sorry, what did you say?"

"I said, good night, Spencer. Sleep well."

"Yeah, you, too." She went back into her room and closed the door behind her. She needed to get a life. She was losing her marbles. When all this ended, she planned on going on a long vacation somewhere warm that didn't have Jameson Drake.

Spencer opened her eyes and had a moment of panic. *Where am I?* Then everything came crashing back. Drake's hotel in Oahu. She groaned and burrowed deeper into her pillows. The bed was divine, all soft and cozy. This was the way to live. She sighed contentedly and closed her eyes again. Just a few more minutes, and then she would get up and deal with everything.

But her eyes wouldn't stay closed. Her Type A personality took over, and she couldn't let everyone else manage what was, fundamentally, her job. Sure, Drake was Kathleen's brother, but Spencer had kept her and Connor safe for all these years, and she wasn't about to step back and let others do it. If they fucked up, the consequences were unthinkable.

She flipped back the covers and slid out of bed. She padded to the bathroom and had a shower, staying in quite a bit longer than she normally would've, but the shower head had a massage feature, and her shoulders were killing her from the stress of the last few months. Plus, the shampoo, conditioner, and body wash all smelled fantastic.

Finally, she got out and toweled off. She brushed out her hair and put it up in her normal bun. Then she looked at her clothing choices. Ugh. Nothing that she wanted to wear. She hadn't been thinking about vacation time when she packed for Hawaii, so she had only serviceable clothing that she could work and move freely in. She hadn't even thought to bring a bathing suit. This wasn't a vacation, even though, thanks to the accommodations, it felt like one.

She shrugged and pulled on a fresh pair of jeans and a navy tank top. At least it wasn't a big sweater. That was a plus.

She walked out of her room and made her way down the hall to the suite they had all used last night, but it was empty. Spencer went back to the hallway and was knocking on Kathleen's door just as one of the Callahan guys rolled up beside her.

She looked up and once again marveled at the good looks of the security team. Where did the Callahan brothers find these guys? This one was tall, dark, and hot. Not quite like the last one, but no slouch either. Good God, why did none of these guys work for Homeland? The job would be so much more interesting.

Spencer swallowed. "I'm sorry. I missed what you said."

The man had the gall to smirk before he said, "They're all on the deck eating breakfast."

"On the deck..." All thoughts of sex left her mind. She

ground her teeth. What the hell were they doing outside? "Where is the deck?"

"Down to the end of this hallway and take a right. You'll see the door."

Spencer turned on her heel and strode down the hallway at full speed. "What the fuck do they think they're playing at?" she growled as she rounded the corner and hit the door for the deck at full speed. The door bounced off the wall, and everyone looked up.

Her jaw dropped open. The view was incredible. The aqua colored ocean sparkled in the sun, but the surprising thing was the tent. They had put up an event tent that covered the whole deck. A dining area where everyone sat was on the left, and off to the right of that was the buffet. To the far left was a seating area that had a firepit with the same color glass as the ocean.

There were guards in all the corners and a few extra hovering by the food tables and close to the entry door. She blinked and walked out farther onto the deck. In front of the hotel, a little way offshore, were two Coast Guard vessels. That wasn't a coincidence. "How did you manage to get the Coast Guard to do guard duty?" she asked as Gage came to a stop beside her.

He smiled. "We have some friends in all kinds of interesting places. I gave them a call and asked if they could do their practice drills out here today. They were very accommodating, especially when I told them Drake would donate the cost of a new boat they've had their eye on."

"I bet they were." It was such a shock to see the tent and the Coast Guard. She'd been so scared that Kathleen and Connor were in danger. She laughed with relief.

"You really need to trust us," Gage said in a quiet voice. "I know it's hard. I understand you've been doing everything pretty much on your own these last few months, and not knowing who to trust just makes it so much harder."

He nodded toward Drake and Kathleen. "They filled us in this morning." He turned back to Spencer. "Trust us. We've got this. We will do our damnedest to make sure Kathleen and Connor are safe, as well as you and Drake. I'd say relax, but I know, in your shoes, there's no way I would do that. But at least try to rest up. Enjoy the downtime while you can."

Spencer nodded. She looked around the deck once more, still awed by what Drake's people had put together. The guy who'd given her the directions came out on the deck.

"Jake," Mitch called and tilted his head in a *come here* gesture. The man walked over and joined Mitch and Logan. Gage walked over as well.

"Aunt Spencer, you're finally up," Connor called. "Good thing, or you would've missed out on the pancakes. These are awesome." He left the buffet and went back to the table.

She smiled as she walked over to the table and took a seat next to Kathleen and across from Drake. "Morning."

"Morning, sleepy head. Nice of you to join us," Kathleen teased.

"Good morning," Drake said and then took a sip of coffee. "I trust you slept well."

"Yes, thank you." She nodded. Suddenly she didn't know what to say or do. She was always the one in charge, worrying about things, but now things were being taken care of by others. She sat quietly and forced herself to admire the ocean view.

"Would you like some coffee?" Kathleen asked as she stood.

"I'll get it in a second, thanks."

"It's no problem. I'll pour you a cup."

Connor stood up. "I want some more bacon to go with these pancakes. I'm coming, too."

"You're going to eat your uncle out of house and home." Kathleen laughed as they walked over to the buffet.

Drake smiled slightly at Spencer. "It's nice to see them relax a bit."

"Yes," she agreed.

"What about you? Do you ever relax?"

She tilted her head. "This from the man that works twenty-four-seven from what I hear."

He shrugged. "You shouldn't believe everything you hear." The phone on the table made a sound, and he picked it up and looked at the screen.

When had he had time to get a new phone? Probably one of his people brought extras.

She studied him. He wore a white button-down shirt with the sleeves rolled up and jeans. The hotel must've provided the shirt, but the jeans were the ones she picked out for him, and she'd noticed how well they fit him yesterday.

He was very sexy and had a reputation for always having a beautiful woman on his arm, but she'd heard rumors that he never dated any of them for more than a month or two. He didn't believe in commitment, or so they said.

Now that she knew him a bit, she decided it was more likely that he simply did not have time to devote to them or their see-and-be-seen lifestyle. But who was he really? A workaholic for sure. She'd observed him for a few days before he went to D.C., and he'd worked eighteen to twenty hours a day. Driven. Smart. Powerful. What did he do in his downtime? Did he actually ever take time off? Somehow she doubted it. She recognized these things in him because she was the same, but she also understood the value of taking a break. Did he?

"Do I pass inspection?" he asked, his voice low.

Caught! Remembering his words about honesty last night, she said, "I was thinking how you work to project the quintessential image of the successful businessman because you assume that is what people want to see, but I don't think that's who you are."

He looked up from his phone. "So"—his voice went softer still—"who am I?"

She was saved from having to answer the question by the arrival of Kathleen and her coffee. She sent Kathleen a grateful glance and then hid her burning cheeks behind her coffee cup. She couldn't have answered the question anyway. She didn't have a clue. Yet. But she was pretty sure she would enjoy finding out.

"Grab some breakfast, Aunt Spencer. The food is super good." Connor sat back down and gobbled a cookie.

"Who has cookies for breakfast?" Spencer asked.

"They do here. Isn't that great?"

"Just great," Kathleen rolled her eyes.

Spencer took another sip of coffee. "What's the plan for today?"

Kathleen smiled. "I'm getting a massage and a mani-pedi." She put her hand on Spencer's arm. "Please don't worry. They are bringing the people up from the spa, and security will be present at all times." She grinned and whispered, "Have you seen these guys? I don't mind them guarding me twenty-four-seven."

Spencer choked on her coffee. She'd been thinking the same thing, but it was odd to hear Kathleen say it. She grinned back at her friend. It was nice to see this side of her. It had been a long time since Kathleen had genuinely smiled.

Connor finished his third cookie. "I'm going to play video games. They have a great setup, and Mom said I could spend the whole day playing if I wanted."

She glanced at Kathleen, who shrugged. "We all need a bit of a lift after what's happened."

Spencer nodded in agreement. *Hell yes to that.* She turned to Drake. "And you? What are your plans for the day?"

"I have some business to take care of and then I have some video game butt to kick over there." He gestured toward his nephew.

"In your dreams," Connor responded, grinning ear to ear.

Drake smiled at his nephew and turned back to Spencer. "What about you? Would you like a massage or some spa treatment?"

She shook her head. "No. I have some calls to make, and then I want to speak with your security team in more depth about certain things."

Kathleen frowned. "Promise me you will at least think about taking one day off. A day to just enjoy this amazing place. Trust me, reality will still be there tomorrow."

She didn't want to kill the mood so she agreed. "Of course. There's a few details I have to iron out. I'll catch up to you all later. I'm going to sit and have a leisurely breakfast and admire this fabulous view."

"Okay then." Connor got up. "Let's go, Mom."

Kathleen stood as well. "Sounds good." She waved at her brother and Spencer and then left with her son. Several members of the security team went with them.

Drake started to say something, but his cell went off. He frowned as he answered the call. "Drake." A few seconds of silence followed and then, "That's not what I wanted to hear."

Spencer was glad it wasn't her on the end of that line.

Drake got up from the table, gave her a small wave, and disappeared inside.

She rose from her chair and went over to the buffet.

Might as well eat. She poured herself more coffee from the large urn there and took a look at all the food laid out. But she'd lost her appetite somehow. "What will happen to the leftovers?" she murmured.

"The hotel donates any leftovers it can to local food banks and homeless shelters. The rest is used for composting. Mr. Drake is keen to be as green as possible," replied the young man who stood by the buffet.

"That's nice." She took a sip of coffee but that, too, had lost its shine. She wasn't used to having free time on her hands. No, not being in charge was what was bothering her. She needed to pack up her ego and put it in her back pocket. It was okay to have some help.

She put her mug down and headed back to her room. A little time to readjust to the new order of things and she'd be fine. She also had to figure out what they were going to do long-term because, no matter how fabulous the hotel was, a gilded cage is still a cage. Kathleen and Connor wouldn't last long in it.

CHAPTER SIXTEEN

Drake put his feet up on the coffee table, rested his head on the back of the sofa, and closed his eyes. He was so tired everything hurt. The stressful business world he usually lived in had nothing on reuniting with his family and being shot at. How the hell did the Callahan clan do this type of thing?

For the first time ever, he was actually dreaming of a vacation. He hadn't thought about taking a real vacation since... He opened his eyes. Since his sister disappeared. All of his downtime had been with an eye on his email and a phone to his ear. That had to change. When everything was sorted, maybe he could convince Spencer to come with him. He smiled. Some R and R with her was just what he needed.

A knock sounded on his door, and he was immediately thankful that Mitch had decided to deactivate all the locks on the rooms they were occupying, at least during the daylight hours. He did not want to move. "Enter."

The door opened, and Gage walked in with Mitch trailing after him. Neither one looked happy.

"Is there a problem?" He immediately sat up straight, his

feet hitting the thick carpet with a soft thud, his heart giving a mighty thump in his chest.

Gage waved at him. "No, no. Go back to relaxing."

He leaned back into the cushions but didn't put his feet back on the table. Every instinct told him he was not going to like what was coming. "What's going on?"

Gage and Mitch settled on the chairs across from the couch. They glanced at each other, exchanging some sort of look before Mitch started speaking. "We've been poking around a bit, trying to get any background on this whole situation." He immediately held up his hands, "Discretely, of course. Logan is in charge, so you know he's being delicate and not making waves."

Drake frowned but nodded. Logan was a damn good lawyer and an even better negotiator, especially when things required a gentle touch. He had even mulled over offering Logan a job, but he didn't think Logan would accept. He'd heard a rumor that the man actually wanted to be a chef. "And?"

"The situation is worse than we thought."

"How can that be, Mitch? Joe wants Connor back and my sister dead. What's worse than that?"

Gage ran a hand through his hair. "A mob war."

Drake sat forward. "What?"

Gage grimaced. "It turns out that Giuseppe Senior, Joe's dad, was in control of a certain bit of territory on Staten Island, a family inheritance of sorts. When Kathleen testified against Joe Junior she put a big dent in the finances of Joe Senior and he lost control of the territory.

"This also tipped off the FBI about the underground gambling ring the Lucchese family had going to the tune of over two billion dollars. She wasn't laundering drug money. She was laundering cash for this gambling ring. She revealed the tip of the iceberg and, eventually, many members of the family went to prison over the ring a few years later."

"Jesus Christ." His mouth went dry. What the hell had his sister gotten involved in? He got up and started to pace. This was so much worse. "Do they hold her responsible for those arrests?"

"Fortunately, no," Mitch said.

"But," Gage cut in, "Joe Senior does hold her responsible for losing his patch of Staten Island. With Joe Junior out of prison, he wants the family patch back. He's appealed to the head of the Lucchese family, Vincenzo Tucci, to get it back. Tucci is an old family friend of Joe Senior, and he is said to be considering giving the business back to Joe. Joe Junior would need to clean up his mess first, though, if it were to happen."

"His mess being Kathleen and Connor." Drake went to the bar and stared at the bottles. It was barely noon, and he was already in need of a stiff drink. He reached for a Big Swell IPA, a local Hawaiian beer instead. He held up the bottle, but both Mitch and Gage shook their heads.

He opened the bottle and took a large swallow. He had rarely drank before all this mess started, but now, he was starting in the middle of the day. He needed to get a hold of himself. Son-of-a bitch, this was such a fucking mess. How could it be this bad?

Gage continued, "The current man in control of all the Staten Island business that now includes Joe Senior's old patch is Angelo Russo, who does not want to give the business back."

"What's the bottom line?" Drake demanded. This was making his head spin.

"Joe wants to kill Kathleen and get Connor so he can get his family's territory back and present an heir. Russo wants to kill both Kathleen and Connor so he closes the door on losing his territory back to the Caridi family once and for all."

Drake nearly drained his beer in one gulp. He leaned on the bar. "So what you're telling me is there are two rival groups, both out to kill Kathleen and kidnap and/or kill Connor."

"Yes." Mitch shifted in his seat and frowned.

"What else? I can tell by your expression there's more."

Mitch gave a small nod. "Joe Senior's other son, Roberto, has spent his life building up the family's ties with the Cosa Nostra. Their mom is Sicilian, and her branch of the family is heavily connected. Joe Senior and his bride, Lucia Navarra, were a match made in mob business heaven. The five families in New York, including the Lucchese's, had their roots in the Cosa Nostra. This marriage helped solidify the relationship."

"So what are you telling me?"

"Roberto is calling in reinforcements from Italy to make this happen for his family."

Drake rubbed his eyes with the heels of his palms as the beer turned sour in his gut. "Jesus fucking Christ!" He took a deep breath. Un-fucking-believable!

"Yes," Gage said in agreement, "but we'll figure all of this out because the alternative is unacceptable."

Straightening slowly to his full height, Drake nodded. What Gage said was the truth of the matter. He wasn't losing his family again. He'd just found them. They would find a way out of this mess because the alternative really was unacceptable.

"Call Spencer. We have to bring her in on this. And get Logan here. I want all heads together. We need to come up with some alternatives. Don't tell Kathleen or Connor. We need to present them with a final plan. All of this will be too much to cope with otherwise. They've been through enough. Let's meet in the other room in thirty minutes."

Mitch and Gage stood up and headed for the door. They recognized a dismissal when they heard one. Drake stood at the bar and watched them go. When the door closed behind them, he let out the breath he'd been holding. He wanted to yell and throw things. Destroy the whole fucking room. The hotel was his, and he could do whatever the fuck he wanted. He let the rage flow through his veins. It washed over him as he imagined all the things he would like to do to Giuseppe Caridi Jr. and his whole family.

His hands shook. He picked up the beer and brought it back to throw it, but put it back down. A violent, childish reaction wouldn't solve anything and would just make his suite smell like beer. His heart thudded in his chest.

He dropped and started doing push-ups. He'd done the same when he'd lost his sister and couldn't control his emotions. Physical exertion brought everything back under control and in focus. He thought he'd outgrown the necessity of this type of release years ago, but this situation was out of control.

He lost count of the push-ups. He just kept going until his arms wouldn't lift him any longer and his body was slick with sweat. His shirt clung to him. But his mind was clear, and the terminal rage had passed. He was going to free his family once and for all from this cluster-fuck, no matter what it took. He stood up and went to shower.

Five minutes later, he walked into the room next door freshly showered with a new white shirt, new jeans, and a new ice-cold perspective on how this was going to work. "Spencer, did they fill you in?" he asked as he approached the table.

Her eyes narrowed, but she shook her head.

"Gage, Mitch, fill Spencer in on the details. Logan, I ordered coffee and lunch. Can you check on it and get an

ETA and then come find me in the kitchen?" With that, he turned and walked into the kitchen area.

This was a larger suite so there was a full and separate kitchen. He opened the fridge and pulled out a few bottles of water. He was setting them on the counter when Logan entered. "Lunch is about thirty minutes out."

Drake gave a curt nod. "I appreciate you gathering all of that information. You did an excellent job. I told everyone at the head office that I am conducting a full review of all my hotels, starting with this one in Hawaii. I will be in and out of touch since this requires my full attention. They understand and will leave me alone, but I need a lawyer from my head office to be here ASAP. I don't want anyone to know he's here. There are reasons for this, but I'll explain later. As far as anyone is concerned, he's over in the Far East on business. Can you do it?"

Logan nodded. "Of course. I'll have him here in the next twenty-four hours."

"Good. I also need to track down Enzo Valardi. He will be easy to find but hard to approach. You might need to go in person. I'm not sure he will accept a phone call. When you do speak to him, tell him 'Uptown Slick' is looking for him. That should be enough to get him to co-operate. And Logan, do this as quietly as possible. I don't want anyone to know."

Logan cocked an eyebrow but said nothing. Drake appreciated the man's understanding. He was smart enough to know now wasn't the time to ask. "Also, I want you and the others to put your whole team on standby, including Lacy. I'm aware her father is officially out of the arms-dealing business, but if this turns into a war, we will need firepower.

Logan's lips thinned. "Do you think that's a likely scenario?"

He shrugged. "I want to be prepared for anything and everything."

Logan gave another curt nod. "Okay then. I'll start making calls. Is there anything else?"

"Not yet, but there will be."

Logan left the kitchen. Drake picked up the water and headed back to the dining room where the team were all seated around the table. Satisfaction grew in his gut, knowing he was taking steps to protect his family, that he had the right people in his corner to do what it would take. He put the water in the middle of the table. "Are we all caught up?"

Spencer nodded. "This is more complicated than I thought. We're going to need reinforcements."

"Agreed, but not the kind you're thinking of." He stood at the head of the table. "We need to explore various scenarios. I want plans A through Z that solve this problem. I don't want to bring in any authorities for many reasons, not the least of which is that there's a mole in the U.S. Marshals Service. And there could be more out there.

"We're dealing with the mob both localized to the New York area, but also the Cosa Nostra. I doubt this is a huge issue for them. I can't see them wanting to get that involved, but if Kathleen and Connor are pawns in a bigger turf war that expands into Cosa Nostra's world, we need to be prepared for anything. To that end, I asked Logan to contact Lacy and her father. We may need firepower in a hurry."

Spencer frowned. "I know who Lacy is, Logan's girlfriend, but who is her father?"

"Armand Fontaine," Gage said.

Spencer's eyebrows went sky-high. "The arms dealer?"

Gage nodded.

"Jesus, do you really think that's a good idea? We don't want to attract attention." She shook her head. "This is getting out of control. An arms dealer. Kathleen and Connor don't need any more exposure than they already have. It's too much." She stood up. "I'll take them, and we'll hide somewhere else. They don't need more danger."

Drake reeled on her. "You won't take them anywhere. They are safe here, and they will remain that way as long as we're smart. Fontaine is the least of our worries. Do you not understand that Roberto Caridi is bringing in the Cosa Nostra? The Sicilian mafia? This is no longer about some small potatoes mob shit on Staten Island.

"This is about the Sicilian mafia strengthening their ties with New York. Their ties extend all the way around the world. They are linked to the Zetas cartel in South America and certain terrorist organizations in the Middle East. Their fingers are in most pies in Europe. This is their way of adding to their empire. It starts with them taking a small bit of territory and business, and then it grows. Kathleen and Connor are just obstacles."

His gut clenched. He knew how ruthless he could be in dealing with issues that stopped him from getting what he wanted. The shitstorm that would ensue if the mob saw his family as just a bump in the road on their way to achieving their goal would be monumental.

Spencer's eyes snapped sparks at him. She was pissed, but he didn't give a fuck. She needed to know that this was no longer her world. This was his. She might know her shit with the witness protection program, but this—this was fundamentally a business situation, and that was his domain.

He held up a hand, staving off her question. "Look, I'm working on limiting the Cosa Nostra's involvement, but until I know for sure, we have to assume they will be a player in this shit-show. We need the extra firepower." He turned back to address Mitch and Gage. "We also need to look at establishing new identities for Kathleen and Connor just in case we can't get this sorted.

"Due to the mob's connections, I would suggest we relocate them to the Far East. I have connections there that can help, but having an American or Canadian or EU passport would be better. Do either of you have any contacts who can make this happen?"

Mitch grabbed his phone off the table. "I think Alex can get them passports. Let me call her and get that ball rolling."

Gage added, "If she doesn't know, I might have a contact that can create something that will be good enough to get them set up somewhere. They would need to stay put after that, though."

Mitch nodded and walked away with his phone to his ear.

Gage leaned back in his chair. "If we go that route, it will be necessary for them to cut ties with everyone again. You understand that, don't you?"

Drake ground his teeth. "We'll see." He would cross that bridge if they had to. "Spencer, we need to figure out who the mole is. We don't want them giving away any more information. It doesn't matter if they don't know where Kathleen and Connor are anymore. We don't want them ratting anyone else out. Lives are at stake."

She hesitated and then nodded. "I have some ideas."

"Good. What can I do to help?"

"Just get me a couple of burner phones, and I should be good."

Drake looked at Gage, who nodded. "No problem. Ask Jake for a few. He has a stash."

"Okay," Spencer sat back down. "But what do we do now?"

"Now?" Gage ran a hand through his hair. "Now we do nothing."

Drake frowned. He wasn't good at doing nothing.

Gage shrugged. "We're in a holding pattern until we can get more information. Spencer, if you can find out who shot at you and which crew they belong to, that would be very helpful.

"Also, if you can find out passenger manifests onto Oahu, we can find out if both sides have people already on the island or not. Every bit of intelligence on this helps. Until we're in possession of all the facts around this, it's crazy to move. Kathleen and Connor are safe."

The sound of rattling dishes reached his ears, and Drake turned to see the carts of food being brought into the room. He moved away from the table so it could be set up for lunch. When he looked at the faces of the waitstaff, he didn't recognize any of them, which made him nervous. Jesus, it sucked not to trust anyone. Would he ever be able to truly relax and trust again?

Gage bumped his elbow. "Don't worry. They're Callahan Security personnel. They are working as hotel staff just in case."

"In case of what?"

Gage hesitated. "If I were Joe or Russo, I would put some of my people undercover as guests in the hotel. There's no better way to find out how the hotel operates. They need that kind of information if they want to do anything on-site.

"Also, they know the odds are against them, but they could catch a lucky break and manage to create an unplanned opportunity to grab Kathleen and Connor. It's a smart play to have someone here."

Drake swore. Gage was right. He did it all the time. He sent spies into other hotels to see how they operated and find out if there was any intelligence he could gather from the staff before making an offer to buy the place.

Sometimes, he got lucky and found out some personal nugget that the world didn't know, and it helped him close the deal. He had to get his head out of his ass and stop thinking of this as Kathleen and Connor, his family. He had to start thinking of this as a business deal.

Seeing it from all angles was crucial if they were going to be successful. And he was damn sure they were going to make this happen. Kathleen and Connor deserved a life free of fear. He would make sure they had one, even if it killed him.

CHAPTER SEVENTEEN

"Uptown Slick. How many years has it been?" Enzo Valardi' s voice came down the phone line. "I have to say, I was quite surprised when your man reached out to me."

Emotion hit Drake like a rogue wave. This man had been his best friend and his lifeline at a point in his life when he needed both. They'd become each other's family in the eighteen months they'd hung out. "Been a long time, Enzo." His voice was thick with the memories.

"Way fucking too long." Enzo agreed. He was feeling it, too. The two men let it settle for a moment, silently acknowledging their shared history. "So, I'm gathering this is not a social call. What's going on?"

"Remember how I wanted to find my sister?"

"The one everyone else said was dead? Yeah, I remember. It's your obsession."

He took a deep breath and fought to control his emotions. "I found her, Enzo. Or rather, she found me." The silence spoke volumes. He knew his friend was concerned for him. "It's really her, Enzo, and she has a kid."

"Well, that's great news, Jamie. I'm happy for you. Family

is everything. We should get together and celebrate."

Jamie. Kathleen called him that and now Enzo. He'd forgotten what it was like to be Jamie Drake. Somewhere along the way he'd become too serious, too caught up in business. Jamie disappeared and Jameson took over. Hearing the nickname now made him smile. "I would really like that, Enzo, but that's impossible at the moment. Kathleen was in witness protection. That's why she disappeared. She got in over her head with the wrong people, and she had to testify against them to get out."

"I see." Enzo's voice changed. It became more guarded, slightly cooler.

He'd expected it, but it still stung. "Hear me out." He went on to explain the whole story to his old friend.

"Jesus, Jamie. That's a tough one. I'm not sure how I can help you."

"I know. It's a fucking mess, Enzo. I wouldn't ask if we weren't up against it. Like you said, family is everything."

Enzo let out a breath. "Jamie, I owe you my life and more, but I can't get involved in this mess. I can't step in and save your sister. I don't have the authority to call off a hit. The Caridis are not my people. Tucci might be in jail, but he's still the head of the family as I understand it, and he's not one of ours either."

"I know, Enzo, and that's not what I'm asking. I need you to stop the Cosa Nostra from being involved. Roberto Caridi is trying to get them to help. He's been working the connection for years. I guess they're all related on his mother's side of the family. I don't want to take on the whole of the Sicilian mob if I don't have to."

"Roberto Caridi. I know him. Unfortunately. He's been doing deals for the guys in Sicily since he graduated college. He's one of their Capos. They'll have to send people out of respect if he asks for help."

"Right, and if we take care of those people, then it will turn into an all-out war between me and them. I don't want that, but I will do what I have to. That's why I need you to broker a deal. Ask them to leave the new world to work things out for themselves. Keep their noses out of it."

"Jamie, it's not that easy. To them, it's a matter of pride. They take care of their own. Roberto needs help, they have to help."

"But, fundamentally, they are a business, and I understand business. So I need you to negotiate."

Enzo asked, "What did you have in mind?"

"What do you think they'd want?"

"From you? Jesus, Jamie, they could want it all."

His gut tightened. "They aren't going to get it." He loved his family, but business and deals were what made his blood pump and his soul sing. He'd worked too fucking hard to give it up to the mob without one hell of a fight. "Open negotiations for me, Enzo. Do it with the top brass so Roberto doesn't find out until it's done. I don't want any more interference in this than necessary."

"Say we get this deal done, what are you going to do about the rest of the problem? Old man Caridi is not going down without a fight."

"I've got ideas. I can handle the local guys, but I just don't want to take on the whole fucking Sicilian mob if I don't have to."

"Okay, Jamie, I'll do what I can. Stay by the phone," Enzo said and then ended the call.

Drake put down the burner cell and smiled. Having Enzo on board definitely gave him an edge. He was far enough up the food chain of the Italian mob that he had clout. They would listen to him and take him seriously. That was all Drake needed. He was confident he could make a deal with the Cosa Nostra without losing his shirt.

CHAPTER EIGHTEEN

Spencer stared at the food and realized two things. One, she was ravenous and, two, she was livid. Being given small tasks to keep her busy but kept out of the main action was insulting.

Drake was across the room talking to Gage. He was so fucking frustrating the way he commanded every room he walked into. It made her want to scream. The fact that it made him even more alluring drove her nuts. He was sexy enough as it was.

She started in his direction and then stopped and turned when she heard Kathleen's voice. There was no need to upset Kathleen by having a blowup with her brother in front of her. Spencer would save it for later.

Kathleen came around the corner, wearing a bathrobe and slippers. Her face had a slight impression of a ring around it. Had to be from the pillow she'd lain on for her massage. She looked happy. It was nice to see, but it made Spencer's belly roll. Soon enough, all of that joy was going to disappear. Once they told Kathleen the extent of the trouble, she would be devastated once more.

"Don't even think about it." Drake's voice was low in her ear.

Spencer whirled around to face him. He was closer than she anticipated, and she had to put a hand on his chest to stop herself from falling into him.

Drake covered her hand with his. "Don't even think about telling Kathleen what we've discovered. She deserves this break. She needs some time to relax. No one can live running on adrenaline for this long. She needs to regroup. Connor is the same. They need downtime."

"I know, but they also deserve to know the truth." She frowned. "Wait. Weren't you the one that insisted on bringing Connor in on all the decision-making in the first place?"

He nodded. "And I stand by that. But we don't have all of the information yet. Let's give them a bit more time. Once we have all the details, we'll fill them in."

He captured her gaze. His green eyes pleaded with her. His heart beat a steady rhythm under her hand. Electricity danced across her skin where his hand covered hers. They were so close his body heat hit her in waves. The scent of the hotel shampoo tickled her nose. Being near him like this was not good for her. His presence made her lose her focus. Those eyes made her want to agree with anything, but she was still so pissed off.

"You need to stop dismissing me. I know what I'm doing. I've been keeping them alive since long before you were on the scene. You send me off to find flight manifests and deal with the mole while you take care of business. Do you think I'm stupid?"

"No. Quite the contrary. I think you've done an amazing job, but I think you're exhausted. You've been doing it on your own for so long you've forgotten how to ask for help. How to be part of a team. You need to relax and recharge, too. You're no good to Kathleen and Connor if you're so tired you can't think straight."

His voice was low, and it sent shivers down her spine. She wanted to say, "No, you're wrong," but in her heart of hearts, she knew he was right. Exhaustion was clouding her thoughts so much so that she'd driven them to the hotel without an escort. Where else on Oahu would they be as well protected? Obviously, Joe had realized that before she did

"Hey, Uncle Jamie. Are you ready to get your butt kicked in *Dark Knight Overlord* after lunch?" Connor asked as he walked across the room toward the dining table. "Oh, great, food! I'm starving."

Spencer stepped back from Drake. She needed some space to get her thoughts together. He was overwhelming to her senses. She turned to find Kathleen staring at her with an amused expression. *Oh, shit.* Kathleen knew her too well. It was bad enough having to deal with Drake, but having his sister cheering for them to hook up from the sidelines would be a nightmare.

Spencer walked to the dining table and stood next to Connor. "Didn't you just finish breakfast? How can you be hungry?" she said. Her voice was a bit husky to her own ears. She cleared her throat. "It all looks delicious." She grabbed a plate and filled it up with random foods in her rush to get out of there. She turned and headed to the door.

"You aren't staying to eat with us?" Kathleen asked.

"Um, no, sorry. I have some calls to make." She gave Kathleen a quick smile and made her exit. She hit her room door just as Jake showed up with several phones in his hands. "Oh, thanks." She opened the door. "If you can just drop them on the counter, that would be great."

Jake did as instructed. "Let me know if you need more." He gave her a nod and then left.

"Need more?" she mumbled as she stared at the four phones on the counter. Just how many burner phones did the Callahan crew bring? She shook her head. Probably better if she didn't ask.

She set her food on the breakfast bar and plopped down on a stool. The combination of foods on her plate was bizarre now that she looked at it, but it didn't really matter because she'd lost her appetite again. Hummus and lettuce? Moving food around her plate wasn't going to cut it. She knew she had to eat if she was going to be able to focus. Her brain and body demanded food.

She took a few bites of the lettuce and added hummus and then a few more of poké. Hawaiians always knew how to make the best poké. It was delicious, for sure. She craved it when she was on the mainland. She tried a few other items and ended up clearing her plate.

She put the plate in the sink and filled the coffee maker. No need to go back over to the other room for caffeine. She didn't want to bump into Drake again because she wasn't sure she trusted herself not to do something stupid like yell at him or kiss him. The jury was out at the moment as to which instinct would win. Better not to engage at all. She called Will and left him a message while she waited for the coffee.

Once her body was fueled and the burnt bean smell was in the air, she focused on the problem of the mole. When Joe Junior had first shown up on Kathleen's doorstep, she'd thought maybe Kathleen had accidentally gotten her picture or Connor's picture in the paper or online somewhere, and he'd found her that way. Then when he found her at the safe house two weeks later, she knew there had to be an inside man. Or woman. There was no other way for it to happen.

All of the law enforcement agencies knew it, too, because all the finger-pointing started. The FBI said it was the

Marshals' fault, but the Marshals claimed it had to be someone at the DA's office in New York that leaked it, although why would the Southern District of New York know where Kathleen and Connor were located?

Either way, it was somebody else's fault. Then the Marshals Service's top brass came out and said the system had been hacked. Someone out there had accessed Kathleen's file remotely.

That hadn't sat right with Spencer, either. If some unknown hacker had accessed the files, then why only take Kathleen's? Why not access them all and sell the information? There was a lot of money to be made for the hacker that they simply passed up.

She didn't buy it.

She poured herself some coffee, then went and sat down on the sofa. There were lots of former mobsters in hiding. Some of them had even turned state's evidence on the Lucchese family, so wouldn't those files have been pulled as well?

She took a sip of coffee and then put her mug down on the low table in front of the sofa. She sank back and rested her head on the couch's cushions. She propped her feet on the coffee table.

So think like a criminal, Spencer. What would you do if you wanted Kathleen's file? Well, if it wasn't a hacker, then it was someone who tried to make it *look* like the files had been hacked. Someone who had access and knew all about Kathleen and Connor's file. Someone smart enough to know how to cover their tracks.

She closed her eyes. Every time a file was accessed, it was noted in a log—date, time, and also who opened the file. If someone knew this and didn't want their name to come up, then hiding their tracks by making it look like a hacker would be a great cover. No one would bother looking back at who else had accessed the file and ask questions about it. An investigation into the mysterious hacker would automatically be started. Pressure would be off.

Her mind swirled as she tried to sort through the order of events and who would have the knowledge and the smarts to cover their tracks so well. She let her mind go and drifted off into a fitful sleep.

Spencer bolted upright on the sofa. Her heart hammered in her chest; her breath came in gasps. Memories flashed through her mind. Little snippets of conversations along with snapshots of people and places. The mole had been put in place a long time ago. The whole picture was right there in front of her, and it was scary as hell.

She glanced at the clock. She'd been asleep for a few hours. It was almost time for dinner. She hopped up off the sofa and grabbed her laptop. She did a little bit of research just to make sure, but she knew it to her very marrow. After confirming her suspicions, she freshened up in the bathroom and then went in search of Drake.

"Hey, we were just about to come looking for you." Kathleen smiled at her as she entered the suite across the hall. "How was the rest of your day? Did you get your calls made?"

Spencer smiled. "Yes, I made a few calls and then had a nap. You look wonderful. Your skin is glowing."

Kathleen tilted her face to catch the light. "Isn't it fabulous? They have all of these wraps at the spa, so I decided to do that instead of the mani-pedi. I swear they peeled ten years of wrinkles off my face. It was so relaxing! I think I might go back tomorrow and do my nails. They said they could fit me in."

"Sounds like fun, but wait, I thought Drake was bringing the people up here to perform the services."

Kathleen blushed. "I know, and he was, but then the

women who were here mentioned about the wraps and I wanted to try them. They couldn't bring all that stuff up so they cleared the spa for me. I know it's wrong, and I feel guilty that all of those appointments had to be rescheduled. It was ridiculous and selfish of me to do that."

Spencer's gut knotted. She'd made her friend feel bad without meaning to. "Kathleen, I am positive your brother made sure these people were more than compensated for any inconvenience they experienced. After everything you've been through, you deserve a day at the spa. Don't feel guilty about it. Just enjoy it."

Relief flashed across Kathleen's face. "Do you really think it was okay?"

"I do, and I bet if you ask your brother, he'll even tell you all the wonderful benefits he gave the people who had to reschedule.

"Oh, that's a good idea." Kathleen's smile was back. "You should join me tomorrow, Spencer. It's so nice to be pampered."

"You lost fair and square! I'm just better than you are, old man. Suck it up." Connor's voice floated into the room as he and Drake rounded the corner.

"I lost by two lousy points. I wouldn't get too excited there, kiddo."

Connor practically bounded over to Kathleen like the young puppy he was. "Mom, it was epic! I smoked him. You should've seen it."

"Two points. Don't let him tell you any different." Drake grinned.

Spencer smiled. They really were a family, and it was nice to see them together. Drake looked relaxed. The tension around his eyes and mouth had eased, and his smile was infectious. His green eyes sparkled with laughter as his nephew explained in excruciating detail what happened during the game.

Her heart gave a small lurch in her chest. To be part of a real family. Someday. She thought she'd been close once, but it had turned into a disaster. Kathleen had helped her through it. Now she was envious, standing here watching them.

It was important to Drake to have his family back together. Although she'd never had a family like that, she understood the joy it must bring him to be close to people who he had a shared history with. The sort of shorthand Kathleen and Drake had fallen back into when they chatted with each other was charming. It was as if the last sixteen years hadn't happened.

Spencer rounded the dining table and pulled out a chair in front of an empty place setting. It made her feel better to have her back to the wall, but it also gave them some space.

It must be horrible to have to have strangers in their world twenty-four-seven. It was exhausting and off-putting and intrusive no matter who they were or how much anyone tried to pretend anything otherwise. She'd had it almost her whole life. Her father had been a senator in D.C. for years and on some of the top committees, and her mother had been an ambassador to several different countries over the years.

She'd spent most of her childhood flying back and forth between them for special events where family was a necessary accessory and, of course, there was always an aide or a staff member to accompany her. Those people saw her parents more than she did. Their housekeeper had really raised Spencer, and she was the woman Spencer had thought of as her closest family member until she died ten years ago.

Lost in thought, Spencer startled when a glass of white

wine was placed in front of her. She looked up to find Drake smiling. "I thought you might like a glass."

She smiled. "Yes, I think I would tonight."

He frowned slightly. "Everything okay?"

She paused. "Um, yes. It's just..." Out of the corner of her eye, she caught a glimpse of Connor and Kathleen laughing. "It's all fine. Thanks for the wine."

Gage and Mitch entered the room, followed by the wait staff pushing various carts. They were overloaded as usual. Dinner was served, and they all spent the next couple of hours chatting and pretending that the world didn't exist. Like they were all friends getting together for a nice meal and good company.

After dinner, Connor pulled Spencer over to his and Kathleen's room for a *Fast and Furious* marathon. She tried to pay attention, but it was too hard to concentrate. Her mind kept swirling around Eddie being the mole. Her former boss and mentor at the Marshals Service, a man who'd sworn to protect a witness had actually been the one to sell out Kathleen. She could barely get her brain around it. Was there a way to prove he was the rat? Did it even matter now? Finally, at a little after ten, she gave up and begged off. In the hallway, she bumped into Dragan. "Is Drake in his room? I need to speak to him."

"He's gone up a floor for a swim."

She blinked. A night swim sounded perfect. She was restless and needed to work off some of her nervous energy. "Um, are we okay to do that?"

Dragan smiled. "You should be fine." He gave her directions, and she went down the hall. Two minutes later, she walked out onto the pool deck. It was breathtaking. An infinity pool overlooked the ocean. There was a slight breeze, and the sound of waves crashing on the shore was music to her ears. She inhaled deeply.

"Did you need me for something?"

She jumped. So enthralled with the view and the ocean, she hadn't heard Drake approach. She whirled toward him and lost her breath again. Drake stood there in a pair of navy board shorts and nothing else. He was every bit as sexy in person as he was in her mind. His chest glistened in the light from around the pool. A lock of hair flopped over his forehead, and she had the urge to brush it off.

"I...was thinking a swim sounded like a good idea. Do you know where I can get a bathing suit?"

Drake lifted his chin to indicate the sliding door. "Back inside, down the hallway, second door on the left. There should be some new ones in one of the drawers. It's a guest bedroom. I keep extras in there."

"Thanks," she mumbled and went in search of the suit. She found the room and took a second to regroup. She really needed to get a hold of herself. Every time she saw Drake without a shirt, she seemed to lose her mind. It was ridiculous. She sighed. Too much time worrying about everything and not enough time spent enjoying life. That was the problem.

She pulled out drawers until she found the one with the bathing suits, and then she sorted through them. There were all kinds of bikinis in a variety of sizes and shapes. She chose an emerald green one in her size and slipped it on.

It was a bit more revealing than she was used to. The triangle top didn't cover as much as she would have liked, but the high-cut bottoms made her legs look nice and long. All in all, it was a good fit. She made her way back to the pool area.

Drake was leaning on the edge of the pool, looking out at the ocean. "Mind if I join you?" she said.

When he turned, she felt, rather than heard, his swift intake of air. His eyes roamed all over her in a way that was far more intimate than she was expecting. His gaze locked with hers, and a frisson of electricity passed between them. Her stomach rolled like she was on a ride at the fair, and every nerve ending tingled.

"I see you found the bathing suits. That one looks spectacular on you. Green is your color."

"Thanks," she said as she stuck a toe in the water. It was warmer than she anticipated.

"I keep it quite warm. Better for my muscles to stay warm while I swim laps."

"It's the perfect temperature." Spencer didn't know what to say. It was like being an awkward teenager again, and she didn't know why. She moved the rest of the way into the pool. It was so warm and inviting, she couldn't resist dropping down immediately so the water was up to her neck. "This is amazing. The view is incredible."

Drake nodded. "Yes, this is one of my favorite places."

"You must travel a lot. Do you have a favorite hotel?" She needed to get back to neutral ground. Anything to feel less...unsettled.

"I do travel a lot but, to be honest, not for pleasure. Hawaii is one of the few places I ever take time to relax a bit. Mostly, it's just business meetings and conference calls."

She bounced around in the shallow end, keeping low in the water. Less exposed and surrounded by warm water, she was content to maintain her distance.

"You seemed to want to say something earlier. Is everything okay?"

That brought her back down to earth with a bang. That's what she wanted. *Right?* "I think I know who the mole is."

Drake's eyebrows went up. "Who?"

"My old boss, Eddie Miller."

"Okay, why do you think it's him?"

Spencer looked out at the waves while she tried to get her

thoughts together. She'd fallen asleep thinking about the problem and woken up with the solution. It wasn't the first time this had happened to her. Sometimes she needed her subconscious to put together the pieces of the puzzle without interference from her conscious mind.

"It was right in front of me the whole time, I think. I just couldn't see it. Eddie was my mentor at the Marshals Service. He took me under his wing and taught me the ropes. He taught me how to be good at my job. When Kathleen called me, he was the first person I turned to. It was automatic. But when I look back at the order of events of what happened with Kathleen, it could only be Eddie."

"Why?"

The weight of Drake's stare was making her heart even heavier. It felt traitorous to even speak the words. "I'd been in the service for a couple of years, and Eddie had been with me every step of the way, mentoring me. Then he assigned me to Kathleen. There was no real reason to make the switch from the other team now that I look back on it, but I didn't question it at the time. He had me get close to Kathleen, closer than we're supposed to get. I did ask him about it, but he said he felt badly for her, and he knew we would connect. I let it go. He was right. We did connect.

"No one was more surprised than Eddie when I decided to leave the Marshals. I usually checked every decision with him. We discussed everything. It was one of the reasons I left, actually. It was like having a big brother always looking out for me. I never truly felt like I was doing the job on my own. It was stupid, but there was pressure from my folks and…" Spencer stopped. Drake didn't need to hear all of her shit. "Anyway, he was quite upset when I told him I was leaving. I thought it was because we were close, but now I'm not so sure."

She turned back to face Drake. "Eddie was passed over

for promotion a couple of times. He said it was because he pissed off his boss. Some sort of in-house political thing, but I'm thinking there's more to it. Anyway, he was not necessarily happy at the Marshals. I wondered why he stayed. He said it was because he liked the work. His explanation always rang hollow for me."

"I don't think I'm following you, Spencer. What does this have to do with Kathleen?"

She moved deeper into the middle of the pool, closer to Drake who was still hanging on the edge watching her. "Sorry, I'm rambling. Eddie's background is in IT. He worked cybercrime before he transferred to the Marshals and got involved in the WitSec program. He would know how to make it look like the system was hacked."

"A background in cybercrime doesn't necessarily mean he's the mole. Maybe he's just unhappy with his job."

"No, I think it's a setup from the very beginning." She floated over to lean on the side of the pool next to Drake.

Drake turned to face her and frowned. "Spencer—"

"Here me out. Eddie's got a background in cybercrime, and he encouraged me to be extra close to Kathleen, which was against the rules. He was the one who picked the original place for Kathleen and then the safe house.

"The worst part is I called him for help when we got to the second safe house. We needed more people to help protect them after Joe found her at the first one. I didn't call him as a marshal, but as a friend. And we barely got out with our lives. I'd called another marshal who was also a friend to come help, too, and he wasn't so lucky. He got shot and is still recovering. He's going to have to take early retirement.

"At first, I thought they planted some sort of tracking device on me or my car, but then the whole hacker theory emerged. I thought the hacker must have found me somehow, but now I think it was me, my fault. I called Eddie, who then called Joe."

"This is all circumstantial."

Spencer nodded. "Well, here's one more piece of circumstantial evidence. Eddie's real name is Eduardo, and his mother's maiden name is Navarra."

CHAPTER NINETEEN

"Son of a bitch! Are you sure they're related?"

Spencer nodded. "I double-checked. Eddie's mom is Joe's mom's sister."

Drake's knuckles turned white on the edge of the pool. His mind was making all of the connections she'd made earlier. It sucked; there was no doubt. His sister and nephew had never been safe, and it was partially her fault.

"And no one caught this?"

"Why would they?" she asked. "He's Eddie Miller. He came from another agency. He had an exemplary record and was well-liked. A background search would only turn up that his mother was Italian. So what?

"I think…from the minute Kathleen testified, they found a way to put Eddie in place to keep an eye on her. There was no point in killing her until Joe got out. Who would take Connor? They didn't want him to be raised in foster care, and Joe would want to kill her himself.

"Eddie fed Joe and his family information over the years about Kathleen and Connor, which he got from me. He used to ask me about them all the time. And then, when Joe got out, the plan was put into play. Joe knew exactly where to find Kathleen and his son, and he made a beeline for them."

"Fuck! Kathleen and Connor had never really been safe. Do you think anyone else is on to him?"

"I think there are a lot of eyes on this now. I'm not sure if anyone else has put the pieces together yet, but they will. His days are numbered, but the question is, how much more damage will he do?"

Drake nodded. "I'm sorry."

"What?" She frowned. "What are you sorry for?"

"I know you kept Kathleen and Connor safe for years. I didn't mean—"

"No, you were right. They were always in danger, and I carry some blame in that."

He shook his head. "No, you don't. You did your job and followed the rules. You assumed your boss was a good guy. That's what you're supposed to do. You've had the rug pulled out from underneath you. Someone you trusted has betrayed you. It's not your fault. None of this is your fault. This situation is…unsettling at best. At worst, it can be catastrophic. Don't let it. Don't let him have the satisfaction."

She swallowed the tears building in her throat. "You know what it's like. Kathleen—"

"It wasn't Kathleen, although there's that as well, but someone else I relied on at work betrayed me, so I get it." He touched the back of her hand. "Don't let them win. If you start second-guessing yourself and your judgment, then Eddie will have succeeded. Take the anger you feel and channel it into something constructive."

"I'm trying. It's just a bit…overwhelming to know that he lied to me and set me up from the beginning."

Drake nodded. "But now you know, and you can shut him down. Is there anyone at the FBI that you trust?"

She tilted her head. "Yes, there is."

"Call them. Fill them in. I have no doubt they will follow up."

She shivered. The breeze was cool, and the betrayal filled her heart with ice.

"Look, Spencer, we're going to get Kathleen and Connor through this. No matter what Eddie did, don't forget you kept them safe for all those years. It doesn't matter what you told him about Connor. When the moment came, you put yourself on the line for both of them and got them to safety. It was all you. You are the reason they are here now. Don't ever forget that. I sure as hell won't."

Goosebumps rose on her skin. It was cool out of the water. A look flashed across Drake's face that she couldn't decipher.

He suggested, "Maybe we should get out of the pool. You're getting cold."

He was right, but she wasn't quite ready to go face up to the shit-storm that was waiting for her once she made that phone call. She dipped back into the water so it was up to her neck. "You go on ahead. I think I'll just stay up here for a bit." She swam to the infinity edge.

Drake called after her, "Spencer, don't overthink things. What's done is done. Now we need to focus on moving forward." He pulled himself out of the pool. "Goodnight," he said and then toweled himself off and left.

Spencer draped her arms over the infinity edge and stared out into the night. Where had everything gone so wrong? She sighed. The better question was, when had things gone right? She'd fought with her parents when she joined the U.S. Marshals Service because she was betraying all their dreams for her, and then she ended up working for a traitor at the job she loved.

Then she finally gave into their pressure and married the man of their dreams only to be abused and lose her baby.

Now, she had given up a job she didn't love to protect the two people who meant the world to her, yet she wasn't sure she would be able to keep them safe. Everything she thought she knew was a lie.

She let out a deep breath and sank lower in the pool so the water was up to her chin. She had to go make a call and accuse a man that had been her close friend and mentor of being a mole. That was going to make a lot of people ask a lot of questions. Her career was definitely over at Homeland. Not that she cared.

Somewhere along the way, she'd stopped living and started existing. Just going through the motions of life. Doing what her parents asked, being the dutiful daughter. It took Joe going after Kathleen and Connor to wake her up. So, what should she do now? After everything was over and done? Find a new job in a new city? Doing what?

It was too much to contemplate at the moment. She was overwhelmed. When she was younger, still at university, when life got too much or too stressful, she and her friends would go out and get drunk and dance the night away. If only that would work now. She needed a few hours of burying her head in the sand and just having fun.

Maybe she should go work out. Her trainer at the gym insisted lifting weights helped with stress relief. Lifting weights sucked. Drink? She could get absolutely wasted. The mini bar in her suite was no doubt fully stocked, and the security was top-notch. Kathleen and Connor would be safe for the night.

Drake. Just his name conjured up images of his rippling muscles and sparkling green eyes. Now *that* was something she'd like to lose herself in. Spending hours in bed with him wouldn't lead to a hangover, and it would definitely be exercise. She smiled. If only.

Spencer cocked her head. Why not? Why couldn't she

spend a few hours having fun with Drake? Unless she was misreading the signs, he'd be up for it. An image of Kathleen flickered in her mind. Did it matter, though? One night, never to be repeated. The way Kathleen had been eyeing Dragan, chances were good she would encourage the whole thing.

She swam to the shallow end and pulled herself out of the pool. Life was for the living. If this whole thing had taught her anything, it had taught her that. Was this a mistake? Probably, but not the first one she'd made and most likely not the last. She needed a break, a way to relieve her stress, and sex was definitely better than lifting weights.

Drake had taken a quick shower and was getting out when he heard a knock at his door. His brain was all tied up on the mole thing. His sister had never stood a chance. The moment she'd decided to launder that first bit of money, her life had been on a crash and burn trajectory. He wrapped a towel around his waist and went to answer it.

"Is everything okay?" Spencer was standing in the hallway still wearing her bikini and shivering. He moved back, and she entered his suite. He closed the door. "Did you need something?"

She looked up at him, and their gazes locked. "Yes," she said, "I need a towel." She moved toward him until they were mere inches apart and then reached out and took the towel off from around his waist.

His pulse quickened as he recognized the desire in her warm hazel eyes. She dropped the towel, put her hands on his chest and went up on her tip toes. She brushed one soft kiss across his lips, and then another.

He knew he should stop her, but she was a grown woman

and knew what she was doing. He wrapped his arms around her and brought her against him as he swooped in and captured her lips in a scorching kiss. She tasted of strawberries and wine, and she was sweeter than heaven. He plunged his tongue into her mouth, rolling and dancing with hers.

His skin seemed to become extra sensitive. He could feel her everywhere, and he wanted more. She ran her hands over his chest as he kissed the hollow of her neck. She groaned and pressed harder into him.

His cock rubbed against her belly and bathing suit. He slid his hands down and cupped her ass, rubbing her across his erection. She kissed him hard as she lifted one leg and wrapped it around his waist. He scooped her up, and she wrapped the other leg around him as he carried her to the bedroom.

"Drake," she moaned as she moved against him.

With one hand he undid her bikini top. She pulled the ties at her neck, and the fabric fell to the floor. He placed her on the bed, and then lowered himself on top of her. He kissed the hollow of her throat. She moaned again and arched her hips up to his.

Groaning, he dropped his mouth to her nipple and tugged it with his teeth. "You are so beautiful," he whispered and then brought his lips to her other nipple. Her moan was a pure animalistic sound as he swirled his tongue around one nipple while he ran his thumb back and forth over the other. She fisted her fingers in his hair and threw her head back, pushing her breasts forward. He took her nipple deeper into his mouth.

She pulled his head away to reclaim his mouth, her tongue rolling with his in a deep kiss. He moved away from her mouth and dropped his gaze to her breasts. Goosebumps appeared on her skin, and he knew it had nothing to do with being cold.

"You're so damn hot." He lowered his head and tugged on her nipple with his teeth. She moaned again and reached for his cock. He groaned when her fingers ran the length of him.

He kissed her again, reaching around to release her hair from the loose bun she had it in. It fell down over her shoulders, and he immediately buried his hands in it as he deepened the kiss.

She rolled the tip of his cock between her fingers. He couldn't stand it. If she kept touching him, he was going to lose it. Growling, he grabbed her hand and held it above her head.

She wrapped her legs around his hips and moved against him. He swore as he slid his hands to her bikini bottoms. She dropped her legs, and he immediately helped her remove the fabric. It hit the floor, and then he covered her luscious body again. He loved the feel of her underneath him. She arched her hips up and locked her ankles behind his back, rubbing her slick folds against the length of his cock. He growled as she rubbed him again. The pleasure from that limited amount of contact was exhilarating.

His hands gripped her ass and brought her closer. She angled her hips so he could slide inside of her, but he pulled back.

"What's wrong?"

"Not yet. I want to taste you."

She gasped. Her cheeks were flushed with desire. He loved that it was for him. She wanted him. He shifted his weight until he was kneeling on the floor and had her thighs over his shoulders. She bit her lip with anticipation.

When he blew on her hot center, her hips jerked in response. He smiled.

"Drake," she gasped as he captured her with his mouth.

His tongue swirled, and she swore. He teased her sensitive flesh with his tongue until she was panting.

Then he put one finger inside her and moved slowly. Her hips strained upward to his mouth telling him it wasn't enough.

"More," she demanded, fisting the sheets.

He alternated between licking and sucking while thrusting his fingers. She yelled his name as her thighs tightened and her body clamped around his fingers. She threw her head back as her orgasm exploded through her. He smiled again.

She caught her breath while he climbed on to the bed next to her. Her gaze locked with his. "My turn," she purred and sat up. She climbed on top of him. She kissed his neck and worked her way down his chest. She played with his nipples and then moved to his belly. She bit his hips and then worked her way over until her mouth was level with his cock.

Her tongue touched the tip, then slowly, she drew more and more of him into her mouth, sucking, and twisting her tongue around his shaft as she went. His growl deepened and rumbled out of his chest.

His voice was rough. "You're killing me." His hips started to move, but then he grabbed her and pulled her back up. "I want to come inside you." He captured her mouth with another scorching kiss.

She moved until her core was hovering above his hard cock. Seconds later, she lowered herself slowly down on top of him. Just a little bit, and then she lifted again. She teased him, taking him into her a little bit at a time until he couldn't take it anymore and grabbed her hips.

"Stop teasing me. You're driving me insane."

Spencer laughed and then took his cock all the way inside her. She tilted her pelvis and started moving.

He moved her more quickly up and down the length of his shaft.

"I feel you. Every hard, hot inch of you." She angled her hips to allow him to go deeper.

She was so damn sexy he couldn't stand it. She felt like heaven, and he plunged as deep as he could inside of her.

Her breath was coming in small gasps. She moaned his name and urged him on, her hips rushing to meet his rhythm, her fingernails raking across his chest as he pounded into her. Nothing had ever felt this good, this right. He slammed inside of her again and again. She bit her lip, and he lost it. He thrust deep inside her and growled her name as he came. She let out a soft moan and flopped down onto his chest. He wrapped both arms around her while they caught their breath.

"That was…incredible." He was still in awe. He'd had sex many times, but never like that. They'd connected in a way he'd never imagined possible. All he could think about was when they could do it again. He needed sex like this all the time. Every day. All day. He hadn't felt this good in forever.

Spencer smiled. "That was good. A great stress reducer. Better than swimming or the gym."

"Much," he agreed. He ran his hand down her back and gently cupped her ass. "I am, however, still feeling a bit of stress. I was thinking maybe we could go for another round. Just to make sure we're as relaxed as we can be."

She chuckled. "I think you're right. We should probably do that again at least once more. Stress has so many negative side effects. We should definitely work to avoid any of those."

He grinned.

She lifted her head from his chest and kissed him quickly. "First, though, I need some water." She peeled herself off him and stood. She walked out of the bedroom and came back a few seconds later with two bottles of water. She threw one to him and then opened her own. She took a long drink.

He just sat on the bed watching her. He loved that she wasn't body conscious and was just as confident naked as she was dressed. Her body was a thing of beauty, and she should be proud of it. So many women weren't. It just bumped her higher in his opinion that she was so confident. It was sexy as hell. He tossed the water bottle on the bed and reached for her. He couldn't wait any longer. He needed her now.

CHAPTER TWENTY

Spencer held the phone to her ear and waited. Her stomach growled. She was starving. All that sex last night left her sore, tired, and hungry—but also happy. She tried to play it off, but it was by far the best sex she'd ever had. Drake was amazing in bed. Generous, thoughtful, and oh so talented. He was fabulous in all kinds of ways.

She shook her head. She didn't need to go down that path. Besides, they moved in two different worlds. Two different places. It wouldn't work. *Would he be up for friends with benefits?* She'd take the train up to New York for sex like that any day of the week.

"Riley." FBI Agent Jack Riley's voice came down the phone line.

"Jack, it's Spencer Gordon."

Jack's voice got quiet. "Spencer, where are you? People are looking for you."

"Are they? Why is that, now?"

"Apparently, someone went out to chat with you on Cape Cod, but it wasn't you."

She swore silently. "Well, you know Jack, I got bored. Anyway—"

"Yeah, that's not going to cut it. Seriously, Spencer, people, as in my bosses here at the FBI and your bosses at Homeland and your old bosses at the Marshals service, are all looking for you. They think you know something about the Caridi situation. Like where his ex-girlfriend and kid are. The shit is hitting the fan over here."

"How come? What the hell is going on?"

Jack's voice dropped. "Half of the Cosa Nostra showed up on Staten Island, and rumor has it that it has something to do with Caridi. Everyone knows they've been loosely affiliated, but now it looks like they are trying to make it a permanent thing. You better come in. It's all-hands-on-deck around here."

Shit. "Actually, I'm on leave so—"

"Your leave has been revoked. My bosses called yours, but no one could find you to tell you. What the fuck is going on? What do you know about all this?"

Fuck! Fuck! Fuck! She was going to have to tread very carefully. "Look, Jack, I'm not exactly sure what's going on." *True statement.* "What I do know is it wasn't a hacker who accessed Kathleen's file."

"How do you know that?"

She played with the pen she was holding. "Because I did my research. It was Eddie Miller."

Silence from the other end of the phone. "That's a big accusation. I wouldn't be throwing it around unless you have major proof. Eddie is well-liked."

"Jack, have you ever known me to throw around baseless accusations?"

"No, but Spencer, Jesus. Eddie? Come on. How do you figure that?"

She started to tell him and then thought better of it.

"You know what, Jack? I'm going to give you a hint. Then I'm going to let you run with it. It's better if you dig it up on your own. If I tell you, it's going to be suspect. If you find it, they'll believe you."

"Spencer, why would it be suspect coming from you?" There was silence for a second. "Wait, what did you do?"

Put a witness in hiding without telling anyone, took a man hostage, took out two killers, and then left them to decompose in a rented house. "Jack, it doesn't matter what I did. What matters is it's Eddie. He's the traitor. Look into his record at the Marshals from the very beginning. Dig around a bit and look into his past. His family. I know you'll make the connections."

"Spencer, it would be better if you came in."

"Yeah, I know, but it's not going to happen. Jack, I need you to keep this call quiet. I know it's a lot to ask, but if you tell your bosses, then it will make everything harder. I don't know if Eddie is the only one. There could be more. Just dig deep and keep your head down. Be careful, because if he finds out you're digging around in his life, he won't hesitate to take you out. Remember, one marshal has already died because of Eddie, and another is in the hospital. I don't want anything to happen to you. Watch your back."

She hung up and put her cell down on the table. This wasn't good. Not good at all. She needed to talk to Drake and his people. Bring them up to speed. She went across the hall to the main suite. The team was already gathered there, and there was a new man with them.

"Spencer," Drake said. "This is my lawyer, Thane Hawkins. Hawk, this is Spencer Gordon."

She offered her hand, and they shook. She had to admit Drake had done it again. How did he always manage to surround himself with good-looking people? Hawkins was six feet with dark hair and blue eyes. He'd obviously spent time at the gym because he was built. His white button-down was crisp, and the crease on his light gray dress pants was sharp. Military training if she had to guess.

"Please call me Hawk. Everyone does."

Drake nodded at Hawk. "Hawk is here to help with some paperwork if I can get a deal done with the Cosa Nostra."

"Well, you better work faster. I just got off a call with a friend at the FBI, and it's not good news."

Gage frowned. "Why don't we all grab some breakfast and then take this next door to Drake's suite. Kathleen and Connor haven't been in yet, and I'm not sure this is a conversation we want to have in front of them."

Drake nodded. "Agreed."

Mitch grinned. "You don't have to ask me twice." He grabbed a plate. The rest of the men fell in line, but Drake took a step back to let Spencer go ahead of him.

The heat from his body behind hers sent her senses into overload. His scent, the hotel shampoo mixed with his own spicy maleness, had images of him naked flashing through her mind. She blinked. She needed to get a grip on herself. Maybe standing next to Drake wasn't the best idea until she got her hormones in check. She moved quickly down the line, adding food to her plate, and then she followed the others to Drake's room.

Images of last night filled her thoughts when she walked into his suite. They'd ended up out in the living area at one point, and she was glad they didn't want to eat at the bar this morning. That would be awkward until the cleaning crew went through.

She glanced up and caught Drake looking at her, smirking. *Shit.* She went to the other end of the table so she had a few bodies between them. Her hormones were so fired up she was afraid if she sat next to him, she'd jump him before the meeting was over.

Five minutes later, Drake said, "Spencer, why don't you fill us in?" and then took a sip of coffee.

"Okay. I just got off the phone with a friend at the FBI. It's all-hands-on-deck over there. Apparently, a large contingent from Italy has arrived in New York. Sicilian mobsters. They're here to support the Caridis. The FBI wants to know what's going on. Why suddenly there's this big group in town."

Gage put down his fork on his plate. "That's not good."

"No, it's not." Drake agreed. "Their arrival means they've already made some sort of deal then with the Caridis. The five families of New York all have to be nervous at this point, not just the Lucchese family. This could easily explode into some kind of mob war."

Hawk leaned back in his seat. "I thought the five families of New York *were* Cosa Nostra."

"They are…sort of." Logan pushed his empty plate away. "The short version is the mob in New York was started by a group that all came from southern Italy, including Sicily. Then in the late twenties, early thirties, the old guard in Italy started telling the young guys in America how to do things. The young crew here didn't like it. A mob war broke out and, eventually, the outcome was the creation of the Commission.

"This Commission divided most of the U.S. up into territories, and each group or family got a section except for New York City, which was too big. The city was divided up between the five families, and there was one main leader who was connected to the Cosa Nostra. The young guys didn't like how it played out so, led by Lucky Luciano, they had the head guy taken out. Now the five families rule equally with loose ties to Cosa Nostra but not anything solid."

"Logan, I'm impressed. I had no idea you were into mob history." Hawk smiled.

"Hawk, you know oh-so little about me." Logan grinned. "Hawk and I overlapped at the JAG corps for a while. Thankfully, we both came to our senses and left."

Hawk laughed. "You were the smart one and stuck with law. I ended up going into…other areas before coming to my senses and coming back to civilian law."

Spencer took a sip of coffee. Hawk's other areas certainly involved special forces of some kind. It was written all over him. He was just the type of guy that would appeal to Drake. Smart and good under pressure. *Well, they'd all better be with the mess they were in.*

Spencer piped up, "This has to be making a lot of people very uncomfortable. The Caridis are upsetting the balance of power of the five families. Why would they risk all of that?"

Drake set his coffee cup down. "Because it's good business."

"Come again?" Mitch asked.

Drake cleared his throat. "The Lucchese family is the weakest of the five families. Their Don is in prison, and they don't have a big crew on the outside. None of them do anymore. The days of the "Dapper Don" and the Gambino family power are over.

"If they want to claim some territory back from the Albanians, the gangs, and everyone else who has carved out a piece of New York, they need more firepower and more pull. By partnering with the Sicilians, they can establish better relationships with the cartels and everyone else the Cosa Nostra deals with and establish themselves as a more dominant power."

"Jesus, this is so out of hand. Your sister is the catalyst for a huge mess," Mitch said.

Drake nodded. "She's just a pawn in all of this. We have to back the Sicilians off. Get them to stay out of it." Drake frowned. "I have someone working on brokering a deal. It's delicate, and it might take more time than we have."

Drake stood up and moved toward the bar. There was a coffee urn placed on top of it. He poured himself another cup and then turned and faced the table. "The arrival of the extra guns means we have to plan for a much larger undertaking. This will no longer be just about saving Kathleen. It will end up putting us all in the middle of a mob war.

"Because of that, I have to ask you all if you want to continue. I will do whatever I have to for my sister, but I don't want any of you to feel obligated. These men won't just stop at killing you if you cross them; they'll take out your family as well. It's a matter of pride. You do not have to follow me down this road."

Spencer's gaze locked with Drake's. Her stomach churned. Drake was right. This was much bigger than anyone had signed on for, but she was all in. Kathleen had been an excellent friend to her and a sounding board whenever she needed it. She'd been Spencer's rock when she needed one most. Spencer wouldn't walk away from Kathleen and Connor right when they needed *her* most. Besides, her career in any kind of law enforcement or government agency was over. It was sort of freeing in a way. "I'm in this to the bitter end."

"Look, Drake," Mitch spoke up, "I'm sure Logan would say this much better, but you've been a client for a year now, and you've stood by us even when you could have walked away. There's no way in hell we would leave you hanging now. We're in this."

Gage nodded, and Logan smiled and cocked a thumb at Mitch. "What he said."

Hawkins cleared his throat. "If you require some help outside of the legal matters, I'm happy to lend a hand."

Gage nodded. "Duly noted and appreciated."

Drake placed his coffee cup down on the table and then straightened, placing both hands on the back of his chair. "I want you all to know I am...grateful for your support." He took a breath. "I... It means a lot to me and my family." His phone buzzed on the table. He grabbed it and flipped it over. "I have to take this." He turned and walked into the bedroom.

Gage took a sip of coffee. "To put it bluntly, this has all the makings of a shit-storm. We need all available bodies here and as many as we can get on standby. We also need to keep Drake and his family as calm as possible. Mitch, we need to work on contingency plans. Where can we stash all of them if we need to? Start with out-of-the-way places here in the U.S. and go out from there. Logan, you and Hawk see if there's anything legal we can do to stop this."

"What did you have in mind?" Logan asked.

"I have no idea. Get creative. They got Capone on tax evasion. See if we can find anything on these people to get them hauled off the street, even if it's just for questioning on something small. Any reprieve will help us prepare."

He turned to face Spencer. "I also have friends at the Bureau. They tell me you're 'headed straight for the top.'. You sure you want to be involved with this? It's going to get very messy, and we're not going by the book. Your career will be over, and your parents... It may cause them difficulties."

She had heard enough. She leaned forward. "My parents are a pair of eels. They will slide through this no problem. Teflon has nothing on them, and I'm not worried about my career."

Gage gave her a hard stare and then a single nod. "Okay then. We'll keep you in the loop."

The door opened, and Jake walked into the room. "Gage, we've got a problem."

"What?"

Jake glanced around and cocked an eyebrow, but Gage nodded so he proceeded. "We have a couple of local detectives downstairs asking questions about three dead bodies and the shoot-out that happened here the night before last. They're asking questions about Drake and Spencer's involvement."

Spencer frowned. "Three? Three dead bodies? There should only be two. Who's the third? And did they ask about me by name?"

Jake nodded. "They said they have reason to believe you are with Drake and that you have two others with you. They want to speak to all of you in relation to the three deaths."

Logan stood up. "Okay, let's go speak with them. I'll get details and stall them for as long as I can, but we can't put them off indefinitely."

"Mind if I join you?" Hawk asked as he rose and pushed his chair in. "Been a while since I had any dealing with police. I kind of miss it."

"The more the merrier," Logan said, and all three left the room again.

Spencer sat rooted to her chair. Who the hell was the third body?

CHAPTER TWENTY-ONE

"What do you mean they won't talk to me?" Drake demanded.

There was a sigh on the other end. "How about thanks for trying Enzo and sorry for the dropped calls?"

"Enzo, I don't have time for playing around."

"I know, I know, and I'm sorry, but Luca doesn't want to be bothered." There was a long silence.

"What is it, Enzo?" He knew his friend well enough to know there was more to the story.

"I think Luca might be the one who is pushing for the expansion into New York. He's the don's son and ambitious as hell. They've already been reviving things with some of the other New York families here and there, so forming another link would only enhance things for them."

"You need to get me to the don then. I need someone who can see reason on this."

"Slick, you're asking a whole lot. We're not even part of the same organization. Just me reaching out is making people nervous."

Drake rubbed his face with one hand. "Enzo, this is life and death."

Enzo grunted. "Stay close to your phone." And then he was gone.

Drake collapsed onto the bed. This whole thing had become a clusterfuck of major proportions. He needed a plan. A way out for all of them. He rubbed his face again and then stood. There was a way out. He just had to find it.

He walked back into the living room. "So, what is the plan? Where're Logan and Hawk?" he asked.

Gage looked up. "The cops are here about the three dead bodies you left behind at the rental house. They're demanding to speak to you and Spencer. Logan and Hawk went to stall them."

"Fuck." Drake sighed. "We knew it was coming, I guess. Wait, there were only two bodies. Who is the third?"

Gage shrugged. "Logan will give us details when he has them. In the meantime, we started making a list of places we can hide you if we need to. Places off the beaten path here in the U.S. that a bunch of mafia guys showing up would draw a lot of attention. So far, we've come up with your spa in Canyon Springs, Montana and—"

"You own a spa in Montana?" Mitch asked. "Seriously?"

Drake sighed. "Yes, it's a very trendy area. The next Aspen."

Gage went back to his laptop. "Also, there's your resort in Colorado."

Mitch groaned. "Don't you own anything anywhere warm other than here?"

"I own a Caribbean island. Would that work?" Drake knew Mitch was just trying to keep it light, but his patience was running low.

"You own a whole island?" Connor asked. "Seriously?"

Drake turned to see his sister and Connor standing by

the doorway. "Hi, you two, and, yes, Connor, I do. We can go visit anytime." Seeing his sister frown, he added, "After you get out of school for the summer."

Kathleen nodded and mouthed *thank you* behind Connor's back. "What are you all up to?"

"We're going over some of my holdings. Doing a review. What are you up to?" Drake had no intention of telling Kathleen anything just yet. It would scare her even more. He wanted to give her a couple of calm days where she could regroup before all hell broke loose.

But his sister wasn't buying the story. He could tell, but she wasn't going to challenge him in front of Connor. She frowned and then gave a small shrug. "I'm going back to the room to get my mani-pedi, and then I think I would like to find a corner and read a good book in the sun."

"I think that can be arranged." He looked over at Mitch, who pulled out his phone and started texting. A second later, he gave Drake a nod.

"What about you, Connor? What's on your list for today?"

"I was thinking I would like to go surfing. Is that possible?"

Drake hesitated. Surfing would be hard. There was a cove they could close, but the exposure was greater. "Connor, that might be a bit difficult."

The boy frowned, and his shoulders sagged. "I get it." He glanced at his mom. "I'm going to go play video games." He turned and left the room.

"I'm sorry, Kathleen. Protecting him while he's surfing would be hard." His gut knotted. He hated to disappoint his nephew, but he also needed to keep the boy alive.

Kathleen shook her head. "It's not your fault. It's mine." Her face grew serious, and her eyes were sad. "I'm off to get my nails done." She left with Jake in tow.

"Shit." Drake dropped the paper he'd been holding onto the coffee table.

Mitch stood up. "Let me see what I can do. We may not be able to do surfing, but we might manage a night swim. I'll see what I can figure out."

Drake nodded. "Thanks, Mitch. Whatever you can safely work out is fine. If it can't be done, there will be other times to surf." As the words left his lips, he said a silent prayer that it was the truth.

Drake spent the better part of the day going over places they could hide Kathleen and Connor. He also discovered he was going to be a liability to them, which hadn't entered his brain before. He was too high-profile. People would notice him. Gage explained to him that he needed to get back to business as usual as quickly as possible.

He rolled his shoulders. His gut churned. It went against every instinct. He didn't want Kathleen or Connor more than a room away from him. He just got his family back. Being across the country from them and having no contact? That would be a crushing blow.

"Thank you, gentleman," Drake said as the men stood to leave the room. He stayed seated on the couch. He put his head back and closed his eyes. He had a pounding headache, and he needed some time to himself. He wondered where Spencer was and what she was doing. He heard the door close, but then someone cleared their throat. He opened his eyes to find Gage standing across from him. "What is it?"

"There's one more thing. Spencer."

"What about her?" If Gage thought he could lecture Drake on who he invited into his bed, the man was greatly mistaken.

Gage sat down in a chair across from Drake. "Her career is over because of this. I just thought you should know."

Drake sat forward and put his elbows on his knees.

"What do you mean, her career is over? I know she's bending the rules by not telling them where Kathleen is, but under the current circumstances, it's the prudent move."

Gage shook his head. "Washington is a political place in more than just government. Spencer was on the fast track up the ladder at Homeland. Her parents, with all of their connections and pull, made it a no-brainer that Spencer would have a solid career, but she also happens to be excellent at what she does. She was headed to the top and, by top, I mean the very top. Her name was being thrown around as someone to watch to run one of the top agencies. She has the right background for it. But she took a leave of absence to help your sister. Instead of working in the community, she's gone outside of it."

"But the mole—"

Gage shook his head again. "Even if she used that excuse, it only cuts so far. She could have brought Kathleen into the FBI, or even to Homeland. Instead, she went rogue. Then she killed those men—"

"One man. I killed the other, and they were trying to kill us."

"Still, doesn't matter. She didn't tell anyone. Spencer is way too far off the playing field to be invited back into the game. Not going down to speak to those cops was the last nail in the coffin. Her career is over and finished. She will never advance past where she is right now and, in fact, she won't have a job when this is over."

Drake sighed. "Why are you telling me this?"

"Because this woman has sacrificed her life for your family. She put them first. Her parents are not going to be happy. You are going to be on their shit list, and as a current senator and a former ambassador, they have a shitload of pull in the world. I thought you should know."

His shoulders were tight and his head pounded. "Well, thanks for the heads-up."

Gage nodded and stood. "Any news from Italy?"

"Not yet. I'll tell you as soon as I hear."

Gage turned and left the room. Drake flopped back into the couch cushions. He felt ill. What the fuck had Spencer done? She screwed up her own life for his family. It wasn't fair, but the more he knew of her, the more he could see why she would do it. It wouldn't occur to her to worry about her own career. She had a bond with Kathleen and Connor, and that was enough for her. She shouldn't have to sacrifice everything. How could he make it up to her? He couldn't. Not ever. But he wouldn't stop trying. She could have any job she wanted. He'd find something that made her happy.

There was a knock on the door, and the woman in question entered. Her face was pale, and the dark circles were prominent under her red-rimmed eyes. He didn't have the heart to ask what was wrong. He didn't think he could take anything else, and then he remembered what she had done for his family. "What is it?" he asked as he stood up. "What's wrong?"

Spencer blurted out, "They killed Will."

"Will?"

"The friend I had protecting Kathleen and Connor. Someone found him and killed him. They tortured him, Drake. They broke his fingers and shot him in both legs before they shot him in the back of the head. It's all my fault."

"No." He shook his head. "No, his death is on them. It's not your fault."

"He was doing me a favor. A favor, Drake, and he died for it."

"He was a professional and knew what he was getting in to. He is dead because someone out there killed him."

She gave him a withering look. “You can sell that to a civilian, but we both know that I brought him into this, so he was my responsibility and I got him killed. I have his blood on my hands.” She closed her eyes and swallowed hard, then looked back at him. “I want the bastards who did this. I want them to pay. They are not getting away with this.”

“We’ll do everything we can—” His phone went off. It was Enzo. “I’m so sorry. I have to take this.” He hit the button on the screen. “Enzo.”

“No, this is Antonio Bacchi.” The voice was heavily accented and sounded elderly. “Enzo says we should speak. I like Enzo, so I’m humoring him. So, speak.”

Drake chose his words very carefully. “Mr. Bacchi, I know you have some associates in New York at the moment. You’ve always maintained loose ties with the families there. A deal here, a deal there. It’s been good for business, I’m guessing.” He paused, but Bacchi said nothing, so he continued. “This business with the Caridis is more complicated than it appears. It might be a better investment to stick to having many friends rather than choosing one best friend.”

“Who are you to tell me who my friends should be, eh? Why should I listen to some *pazzo*?”

Drake silently cursed his own heavy handedness. “Mr. Bacchi, I don’t mean to tell you who your friends should be, but I’m a businessman like you. I understand the needs of a business. I want to make sure your business grows in the best way possible.”

“And why would you care about my business, eh?”

“Because it’s my sister Giuseppe wants to kill, and I can’t let that happen. I would like it if we could be friends rather than enemies.”

There was silence for a long moment. “And why would I care if you want to be my friend? Everyone wants to be my friend. I don’t need more friends.”

Drake had a call to make. He ground his teeth and checked his gut. He'd been placating until now. He let his eyes roam around the room until they landed on Spencer. He was leading with his heart. It was time to get his head in the game.

He dropped his voice. "Because you don't want me as an enemy."

There was a moment of silence, and then Bacchi laughed. "You have *palle,* balls, but maybe not too many brains."

"Mr. Bacchi, I don't know what Enzo has told you about me—"

"He said you own a few hotels. You're a good businessman, but I think he's wrong. I don't see any good business going on here."

"Mr. Bacchi, I own a great many hotels. I have more money than the GDP of many small countries, and I'm willing to spend every last cent to keep my family safe. If that means I have to take on you and all of your friends, I will do it with a literal army. I can afford to hire, arm, and train them without breaking a sweat. I could invade your small island and take it over if it pleased me, and I can do it tomorrow." His voice was cold as steel.

"Or"—he made his voice friendly again—"we could be friends as I mentioned before. I, too, am a great friend to have. If, for example, you were to call your people back home, I could provide you with some real estate.

"Spain is lovely this time of year. I understand you have many friends in South and Central America that often like to come to Spain to discuss business. A small boutique hotel in Barcelona or Madrid might just be the thing for them. A place to stay where you could conduct your business uninterrupted and with the environment totally controlled by you."

Bacchi remained silent. Drake held his breath. It was a

huge gamble. He insulted and threatened the man, but he also offered him an out.

"I want to have the contracts for the cleaning in all of your hotels."

Drake chuckled. "No, but we could come to some arrangement as to you buying several hotels for a very low cost."

"How many hotels do you have?"

"The more appropriate question is how many hotels would make you happy?"

"Twenty. I want twenty of your biggest hotels."

He smiled. He had Bacchi now. *Yes!* "Mr. Bacchi, you don't want large hotels because they are difficult to run and attract a lot of attention from the tax people. You want small hotels. They are easily controllable and less likely to draw attention. I will sell three hotels for a very good price. Which cities would you like them in?"

"You make a good point. Okay, ten of your small hotels."

"Three."

"You love your sister. You need to think about that."

"You love your lifestyle. We all have things we love and don't want to lose, but that shouldn't stop us from being good businessmen. Three hotels."

Bacchi chuckled. "Okay, alright, why do I need to be involved in this mess in New York for, eh? Three hotels. Madrid for my friends overseas, Rome so I can visit my friends in the north, and New York City so I can visit my American family."

"Done. I already have the paperwork drawn up. Have your men on the next flight home to Italy, and I will have it faxed over to you."

"I think that will be good. Enzo said you are slick. He is right. I like Enzo. We're friends. You and me, we can be friends, too. But take care, my friend. Sometimes things can go badly. I cannot control my American friends. They do their own thing."

"Mr. Bacchi, I am honored to be your friend. I will handle your American friends on my own. There's one more thing that I think might interest you."

Ten minutes later, Drake hung up. When his knees started to buckle, he grabbed on to the back of the chair and hung his head. He sucked in oxygen like he'd been underwater for days, and finally the tension eased along his spine. There just might be a glimmer of light at the end of this long, dark tunnel.

"What is it? What's wrong?" Spencer came to stand beside him. She put her hand on his back and started rubbing it in circles.

Drake absorbed the warmth and energy from her touch. It grounded him. He took another deep breath and exhaled. His legs were solid again. He straightened up. "Something is right for a change. The Sicilians are going home. They won't interfere."

"Oh, my God, that's wonderful news." She threw her arms around his neck and squeezed.

He hugged her back. It felt so good to have her in his arms. They needed this victory. It didn't solve everything, but it made a significant impact. He eased his grip and then dropped his arms. "I have to tell the others. Now we can make some better plans on how to deal with the rest." He smiled at Spencer and kissed her hard on the mouth. He would love to spend the rest of the afternoon in bed with her, but they had to move forward now.

"You go share the good news. I'm going to go back to my room for a bit. I'll catch up with you later."

"Are you sure? I know you're upset about Will." He pulled her in for a hug.

"Thanks." She squeezed him back. "But I need some time alone. I need to...process everything."

Drake dropped his hands to her waist. "Spencer, it's not your fault."

"I know." She nodded. "I do know. I just need some... space at the moment. Go on, fill everyone in. I'll catch up with you later." She touched his chest and then turned and left the room.

Drake watched her go. She was blaming herself. He knew it as sure as he knew he would do the same thing in her position. He'd give her a bit of time to herself, and then he'd make sure she was okay.

He strode across the room and out into the hallway. "Jake, is everyone in there?" He pointed to the main suite.

"Kathleen and Connor are in their room, but rest are in there, yeah."

"Great. Thanks." Drake entered the suite and smiled. "Good news. The boys from Italy are going home. I struck a deal with their don, and they won't interfere with this issue any longer."

"Should we ask how you managed it, or is it better left undisclosed?" Logan asked.

"We negotiated a deal. Hawk, I'm going to need you to go over those contracts one more time before you send them off. Three copies. One for Rome, one for Madrid, and one for New York."

Hawk's eyebrows went up. "Do you have specific ones in mind?"

Drake paused. *Did he know which hotels he wanted to get rid of in each city?* He wasn't entirely sure. He'd spent most of the last few years setting things up in the Far East. It had been a while since he'd reviewed his entire portfolio. "Call Marty in acquisitions at head office in New York. Ask him which boutique to mid-size hotel would he sell in each city and then use his choices. Marty knows what's what in Europe and the U.S. better than I do at the moment. Don't give him details. Tell him I'll call him and explain next week. You're going to need to work with the numbers."

Hawk nodded. "I will speak with Reg Henderson in accounting on that. I prepped him, and he has some ideas how we can justify the prices and make it legit. He says he might even be able to get you some kind of tax break on it."

"Good." Drake pulled out a chair and sat down at the table. "Keep me posted on your progress."

"Do you mind if I get Logan to give the contracts the once over? It's always better to have a fresh set of eyes."

Drake looked up at Logan. "Do you mind reviewing some contracts?"

"I would be happy to help. My talents are better spent on contracts than troop movements."

"Great." Hawk smiled. "I've got them back in my room." The two men headed out the door.

Drake turned to Gage and Mitch. "How do we move forward from here?"

"That's a good question." Gage looked at Mitch.

Mitch shrugged. "It depends on what you want to do. Logan and Hawk managed to hold the cops off for a little bit, but Spencer is supposed to go down and answer questions tomorrow, first thing. If she doesn't show up, they may come and try to arrest her."

He ground his teeth. "It's one step forward and two back at this point."

"You can't blame them. They have three dead bodies." Mitch reached out, grabbed a stir stick, and then proceeded to stir the coffee he had in front of him.

"How did they get our names in the first place?" Drake demanded.

"Prints. They ran fingerprints, and I would imagine their

phones lit up like it was Christmas. They must have hit every red flag out there."

He swore long and loud in his head. They hadn't had time to wipe the place clean, not that he would have even thought of that, but Spencer must have known. "So now every agency knows we are in Hawaii, but how did the police know to look here?"

"Traffic cameras, plus the whole shoot-out thing." Mitch moved the stir stick through his fingers as he spoke.

"Shit. Do they want to speak to me as well?"

Gage spoke up. "They're not sure how you're involved, or even *if* you're involved, so they're being more cautious with you. Your prints aren't on file, so they don't know you were at the house. They didn't get faces on the traffic cams, just the vehicle, and they don't know exactly what is going on with the whole Kathleen and Connor situation. They know a woman and her son lived at the house, and they know Spencer was there. There are now three bodies attached to it. Spencer is the only name they have. Kathleen and Connor's records are sealed."

Drake tilted his head. "You must have a source in the police department here."

Gage smiled slightly. "Something like that."

"So where does that leave us?"

Mitch took a sip of his coffee. "Trapped, or at least they're hoping that's the case."

"Who is hoping?" Drake wondered.

Gage leaned back in his chair. "Both sides. All sides. The mob hopes we are trapped here and so does the FBI and the Marshals and whoever else has a hand in this."

"And are we trapped here?"

"No. We're making plans to move tonight if that works for you." Gage looked at his brother, and Mitch opened up a laptop and turned it around so Drake could see the screen.

"Tasmania? You want us to go to Tasmania?" That was unexpected, to say the least. "Why?"

Mitch laughed. "For the reason your face just crinkled into that look of horror. No one would expect us to go there, and it gives us room to move. We can regroup and form a solid plan on how to move forward. You want this sorted once and for all, right? You don't want Kathleen and Connor on the run for the rest of their lives. We can make that happen, but it takes planning and research on many levels."

"But Tasmania? What's wrong with Australia or New Zealand?"

"Tasmania is part of Australia," Gage pointed out.

"You know what I mean."

Gage held up his finger. "One, you have hotels in Auckland and Sydney. Two, we don't have as many friends in either of those cities in case we run into trouble—"

"You have friends in Tasmania?"

"Yes," Gage continued, "and, three, you have a much greater chance of being recognized. Your face is all over the place. You have friends in each city, and you even flirted with the Prime Minister of New Zealand. It was all over the news. If you show up there, the world will know."

Drake caught a look exchanged between the two brothers, and Mitch opened his mouth to speak, but Drake cut him off, "From that look, I know you are about to tell me something I don't want to hear. I can tell you I know what it is, and I really don't want to hear it."

Mitch grimaced. "You can't see them if we take them to Sydney or New Zealand or anywhere else that's popular."

"If I want to see my family, I have to ship them off to Tasmania?"

Mitch grinned. "It's actually a great place. Connor can take up cricket or rugby or Australian Rules Football."

The thought of not seeing Connor and Kathleen was too

hard. He wouldn't do that again. Not ever. He let out a big sigh. "Fine. Tasmania. How are we getting there?"

"You aren't going," Gage stated, but held up his hands to ward off Drake's angry response. "At least, not yet. It's better if you stay here and go back to normal life. We will, of course, beef up your security and make sure you are safe, but Joe will be watching you closely. For the next couple of months, you will have to stick to video conferencing."

Drake rubbed his temples. His chest hurt. He hadn't seen his sister in sixteen years. He hadn't even known he had a nephew, and now he wasn't going to be able to be with them again. His shoulders drooped. It was only for a few months. He could do it. They all could. It was a hell of a lot better than them being dead.

CHAPTER TWENTY-TWO

Spencer rested on the bed in her room. She needed some time to herself. After speaking to Logan she understood the cops wanted to speak to her. The chances of her getting arrested were great because she couldn't tell them anything. They weren't aware of the background on this, and her hands were tied by bureaucratic bullshit.

At this point, she had pissed off so many people she didn't know if any of them would go to bat for her. Eventually, the local cops would release her. She'd acted in self-defense as Logan had said. She could even argue it was in the auspices of performing her duties as an officer of the law that the event occurred. Logan remained confident he could get her out of any trouble they might want to throw her way. He had been less confident he could do anything about her career.

She rubbed her face. The deep-down-at-the-bottom-of-her-soul truth was she honestly did not have any fucks to give now. Working at Homeland didn't bring her joy. She had been much happier at the Marshals Service, but still not the way other people loved their jobs. She wanted to love her job. Mostly, she just wanted to stop feeling like utter shit inside.

Will's death put her career in perspective for her like nothing else had. He was a good man who just wanted to make some money on the side to support his family. Now, they were all alone.

Tears streamed down the side of her face into her hair. She bit her lip. She would find a way to tell them how great Will was and to make sure they were taken care of. She would ask Drake. He could afford to set them up. Will gave his life to help Drake's family. She knew he'd be happy to help. It wasn't enough, but it was a start.

Frustrated and heart-sore, Spencer wiped her eyes and sat up. She looked at the pile of burner cells Jake had given her. Could she risk another call to Jack Riley? What was the danger for her at this point? She picked up the phone and punched in the number.

"Riley."

"Jack. How's it going?"

"Jesus, Spencer, are you trying to get me fired?" he hissed.

"What are you talking about?"

"I poked around in Eddie's life like you suggested, and I stumbled into a hornet's nest. The guy is under investigation already. They wanted to know what I was looking for and why."

"What did you tell them?"

"The truth. What else could I tell them? I had no reason other than your suspicions." Jack kept his voice low. "You were right, by the way, in case you hadn't figured that out. Everyone else was a step behind you. Eddie was definitely the one behind the leak."

"So, did they arrest him?"

"No. He skipped town before the net closed in."

"Shit. Does anyone have a line on him?" Eddie on the

loose meant one more person who might be gunning for them.

"He's in Hawaii where you are, I hear."

"Fuck. That's not good." *Understatement of the century.*

"No, it isn't. Look, Spencer." Jack's voice changed. It dropped lower and filled with sympathy. He had bad news. "They had a trace on Eddie's phone. When you went off-grid, Eddie called everyone he could think of to find you. Will called him back."

She closed her eyes. Tears leaked out from under her lashes. "Eddie tortured and killed Will."

"I'm so sorry, Spencer. I know you were close with Will. I remember going for drinks with you guys at the last conference in Virginia. I liked him."

She opened her eyes. "Yeah, he was a good guy. He didn't deserve this." Feeling sorry for herself wasn't going to change the fact that a good man was dead, a family bereft. "Are there any leads on where exactly Eddie is located on the island, or who he's with?"

"If they have any, they haven't told me."

"Okay. Thanks, Jack."

"Spencer?"

"Yeah?"

"They're not happy about all of this. I... Just watch your back. They need a fall guy for this mess, and Eddie won't be enough."

"I know, but thanks for the warning. Take care." She disconnected the call. So, Eddie was on the island and hunting for her. Good. She wouldn't mind having a word with him either. Preferably with a Glock in her hand. She got up off the bed and went in search of everyone. They weren't in the main suite, so she went and knocked on Drake's door.

"Enter."

Spencer opened the door to find Drake sitting on the

sofa with his laptop open in front of him and a plate of food beside it. "Oh, sorry. Are you doing a working dinner? You want me to leave you in peace?"

"No. Come in. I'm reading some emails. How are you doing?"

She crossed the room and sat down in one of the chairs opposite him. "I'm... I don't know what I am. What about you? How are you doing? Where is everyone?"

He leaned back on the sofa. "Gage and Mitch are getting things ready for tonight. Hawk and Logan are going over some contracts for me. Kathleen and Connor are having dinner in their room, and then they're going to pack."

"Pack? Where are they going?" Her hand's fisted, and her body went rigid.

"We're moving them to a new location. Tasmania."

"Tasmania? Seriously? Why?"

"Mitch and Gage think it's the best location for them for the time being until we can figure out a permanent solution. Technically, they aren't obligated to stay here, so we can move them out of the country."

"Why didn't anyone consult me? I've been protecting them for years. This is as much my call as anyone else." She was on her feet, fists on hips. Rage pumped through her bloodstream. Fucking hell. Where did they get off making decisions without her?

"I told them not to discuss it with you at the moment."

His admission was a gut punch. "Why?" She could barely get the word out through her anger.

"Because you can't go with them." He held up his hands. "Believe me, I know how much it stings to hear that, but you can't. You have to stay here and sort out this mess with the police, the FBI, and your boss at Homeland."

"I will decide who I have to speak to and what I have to do, and I don't have to do any of that." How dare he? Her breath came in gasps. She wanted to reach across the coffee table and snap his neck.

"Yes, you do, unfortunately. You must sort this. They'll issue a warrant for your arrest, if they haven't already and then we can't get you into any country. You will need to get a fake passport and all the rest of it. And the mess will all still be there when you decide to come back to the U.S. Plus, Australia has extradition, so even if you did accompany them, and were later charged with a crime, Tasmania would send you back." His voice remained calm, but the storm in his eyes told another story. His anger was just as raw as hers.

"You aren't going either," she stated.

He shook his head. "Not yet. Not for months, by the sound of things. I am thoroughly pissed off about it, but you and I don't really have a choice. We need to stay here and see if we can figure out a way for Kathleen and Connor to get their lives back permanently."

She closed her eyes. She wanted to throw things and scream, but it wouldn't do any good. Anger left her body. She opened her eyes and flopped down again in the chair. "We also need to find Eddie and make sure he gets what he deserves. He tortured and killed Will. He's also here on the island. I'm guessing, by now, they all are."

"Son of a bitch. I'm so sorry. I know that's eating at you."

She nodded.

He leaned forward and started typing away on his laptop. A minute later, he sat back again. "I instructed my assistant to find out what, if anything, Will's family needs. I also asked her to create a fund to send his children to college if he has them and, if not, or if they've graduated, we'll turn it into a fund for his grandkids or something. I know it won't make up for losing Will, but I will do my best to take care of his family and the family of the other two men who were injured or killed while guarding Kathleen."

She bit her lip. She knew that under his granite exterior, Drake was a good man. He was Kathleen's brother, after all, but the fact that she hadn't even had to ask him to help Will's family hit her in the heartstrings. She blinked rapidly, but she couldn't keep the tears from falling.

Drake got up from the sofa, walked around the table, and pulled her up to her feet and into his arms. He held her tight against his chest. She didn't resist. She needed the feel of his arms around her at the moment. She needed his strength and determination. She rested her head on his chest. His heartbeat was slow and steady. The calm cadence helped ground her. She looked up at him, and their gazes locked. He bent down and captured her lips in a tender kiss.

She responded and, seconds later, what had started as a gentle, comforting tide was building into a gathering storm of heat and fire. She deepened the kiss, opening her mouth to allow their tongues more space to dance. She sunk her hands into his hair and held his mouth to hers. She needed him at this moment, and she was going to be selfish and take him.

She let go of his head and started unbuttoning his shirt. She undid the first three buttons when he broke the kiss. He reached back with one hand and grabbed the shirt, pulling it over his head in one move. Then he quickly pulled her shirt over her head as well. Her bra followed. When he picked her up, she wrapped her legs around his waist and let him carry her into the bedroom.

This was probably all kinds of wrong, but it was exactly what she needed at this moment. She kissed him hard, and he responded in kind. They were two people outside of their normal world, looking for comfort wherever they could find it.

More than an hour later, Spencer sat up and leaned

against Drake's headboard. She took a sip of coffee from the mug he handed her. "I needed that."

He grinned. "The coffee or the sex?" he asked as he climbed onto the bed and leaned on the headboard beside her.

"Both," she laughed, pulling the sheets up to cover her chest. The air conditioning felt cool now that all the physical activity had stopped. The smile slowly slid from her face. Kathleen and Connor had to leave that night. She wasn't prepared. They'd been a part of her life for the last ten years, in some ways the best part.

Drake sighed as he sipped his coffee next to her. She reached over and grabbed his hand. "Here I am lamenting them leaving after ten years. You just got them back, and they have to leave again. I'm so sorry. You should go spend time with them." She started to get up.

He squeezed her hand and held her in place. "I will, but I needed a bit of time to adjust my thinking. I don't want to be upset in front of them. It will only make it harder.

"I keep telling myself it's for the best. If Kathleen and Connor will be safe in Tasmania, then that's where they need to be. In truth, I don't think the Caridis will bother to follow them in the end, but what does that mean for their futures? What if they stay there, and life is fine? Will Kathleen ever be able to come back? Will Connor ever be able to use his own name and travel freely without always looking over his shoulder? It is a never-ending nightmare for them at this point. We have to find them a way out."

He was devastated, something she understood. "I feel like I've failed somehow."

"You've done nothing of the sort! You kept my sister and my nephew safe for ten long years. Nothing else matters. Things moved beyond your control. There is nothing more you could have done."

She smiled briefly. "We're like a mutual pity party over here."

He squeezed her hand again. "It's a tough one to get through. And if we feel this way, imagine how Kathleen and Connor are feeling."

"Kathleen is such a good person. She saved me in so many ways."

"How do you mean?" Drake asked.

She fidgeted with the sheet. She didn't know if she wanted to have this conversation with Drake just yet. Six years after the fact, the tale was still so raw and emotional. Although, in some way, she felt she owed him. He missed out on sixteen years with his sister.

She took a deep breath. "When I got a promotion to WitSec and Eddie assigned me to Kathleen, I was in a dark place. My parents were horrified that I joined the Marshals a few years before, and they weren't speaking to me. I went up to D.C. from Phoenix for my father's birthday to try to mend some fences. They had a dinner party where I met Josh, a young up-and-comer in all the right political circles. My parents loved him and were thrilled when we started dating.

"Looking back, I'm pretty sure I dated him and subsequently married him because that's what they wanted, and I wanted their approval in one form or another. Anyway, after the wedding, my parents and Josh wanted me to move back to D.C. and give up my job with the Marshals. They would find something more suitable for me—that's what they said.

I resisted. I would put in for a transfer to Washington or Virginia or somewhere around there, but I wouldn't quit. Mother and Father weren't pleased, and neither was Josh. How would it look for his career?

"I traveled back and forth at that point from Arizona to D.C., but Josh didn't like that either. Things would be fine when I arrived in town on Friday night but, by Sunday, he would be screaming at me. About six months in, he hit me for the first time."

Her breath caught in her chest. The pain and humiliation still got to her even now after all these years. Drake squeezed her hand, but she couldn't turn and look at him. She wouldn't be able to finish her story, and if he gave her a pitying look, that would be the end of their...whatever this was...because she wouldn't take pity from anyone.

"I flew back to Phoenix, and by the time I landed, my eye had turned black and looked ugly. I had to lie and say I got an elbow to the eye during a game of basketball."

She took a sip of coffee, mostly to wash down the anger and sadness that clogged her throat. "Josh called and apologized over and over again. He sent flowers and candy and even flew down the following weekend. Work stressed him out he said, and he lost control, but he would never hit me again. And like an idiot, I took him back.

"He did keep his word for a while, but about a month later, he hit me again. I knew then he would never stop, but I felt trapped and hopeless. Keeping my job was my only defiance. He kept saying if I moved to D.C., then it would all stop because he wouldn't be so angry all the time. I would be with him, and life would be good. I recognized it as a pack of lies. I think I knew he wouldn't change, but I wanted to believe him.

"Anyway, I arrived in D.C. one Wednesday night all excited to tell Josh I was pregnant. I flew up early so we could celebrate. I knew being pregnant meant that the pressure would increase for me to quit and move permanently to D.C. I had resigned myself. I thought that me being pregnant, us having a family, would make things better. When I arrived at our apartment, he was having sex with his assistant in our bed." Drake swore beside her, but she still wouldn't look at him. Humiliation crawled up from her belly and bloomed across her cheeks.

"Josh was livid, angrier than I had ever seen him. What was I doing there? How could I come without telling him? Then he blamed me for his affair. It was all my fault because I didn't live in D.C. with him fulltime. I refused to be a good wife to him. He railed at me for what seemed like hours in our bedroom as the mistress slunk out of the room and left the apartment.

I made the mistake of fighting back finally. I yelled at him. Told him how worthless he was as a man and a husband. That he was a coward and a cheat. I remember leaving the room. He came after me and yelled at me for turning my back to him and grabbed me. He whirled me around and hit me so hard he lifted me off my feet. I flew backward and fell down a flight of stairs. I woke up in the hospital, and I wasn't pregnant anymore."

Drake slammed down his coffee cup on the bedside table and moved so he sat in front of Spencer. He took both of her hands in his. "Look at me," he demanded.

She gritted her teeth and braced herself for the pity she expected to see. She looked up slowly. Rage was etched into every line of his face. Pity didn't exist.

"I am so sorry that happened to you, Spencer. I will gladly kill the man for you if you want. Just say the word."

She blinked. He meant it. He actually meant every word. She gave a choking laugh. "I don't need you to kill him, but thanks for the offer. We're divorced, and I never have to see him again."

He pulled Spencer into his lap. "I wish to God I could find a way to make this better. To make you feel like it never happened."

She looked at him and shook her head. "But it did happen, and I learned so much from it. I'm stronger now, and I know how to take care of myself. And because of Josh, your sister and your nephew became my family. Kathleen gave me the support I needed to get back on my feet. She'd been through it, so she understood. That's the best gift anyone could have given me at that point—understanding. I will be eternally grateful for it."

"Still..." He shook his head. "Are you sure I can't kill him for you?" He tried to make light of the situation for her sake, and she appreciated it, but the rage was still there in his eyes.

She put a hand on his chest. "It's okay. I'm okay, and it's over. Josh is still in Washington, but his career has stalled out, thanks to my parents. To him, that was a fate worse than death. They never truly acknowledged what had happened because then they would have to admit they'd made a mistake in judgement, but they quietly put out the word, and Josh's career went up in flames. That's how it's done in those circles."

The pulse in Drake's jaw jumped to a lively beat. He was still angry. She leaned in and kissed him, hard, and then more softly. Having his arms around her made her feel safe but more, his anger on her behalf made her feel loved, which was something she hadn't felt in a very long time.

CHAPTER TWENTY-THREE

Spencer stepped out of her room and closed the door behind her. She'd had a quick shower and thrown on a navy T-shirt and a pair of jeans. She'd pulled on her sneakers and tucked her gun into her waistband, under her T-shirt before she'd entered the hallway. Her blond hair was pulled up in a messy bun so it could dry a bit but not be in her face. "Hey there, stranger," she called as Kathleen came out of her room.

"Hey, yourself."

Spencer walked over to stand beside her friend. "Where's your luggage and where's Connor?"

Kathleen lifted her chin. "He's there in the main suite, and they came and got the luggage a while ago."

"Are you ready for this?" Spencer asked. The fine lines across Kathleen's forehead were back, and her mouth was turned down at the corners. Anxiety came off her in waves. Spencer reached out and squeezed her friend's arm. "You and Connor are going to be fine. These men know what they're doing. You will be safe. Much safer than you are here."

Kathleen gave her a quick smile, but it didn't reach her

eyes. "I know. It's just...moving again is upsetting Connor. He just found out he had an uncle, and now we have to go away again. It's not fair, and it's hard on him."

"Kids are resilient. He will be fine. All this will be over soon, and you both can have your lives back."

"From your lips to God's ears."

They both turned at the sound of approaching footsteps.

"Are you ladies ready?" Mitch asked.

"We are," Kathleen answered. Connor appeared at his mother's side.

"What about you, Connor, are you good to go?" Mitch asked.

Connor nodded.

Mitch turned and gave a wave. The others all piled into the hallway. "Off we go," he said as he followed some of his men. Everyone fell in line, and they headed down the hallway to the stairwell.

"We're taking the stairs all the way down?" Kathleen asked as she looked down at her wedges. "I should have worn sneakers."

Spencer laughed. "It won't be that bad."

Connor walked alongside Drake and talked a mile a minute about video games. He was nervous. Drake listened and asked questions. He put an arm around his nephew's shoulder and gave him a sideways hug and then let Connor go first down the stairs. Spencer glanced at Kathleen, and their gazes met.

Kathleen smiled. "He's so good with Connor. It surprises me every time. He certainly has more patience now than he did when he was a kid."

"Don't we all, " Spencer replied. She glanced up as she turned the corner in the stairs and saw more security behind them. There had to be at least ten guys. She spotted Kathleen and Connor's luggage up ahead with a couple of the men who were carrying everything. Everyone was well-armed and on full alert. The butterflies in her stomach settled somewhat. This was a well-trained and well-prepared group of professionals. It would be fine.

They hit the lobby level but continued down another flight. They reached the bottom and exited into the back hallway of the hotel. A few twists and turns later, and they left the building. She knew they were steps away from the beach because the sound of the waves breaking on the shore was loud.

The whole security team went on red alert. Spencer's skin tingled. It was always like this on an op. Adrenaline took over and her senses were heightened. They walked for about two minutes in silence. Even Connor seemed to sense the tension of the moment.

They went through some undergrowth and came out on the beach. Spencer looked around but didn't see anything. No transportation whatsoever. She looked up and caught Drake's eye. She raised an eyebrow. *What's going on?*

He shrugged slightly, but he was frowning and his hands were fisted, a sure sign he wasn't relaxed either. She cocked her head at a buzzing noise. She looked out at the water. There was a storm out at sea heading their way so the waves were on the bigger side and they pounded the beach.

She thought she saw movement. She squinted. Some sort of speedboat came out of the darkness. It had high rubber sides and benches in the middle. It was similar to what the Coast Guard often used. Was it an actual Coast Guard boat? She didn't think so because the three guys on it she recognized from the hotel. They were part of Callahan security. Maybe they borrowed the boat then. Or maybe this was the one Drake agreed to buy the Coast Guard. She'd ask him later but either way, damn, it was good to have friends. She grinned.

The boat came right up onto the beach.

Connor pointed. "Is that our boat? How bad-ass is that?"

"Connor, watch your language," Kathleen rebuked him, but Spencer could tell her heart wasn't in it.

The team immediately made sure to surround everyone and the boat, guns pointing outward. It was fast and well done. They were truly professionals.

"Well"—Spencer turned to Kathleen—"you and Connor be safe—"

Kathleen threw her arms around Spencer. "Don't say another word, or I will bawl like a baby. I can't thank you enough for all you've done, so I won't even try. What I will do is say, 'I'll see you soon.'"

She swallowed the lump blocking her throat. "That you will. Promise." With one final squeeze, the women broke apart. Then Kathleen hugged Drake. She whispered something in his ear, and he squeezed her even tighter. Then they broke apart. Drake's eyes were bright.

Connor busily peppered the men on the boat with all kinds of questions. "Connor," Spencer called.

He turned and looked at her, then realized everyone was waiting on him. He quickly came over and gave her a hug. "See you soon, Aunt Spencer. Thanks for everything."

She smiled as she let him go, but she blinked hard for a few seconds. "Be good and listen to your mom."

"I will." He turned to Drake and gave him a big hug.

Drake crushed the boy in his arms. "I will be to see you just as soon as I can."

Connor stepped back, and his eyes were red-rimmed. "That would be good. We can play online in the meantime. Practice up, old man!"

"Okay, we have to go." Mitch signaled to the crew. He helped Kathleen and Connor onto the boat. Gage got on, and five more Callahan guys followed suit. Two of the remaining Callahan guys standing on the beach pushed the boat off the sand. Drake came to stand beside Spencer, took her hand in his, and squeezed.

The boat backed up and turned to go out of the cove. Connor waved. He had been sitting on one of the benches inside the boat, but he shifted so he was half standing, half leaning against the big rubber side of the boat. He craned his neck. He was trying to see something ahead of them.

Spencer had a sinking feeling in her stomach. "Sit back down, Connor," she mumbled. Kathleen leaned over and tried to get Connor's attention, but the boy was too focused on what he was doing. Gage reached over to grab Connor just as the boat hit a huge wave and Connor went over the side.

The seconds ticked by, each one seeming like an eternity. Especially since Connor didn't pop back up. The boat circled around, and Kathleen screamed Connor's name, but nothing. Mitch and Gage both went into the water.

Spencer dropped Drake's hand and kicked off her sneakers. She hit the water at full speed and dove deep. She came up and swam for all she was worth toward where Connor had disappeared. He was learning to surf, but he always wore a life jacket because he wasn't the strongest swimmer. She pulled herself through the water. Drake was swimming right behind her. She reached where Connor had gone in and ducked down under the waves, but it was nighttime, and the water was pitch black. She couldn't see a thing.

She surfaced. There was a strong current so maybe Connor got swept up in it. She swam in the direction of the current but there was nothing. She dove down again and saw a faint light and dark shapes. She pushed through the water toward the light, but it moved away from her. Then the light shifted to the right, and she saw Connor. She tried to swim to him, but her lungs were screaming for oxygen. She broke the surface and gasped for air. There, in the distance, was another boat.

Gunfire ripped through the night. Bullets flew over her head. There was yelling. She heard Drake's voice, and she turned to see if he was okay. He was waving frantically at her, but Mitch pulled him underwater, and the surface exploded right where they had been. She yelled, but her voice was lost in the cacophony of sound. She was torn. Connor or Drake? They were in opposite directions.

Drake and Kathleen would want her to save Connor. She turned and started swimming in the direction of the other boat. She pulled herself through the water. Connor was being hauled on board the other boat. She swam faster. If they didn't notice her, she might be able to—to do something. She'd figure it out once she got there.

They had Connor standing on the back of the boat with a gun to his head. All the shooting had stopped. She turned to look back at Drake. He was now on the boat, but Gage and Mitch were holding him back, trying to put themselves between him and the shooters. Kathleen's face, just visible over the side of the boat, was filled with anguish.

Spencer turned back toward Connor and screamed as a man popped up inches in front of her. He was in scuba gear. He grabbed her left arm, and she slugged him as hard as she could with her right. She hit the exposed part of his jaw and his head snapped back, but he didn't let go. She tried to hit him again but someone else grabbed her other arm, and she couldn't move. The first guy hauled his fist back. She tried to avoid it, but she was out of options. The whole world went black.

CHAPTER TWENTY-FOUR

"Can someone please explain how this happened?" Drake sat very still at the head of the dining table in the main suite. He controlled his voice so he sounded calm. He measured every breath and counted silently—one, two, three, and then release. He was on the knife's edge of losing control, and it scared him. For the first time in his life, he actually knew for a fact he was capable of killing. If he lost control now, he would likely kill someone in this room. Logically, he knew that wouldn't be helpful, but the rage in his veins and the pain in his heart demanded some relief.

Mitch stood at attention about three feet away. "There was a leak. The person we procured the boat from was approached by one of Caridi's people. He provided them with a copy of every boat he sold. Despite paying cash, or perhaps because of it, in combination with the type of boat purchased, was enough to tip our hand.

"We discovered a couple of houses further up the beach that had security cameras. The owners were kind enough to let us see the video footage. The kidnappers were waiting offshore for hours and watching the cove. The boat was disguised as a fishing vessel. It didn't stand out to anyone as being out of place. The kidnappers knew this was the only spot where we could do an extraction without major exposure. None of this would have mattered if Connor hadn't fallen out of the boat. We would've exchanged gunfire, and that's all. Our boat was superior, so they had no chance to catch us.

"They had divers in the water in case an opportunity arose to grab Connor and Kathleen. Once Connor fell overboard, they grabbed him and took him to their boat. We assume Spencer was looking for Connor when she must've spotted the divers underwater. She was already close to the other boat when they started shooting at us. She got caught in the crossfire. Again, we assume she decided to swim to Connor, and they grabbed her as well.

Drake's hands were gripping the arms of the chair so tightly his fingers throbbed. He'd followed Spencer into the water but had lost her. Mitch had grabbed him to keep him from being shot, and he'd had no opportunity to get to Spencer after that. He closed his eyes.

A flash of Connor's terrified face danced behind his eyelids, and then Spencer being pulled onto the other boat, her limp form thrown on the floor like she was garbage. Kathleen's cry of anguish filled his ears.

Mitch cleared his throat, and Drake focused on him again. Mitch met Drake's white-hot rage head on. "I take full responsibility for this. We lost Connor and Spencer on my watch."

Drake ground his teeth. He was having trouble marshaling his thoughts into a coherent stream. He wanted to kill this man who let his nephew be kidnapped. "I—"

"It's not his fault, Jamie."

Drake started slightly at the sound of Kathleen's voice. He'd been so lost in his anger that he hadn't realized she was in the room. "Kathleen." His tone was harsh. She didn't deserve to bear the brunt of his anger. He took a breath and started again. "Kathleen, please leave this to me."

"No, Jamie. You're going to yell and rage at Mitch, and that's not fair. It's not his fault. He and his brothers did everything they could. They did their jobs." She approached the table. Her hair hung limply, and her eyes were red-rimmed. Her breath caught in a hiccup. She'd been crying for hours. His chest hurt to see her this way.

"Kathleen, why don't you go lie down?"

"There's no point. I won't sleep, and I can't stare at the ceiling any longer." She moved over and put her hand on Drake's arm. "Jamie, it isn't his fault. It's mine."

"Kathleen—"

"Stop. Both Mitch and Gage spoke to Connor when they were helping him on the boat. They told him to stay low and stay seated. They also told him he had to listen to everything they said if he wanted to stay safe. They were both at their posts doing their jobs when Connor fell.

"I saw him stand up, and I let him. He was so excited." Her voice broke. "He'd never been on a boat like that before. I thought it wouldn't hurt if he stood just for a second. I leaned over to tell him to sit down when we hit the wave, and he fell. It's on me, Jamie, if it's on anyone."

"Ma'am," Mitch said, "I respectfully disagree. You and your son were my responsibility, and the buck stops with me. You did what any mom would do and let your kid have a moment of fun."

Kathleen reached out and gave Mitch's arm a squeeze. He gave her a smile of encouragement before making his face blank once more.

Drake's heart squeezed. He should be the one comforting his sister, and instead he was in corporate mode, trying to lay blame. Stupid. He could hear Gus, his old mentor's, voice in his head. *Sometimes, Jamie, things don't break your way. Nobody is at fault. It's just the way of things.*

He studied Mitch. The man's expression was blank, but fatigue and worry were etched in his face. Mitch was suffering. Gage would be the same. They all would feel horrible about what happened and do their damnedest to get Connor and Spencer back. *Spencer.* His heart gave a big thump in his chest, and pain radiated outward. He rubbed it absently as if he could rub the pain away.

He stood up. "No one is at fault. Sometimes things just don't go the way we want. Now we need to focus on getting them back." He reached over and pulled Kathleen in for a big hug. He looked over her head at Mitch and offered him a hand.

Mitch seemed surprised but recovered quickly and shook Drake's hand. "We will get them back."

"I know. We're counting on it." He released Mitch's hand and let go of Kathleen. "Why don't you go grab a shower. The sun will be up soon, and the cops will be wanting to speak with all of us."

Mitch grimaced. "Are you turning this over to them?"

"No way in hell. I want you all working on getting them back, but we can't ignore them or they will cause us more problems. The big question is, can we keep the cops out of the kidnappings?"

"Yes," Logan said as he walked across the room. "The FBI won't want them involved any more than we do and, in this case, they will demand the locals stand down. The hard part is keeping the FBI at bay. We can turn down their help, but we can't stop them from being involved. They've invested too much in this since it involves one of their cases, albeit an old one."

Kathleen frowned. "I know you are all doing your best, but are we sure we don't want them involved?"

Drake rested his butt on the dining table. "It's really up to you, Kathleen. If you want them involved, then we let them run the show. Connor is your child. You get to make that call."

Kathleen's shoulders drooped under the unseen weight of the situation. She rubbed her face. "What happens if they are involved?"

Mitch folded his arms across his chest. "They will run everything and decide how to handle the situation. If a demand for money or—"

"Or what?" Kathleen asked.

Mitch glanced at Drake, who gave a small nod. "Or an exchange, then they would lead that. Or say no, as the case may be."

"Say 'no'? What do you mean?"

Drake cleared his throat. "Spencer." It hurt him just to say her name. "She is of no use to the kidnappers. They don't want her. Our hope is they offer her in exchange for you, not that we would actually go through with the exchange, but it's what we want them to ask."

"What if they don't ask? What if they take Connor and run back to New York or somewhere else?"

"Then...then they'll kill Spencer."

Kathleen paled. Logan touched her arm and handed her a glass of water he poured from the pitcher in the middle of the table. "Thank you," she said out of reflex.

"There is one other thing to note here," Logan stated. "Because Joe is Connor's father, he may have certain parental rights. Usually they make him sign those away while he is in prison, but I can't find anything on file anywhere, which means there may be an argument to be made that he should be allowed to see his son. Obviously, we know he's behind the kidnapping but, at this moment, we can't prove he's really done anything wrong."

When Kathleen swayed on her feet, Mitch and Drake guided her onto a chair. Logan squatted down beside her. "I'm not saying anything is going to happen, but you do need to be aware that it's a possibility. If we can make sure Joe is arrested for Spencer's kidnapping or anything else, then the problem goes away."

Kathleen looked up at Logan. "So you think we should let the FBI be in charge?"

Logan tilted his head. "As your lawyer, I would advise you to be prudent. But as CEO of Callahan Security, I would tell you you're in good hands, and it might be better to be on our own where we can exercise a wee bit more flexibility than the FBI would be allowed to do."

Kathleen frowned.

Mitch sighed. "What my big brother is trying to say, but not say because he's a lawyer, is if we handle this on our own, we can handle the situation our way. We can break the law and do whatever is necessary to bring them both back. The FBI can't do that."

Kathleen's response was immediate. "I want you in charge."

"Done," Drake stated. "We will tell the FBI, 'No thanks, we can handle it ourselves.' They will investigate, but we'll maintain control. So, how about that shower?" he asked his sister. "I'll have breakfast brought up."

Kathleen nodded as she stood. "We're going to get both of them back." She looked at every man in the room. "I am counting on you to make that happen." She walked out the door.

"So how do we do this?" Drake asked as he sat back down in the chair.

Logan and Mitch grabbed chairs as well. Gage entered the room. "I took the liberty of ordering breakfast."

Drake nodded. "Thank you."

Gage sat at the other end of the table. "Just got off the phone with an informant. We think we might know where Joe and his people were staying."

"Where?" Mitch asked.

"They've left, but some of our guys are going over to check out security footage so we can get an idea of numbers and check things out in case they left something behind. I'm assuming they haven't contacted anyone yet?"

Drake shook his head. "Not yet." He clamped his jaw together. He refused to give up hope that Spencer was still alive. "Is there any way of knowing if they are still on Oahu?"

"They haven't left," Gage replied. "The airports and major water ports are being monitored by law enforcement. Mitch and I both contacted some old military friends that live here on Oahu, and they've agreed to help us. The message has gone out. There will be a bounty on the head of any man, woman, or child who even thinks about helping them get off the island. There's also a reward for any information about their whereabouts."

"Let me know if you need more money." Drake poured himself a glass of water. "Spend whatever you need to make this happen."

Gage nodded. "We're good for now. People understand what's at stake. We'll hear something soon."

He braced himself before asking, "Is there any word about Spencer?"

"No." Gage's phone pinged, and he looked at the screen. He clicked it a couple of times and then typed something.

"What's wrong?" Drake asked as Hawk entered the room.

"Ah, sorry is this a bad time?" Hawk asked.

Drake shook his head. "Is it done?"

Hawk nodded. "Yes, all sent and signed, and we have the copies back. Money is taken care of as well."

"Great, Hawk. I can't thank you enough for making that happen."

"No problem, sir. Is there anything else I can do?"

"You are free to go back home. I'll make sure the jet is ready at the airport for you."

"If you wouldn't mind, I'd like to stay and help out."

Drake looked at Mitch with one eyebrow cocked in a silent question.

Mitch nodded. "Happy to have you with us. We can always use a man of your skill, but you should know what you're signing on for. It may not be pretty. In fact, it could get ugly."

Hawk grinned. "I kind of hope so. It's been a long time since I've done ugly, and I miss it." He quickly whirled to face Drake. "I didn't mean—"

Drake waved him off. "I know exactly what you mean. Sometimes it's nice to get down and dirty in the fight. Makes the heart pump a bit."

Hawk nodded.

"Then take a seat."

Hawk walked around to the far side of the table and sat down.

Gage leaned forward. "That was my guy at the hotel. Eddie Miller, aka Eduardo Navarra, Spencer's old boss, is definitely with Joe and his crew."

"Is that a good thing or a bad thing?" Drake asked.

Gage shook his head. "I have no idea."

CHAPTER TWENTY-FIVE

"Last chance, bitch! Tell me where the money is, or you die!" Joe had his gun pushed against Spencer's forehead.

Blood roared in her ears and her heart was trying to break out of her chest. She was bound to a chair with her hands zip-tied behind her back and her legs fastened to the chair legs. She tried to wiggle her fingers, but she'd lost sensation in them a while ago. Her shoulders ached from being pulled back so hard, and her face hurt from all the blows she'd had to absorb. She took a deep breath and let it out slowly. Pain radiated across her body, and she used the pain to focus her mind.

"As I said, I don't know what money you're talking about," she answered in a calm voice.

Joe jammed the gun hard against her forehead. "Then die, bitch!" he yelled and pulled the trigger.

A dry click echoed through the warehouse. Her heart stuttered in her chest for a fraction of a second and then took off again at lighting speed. Was she really still alive because the gun had misfired? *Holy fucking* shit! Death just didn't get any closer than that.

"Fuckin' gun," Joe screamed. "Water got in it, and now it doesn't work." He looked around. "Eddie, give me your gun. I want to kill this bitch."

"Joey, let me talk to her. I'll get it out of her. She'll tell me where the money is." Eddie moved forward and stood beside Joe in front of Spencer. "Why don't you go in the office and talk to your son?"

"Fuckin' bitch. You better tell him, or you're dead." Joe pointed in her face and then stomped off toward the office.

Eddie stood directly in front of Spencer. "I just saved your ass, so you'd better start talking."

"Look, Eddie, I don't know anything about any money." She glared at her former boss. "And even if I did, I wouldn't tell you, so go ahead and kill me."

"Come on, Spencer. You're close with Kathleen. She must have told you what she did with the money she skimmed from Joey."

She snorted. "Funny. She didn't mention it. Just like you didn't mention that you were part of the mob or a murderer. I guess we all have our secrets."

Eddie's face hardened. "I'm trying to be nice here, Spencer, but if you don't start talking soon, I will be forced to find other methods of coercion."

She refused to be intimidated. "You can do what you want, but it's not going to change my answer any."

She heard a door slam, and she turned to see one of Joe's goons crossing the warehouse floor. Joe had sent him out to do something earlier. She thought of him as Tweedle Dee, but they called him Tony. He walked into the small office at the back of the warehouse, and when Joe looked up, Tweedle Dee shook his head. Joe slammed the old metal desk with his fist.

"Hey, look at me when I'm talking to you," Eddie bellowed and followed up the yell with a backhand to Spencer's cheek. It wasn't the first one and wouldn't be the last. Her head ached and her cheek throbbed. Eddie seemed like he was just getting warmed up. The one benefit she'd taken away from her abusive relationship years ago was she'd learned how to tolerate pain. It came with the territory. *Go ahead asshole, you're not going to break me.* She wouldn't let this traitor win, no matter what.

"Where's the money?" Eddie leaned down so his face was inches from hers. She wanted to bite his nose off. She could do it, too. Wouldn't bother her in the slightest. She didn't care what they did to her. But Connor was here, and if they killed her, no one would be here to keep an eye on him. Not that she could do much at the moment. He was in the office with Joe.

"I. Don't. Know. I didn't even know the money existed. I never heard anything about it. Kathleen never mentioned it."

Eddie smoothed his black hair back as he straightened up. He wiped his face and then folded his arms over his chest. His wrinkled black T-shirt hung over his stained blue jeans. This was not the Eddie she knew. Eddie dressed well and was always neat. This Eddie embodied an altogether different animal—a desperate one—and she wasn't sure quite how to manage him just yet, but she would learn. Her life might depend on it. She recognized this as his *I'm getting frustrated* stance. Well, that made two of them.

"Spencer, I told my cousin you would be useful. That we didn't have to kill you, but you're making a liar out of me, and I don't like that." Eddie walked over to a table that had water bottles on it and assorted tools. Eddie's torturing devices. *Great.*

If she got out of this mess—*when* she got out of here—she would find a career that made her happy. She also planned on telling her parents to piss off. She was done with feeling guilty for not living up to their expectations.

And she would tell Jameson Drake that they needed to keep doing what they were doing. Life was too short, and the sex was too good to pass up. The truth was, she might even be just a bit in love with him, not that she would tell him that. He probably already knew. Smug bastard. Her heart gave a little lurch in her chest when she thought of him.

"If you aren't willing to do it the easy way, then I guess we'll have to do it the hard way," Eddie said as he approached her again. She didn't like his feral smile, and the fact he held pliers in his hand didn't help matters. Her mind went to Will. Eddie had tortured him, and now she understood he had enjoyed every minute of it.

"Eddie, come in here and bring her," Tony yelled across the warehouse. "Joe wants to talk to her."

Eddie leaned down in Spencer's face again. His breath was hot and stale against her skin. "You're awfully lucky today, but soon your luck will run out." He rubbed her cheek with the pliers and then bent down and cut the ropes that bound her legs to the chair. He pulled her up by her T-shirt and shoved her. She stumbled but caught herself.

Her feet were bare. She's taken off her sneakers at the beach and lost her socks in the water. Her kidnappers had yanked her out of the trunk of the car and made her walk into the warehouse, but she'd stepped on a piece of glass so now her foot hurt and bled as she made her way to the office.

Tony opened the door, and Eddie shoved her in. Connor sat on the farthest corner of an old green couch. His eyes were the size of golf balls and his skin as white as a snowflake. His lip trembled. She tried to give him an encouraging smile, but Eddie shoved her again until she bumped into the old desk directly in front of Joe.

Joe looked her over. "Where's the money, cunt?"

"I don't even know what money you're talking about."

"Kathleen stole a bunch of money and hid it from me. I want it back. He"—Joe lifted his chin to indicate Eddie—"says you're close with Kath, so where is it?"

"I don't know." And she didn't. She had no blessed clue what the fuck he was talking about. She did know that Kathleen absolutely hated being called Kath, and now she knew why.

She also understood why Kathleen had fallen for Joe sixteen years ago. Joe had beautiful, dark eyes and a rugged jawline. He was handsome by anyone's count. He could also be charming. He had tried flirting with several of the jurors across the courtroom, but the prosecutor stopped that in a hurry. They only got him on tax evasion and money laundering. They couldn't find the body of the man he killed, and Kathleen didn't know enough to offer any help.

Still, his time in prison hadn't been kind to him. His dark eyes were watery, and his jawline, although still there, didn't make up for the receding hairline or the general meanness stamped on his face. The prison tattoos on his arms and hands didn't help either. Spencer normally liked tattoos, but prison tats were a whole different ballgame. At least, these were.

Joe had been staring at her this whole time, so she stood there and stared back.

"I'll ask one more time and you'll tell me, or I'll hurt the kid."

Her knees went weak, and fire burned in her stomach. Would he really hurt Connor? Probably. Tony went over and sat down on the sofa with his gun out and aimed at the boy.

"Where is the money?"

She glanced at Connor. Should she lie and say she knew? She could make something up now, but how long could she continue the ruse? She looked back at Joe. It absolutely killed her to say it, but she had no choice. "I honestly, sincerely don't know anything about it."

Joe nodded. "I told you this one is useless. She doesn't know anything. Kath was good at keeping secrets. She didn't tell nobody about the money. We need her if we're going to get it back. Take this one out behind the warehouse and shoot her. Dump her body in a dumpster on the other side of town."

"No!" Connor said and started to get off the sofa. Tony pushed him back.

"I agree with the kid. She might have a use," a new voice said.

Spencer craned her neck to see who arrived. The dark warehouse didn't help, and the voice came from outside the office where the door blocked her view.

"Oh, yeah? What use is that?" Joe asked. "If you want to have fun with her first, be my guest. She's not my type."

"No, Joey." Roberto Caridi strode in. Spencer recognized him from his picture in Kathleen's file. He wore a lightweight navy summer suit. He had gotten the looks in the family and still kept them.

Roberto Caridi was known as a heartbreaker on top of being a mobster. He had even made Page Six in one of the New York papers a couple of times. The star of the gossip columns. The most eligible mob bachelor. "We can trade her."

"Trade her for what? She's too old to be in the trade, and no one is gonna wanna buy her."

Spencer was sure she heard Roberto's teeth grind. It seemed the brothers weren't the best of friends.

"Joey, Joey...Joey! You want Kathleen dead, but you want to keep the boy, yes? So you offer to trade this one for Kathleen."

"Why would they trade this one for Kathleen? Her brother is not going to do that."

Roberto smiled. "Oh, I think he will. Didn't Connor tell you this one"—he pointed at Spencer—"and Drake have been playing hide the salami?"

She glanced over at Connor. He was studying his shoes, and his cheeks were red. She and Drake hadn't been as careful as they'd thought. Didn't matter now. Her shoulders dropped a notch.

Joe leaned back in his chair. "Yeah, he mentioned it, but I still don't think Drake would trade his sister for a lay, no matter how good she is."

He had a point. She didn't like to agree with the guy, but Drake would never give up Kathleen and Connor again. Not for anything, including her.

"So then make it worth his while. Throw in the kid."

Joe looked over at Connor. "I want my kid. He's part of the family. He needs to learn our ways and be a part of the crew."

Roberto leaned on the doorjamb. "Joe, do you want the money or the kid? You're not going to get both here."

"Why not? I can ransom the kid to the uncle. He'll pay, and then I just won't hand the kid over."

"And how are you going to get Kathleen? I thought the whole reason we're doing this is so you can kill Kathleen and get your money back, thereby restoring your honor. That's the line Pop's been selling. You don't want that?"

Joe glared at his brother. "Fine. Trade her for Kathleen. I'll give the kid back, but I want more money. I want the money she stole plus another five hundred G's for the kid. They can have these two, but I want that bitch!"

Roberto smiled. "Now you're making sense. We need to plan where we want this to go down."

Joe stood up. "We also need them to supply a way off the island."

Roberto shook his head. "No, but we do need them to call off the bounty. No one is going to help us as long as that's in place. Get the men together. We need a plan. Call that guy you hired for the kidnapping. We're going to need his help again."

Joe pointed to Spencer and jerked his head to the warehouse. Tony stood up and grabbed her by the arm. He pulled her out of the office and back to the chair. He tied each foot to a leg of the chair and put a gag in her mouth. Then he went back to the office. She watched him go. She tried to listen, but the office was too far away. Eddie saw her watching through the glass. Their eyes met. He went over and closed the office door.

She sighed. The zip-tie bit into her wrists. She couldn't break it no matter how hard she tried. Exhaustion washed over her. The guard by the door went out for a smoke. He stood just outside the doorway and kept one eye on her and one eye on the pier. She was stuck.

She turned back toward the office. Connor came out. One of the guards had him by the arm. Where were they going? She struggled harder against the zip-tie, but it was no use. They walked past her to the front corner of the warehouse. Connor opened the door and went in by himself. Must be the bathroom. *Thank God.* The guard went over and started chatting with the guy having a smoke.

Connor opened the door and looked around. He peered around the corner and saw the guard. He backed up and moved along the wall. When he was opposite to Spencer, he moved over in her direction. "Spencer," he said in a quiet voice, "I'm so sorry. This is all my fault."

She shook her head. She couldn't speak because of the

gag. She tried to smile at him but with the gag in her mouth it was impossible.

"I'm scared."

She nodded.

"I know Uncle Jamie and the guys will come for us though, right? They won't really trade mom for me, will they?"

She didn't know whether to nod yes or shake no.

She nodded. He started moving toward her when the guard yelled. They both turned to look at him.

He jogged in their direction, waving his gun. "What the hell do you think you're doing?"

Connor's face lost all its color again, and he stammered. “I—I—”

The guard just grabbed him and pulled him back to the office. Spencer sat there and watched it all unfold. There was nothing she could do.

Yet.

There would be a moment where she could act. She would just have to be ready.

CHAPTER TWENTY-SIX

"Any news?" Kathleen asked as she entered Drake's suite.

Drake looked up from his spot on the couch and shook his head. "You will be the first to know if there is."

Kathleen came over and flopped down beside him. "I can't take the waiting, Jamie." Her eyes filled with tears. "The not knowing if my baby is okay is killing me."

He leaned back and put his arm around his sister. He understood how much she hurt. He'd spent years not knowing what really had happened to Kathleen. "The not knowing eats away at your soul."

"Yes, exactly. I..." She looked up at her brother, and tears spilled down her cheeks. Her mouth formed a perfect *O*. "Jamie, I'm so very sorry. I had no idea of the agony, what you felt all those years. It's unconscionable what I did to you."

Deep down, he *had* been mad at his sister. Really livid for what she'd done, but he never wanted her to experience the agony. The anger seemed to burn itself out. Now he was just sad she had to live through it, too. "Kathleen, you made choices. You did what you thought was best, and it probably was best for you and Connor. It's over now. We're back together, and we'll get Connor and Spencer back as well. Then we can be a family again with nothing hanging over us."

Kathleen leaned on his shoulder. "I'm so tired, Jamie. I feel one hundred years old."

"I know. When this is over, we'll all go on a real vacation. Pick a spot on the globe, and we'll go and have fun. We can find tutors for Connor. We can spend the next months catching up, and you and Connor can decide where you want to be permanently."

"That sounds like heaven." She sniffed. "Please let it happen."

"It will." He was determined to remain positive for his sister. There was no point in doing otherwise. The blow would be just as bad no matter what they said now, so might as well keep her spirits up as much as possible.

"What about you?"

He glanced at his sister. "What about me? What do you mean?"

"Will you live with us?"

"Ah, I don't know. I guess that depends on where you settle. I work a lot, and my headquarters are in New York, so I'm usually there if I'm not traveling. I'll come visit you no matter where you are."

"At least New York is close to D.C. so that's good."

He frowned. "Why is that good? Why do I need to be close to D.C.? What are you driving at?"

"Spencer lives in D.C. I assume you'll want to continue to be close to her."

He was speechless. He didn't realize he and Spencer were common knowledge, although he probably should've known. "Spencer and I currently enjoy each other's company. I wouldn't read too much into the relationship." Even as the words left his lips, he knew they weren't true.

He had admired Spencer almost from the moment he met her. Her determination, her intelligence, her drive—she was impressive, and she could handle herself. She was an amazing woman. Had he met her in any other circumstance, he might relentlessly pursue her, but given the current situation, he wasn't sure trying to date her was a good idea.

She seemed to be in a vulnerable spot, exhausted from all the stress of looking after his sister and nephew and maybe a bit lost in her own life. He worried he might've taken advantage of that or, at the very least, she might feel he did. He closed his eyes. "Regardless, we need to get her back first." He absently rubbed his chest over his heart.

A knock sounded, and Mitch opened the door and walked in, followed by his brothers. He held out a phone. "This was dropped off at the front desk with instructions to give it to you. Don't worry, we've had it checked out. It's just an ordinary burner phone."

Drake took the phone. "Are there any numbers programmed in or anything?"

"No. Presumably, they want to talk about something, though, so it's a good sign." Mitch gave Kathleen an encouraging smile.

Gage sat down opposite Kathleen, and Mitch took the seat across from Drake. Logan stood between them.

"What's wrong?" Something was wrong. He could tell just by the looks on all three of their faces. Was it Spencer? Was she dead? Did someone find her body? His heart thumped against his ribcage. He had trouble breathing. He couldn't bring himself to ask those questions out loud.

Gage leaned forward. "We've just had word that Russo is downstairs, along with ten of his closest associates. He wants to speak with you."

"Why does he want to speak to Jamie?" Kathleen had leaned forward as well.

Logan shook his head. "We don't know. It doesn't make much sense to us either."

Drake stood up. "Tell him we'll meet."

"Wait a minute," Mitch said as he stood, too. "Let's come up with a bit of a plan first."

"Mitch, I'm sure your men are ready and able to defend me. Pick a spot in the hotel where you want us to meet and dictate the terms to him. If he doesn't go for the deal, he's not serious. If he agrees, then he is." Drake moved around the coffee table and headed over to the bar area. "Anyone want coffee?" He got himself a cup out of the urn.

"Okay, let's say we do this. What is our goal?" Gage asked.

Logan responded before Drake could, "To find out what he knows and what he wants and to see if we can make some sort of deal."

Drake smiled. "The enemy of my enemy is my friend."

Gage took a deep breath. Mitch shrugged. Kathleen stood up. "Are we sure Jamie will be safe?" She directed the question at Mitch.

He nodded. "We'll make sure everyone is safe. I promise."

Drake said, "Okay then. I'm going to grab a shower while you figure out the details." He turned and went into the bedroom, closing the door behind him. He put the coffee on the dresser and then got the shower running. He stripped off and got inside. Then he stood under the spray and let it pound on him.

He had done his best to keep his emotions together in front of his sister, but her questions about Spencer hit home. What if they'd decided she had no value and had killed her already? He leaned against the shower wall and rubbed his aching chest.

He had to rein in his thoughts. He couldn't function if his brain was caught up in the what-ifs. He knew this from every business deal he'd ever made. No matter how big or how small, business was just business; no emotion should be involved. Damned hard to do with the lives of people he cared so deeply about hanging in the balance.

He straightened and reached for the shampoo bottle. He'd had his moment. It was all he would allow himself. If he wallowed any longer, he might not be able to pull himself back together. He had taken months after his grandmother's death to get his shit together. A good year, in fact.

He started hanging out with the "wrong crowd," as she would have said. Drugs were never his thing, but he'd drank heavily and gambled a lot. Turned out he was good at both. He managed to party a year away, traveling around, drinking and gambling. He and Enzo had met up in Europe, and they'd instantly become friends. Going from party to party, poker game to poker game.

It wasn't until he won those run-down hotels that he had bothered to take his head out of the sand. Thank God, he had. They'd been his saving grace. He hadn't realized it at the time. They were just another gamble he'd been willing to take, but they'd paid off in a big way, and they'd whet his appetite for more.

Damn good thing, too. He could now afford to do whatever the hell it took to bring his people back. He also had hotels in many countries that didn't have extradition treaties with the U.S. If getting Connor and Spencer back meant having to run his empire from Morocco or Dubai, he was happy to do it because the legal system wasn't going to stop him from bringing his family together again.

He finally got out of the shower and toweled himself off.

He pulled on a navy and white pinstripe suit with a light blue button-down shirt and a red tie. Spencer had said the shirt matched his eyes. He pulled on his blazer and took a moment to center himself. Then he walked out of the bathroom into the main room of the suite as Mitch walked in from the hall.

"Ready to go?" Drake asked.

Mitch nodded. "We're meeting in the Hibiscus room. You okay to go?"

"Yes, let's see what they want." He moved out the door into the hallway and started toward the elevator. "I assume no one called on the burner phone yet."

"No. Logan has it and will find you if anyone calls."

They got on the elevator and went down to the lobby. When the doors opened, he was surprised to see that six of Mitch's men were already there in a semi-circle, facing out. There were four more with him in the elevator along with Mitch. They left the elevator, and all moved as one pod down the hallway to the room. It was slightly surreal. People stared, and Drake wondered when his life had become such a bizarre circus.

The first man opened the door, and the rest filed in. Then Drake entered with Mitch, and the other three members of his security team entered behind him. Gage and four other men, including Dragan and Jake, were already waiting in the room. Drake had lost count of how many men were present, but it had to be a new record. *This should be interesting.* He was glad Logan was staying with Kathleen. If she saw this, she might freak out.

There were two chairs on opposite sides of a table. The man already seated in one slowly stood. He wore a navy suit jacket over a white button-down and a pair of light gray pants. He had brown hair and eyes. His skin had a slightly olive cast and was scarred from acne across his cheeks. He looked like a typical middle-aged man from New York. He could be working in an office building in midtown. Drake had found that most criminals usually did resemble ordinary folks.

"Mr. Russo." He offered his hand. No need to make this adversarial right out of the gate. Plus, it always threw his enemies off when he was cordial to them, and off-balance was good.

Russo hesitated and then shook hands. He read the cues correctly and rolled with Drake's atmosphere of friendliness. "Mr. Drake. Thank you for meeting with me."

Both men sat down at the table. One of Mitch's men brought over two bottles of water and placed them in front of the men. If it weren't for the extra thirty or so men in the room with all manner of weaponry, this could be a regular business meeting.

"So, what can I do for you, Mr. Russo?"

"You can give me the money your sister stole from Joey."

He froze. Stolen money? Kathleen had never mentioned any stolen money. "How much money and what makes you think Kathleen has possession of any stolen money?"

"Five hundred large. When Joe went to jail and the feds closed everything down, the money was missing. The only ones who knew where the money was hidden were Joe and your sister. Joe doesn't have it."

He nodded. "I see. Mr. Russo, there are several other people who may or may not have that money besides my sister, assuming of course that Caridi is telling the truth."

"Maybe your sister's not telling the truth."

"If my sister had the money, do you think she would've spent the last sixteen years working as a school secretary, hustling to make ends meet? I'm guessing she would have supplemented her income with the money so she didn't have to say 'no' to her child quite so often. Why is it important for you to get the money back?"

"That's none of your business."

"Actually, that's the only business that matters. Tell me if I'm wrong, but my understanding is you would like to hang on to your business that you've been growing over the last sixteen or so years. Joe Caridi is now out of prison and trying to get it back. Your top boss said 'yes,' to Joe Caridi Senior since it's a long-standing family tradition, but only if Joe Junior cleans up his mess, by which he means my sister and the missing money. You don't want that to happen, so if you take care of things, then your business stays yours."

Russo's eyes narrowed. "You are well informed."

Drake inclined his head slightly. "I have a proposition for you. I will give you the money, but we'll add interest as well, say ten percent over sixteen years, so that's a little over two million, but you leave my sister out of it."

"I'll take the money, but it's a matter of honor about your sister."

"Not your honor. That part has nothing to do with you."

Russo shook his head. "The money isn't enough. I need reassurances that Caridi and his brother won't keep pushing for their piece of the pie. As long as they're around, it's a problem for me. And he has a son. That kid will have a claim to my business. I can't have that."

Ice poured through Drake's veins at the mention of Connor. "Connor is not interested in claiming anything."

"You say that now, but down the road..." Russo tilted his head and shrugged. "The kid could change his mind."

"He won't. I guarantee it."

Russo chuckled, "And how are you going to guarantee that? It's a lucrative piece of the action."

"Mr. Russo, I will be leaving most of my empire to my nephew. He has no need for yours, but if you like, I will put it in writing. Should Connor ever attempt to become involved in your business, he will lose any and all claims to mine. Does that sound fair?"

"Caridi and his brother are still a problem."

"You let me worry about that. Do we have a deal?"

Russo narrowed his eyes. "I heard you have some friends in the old country. You struck a deal with Don Bacchi."

He nodded. Where was he going with this?

"And Valardi vouched for you. Having Enzo Valardi vouch for you is no small thing."

"I am aware."

"If Bacchi and Valardi trust you, then I'll take your deal, but at twenty percent interest." He offered his hand across the table.

Drake smiled and shook Russo's hand. Russo squeezed his hand and pulled him in. "But remember I'm not a man to be played with. It won't end well for you if you try to double-cross me. I don't care how many guards you have."

Drake leaned in as he squeezed Russo's hand back. "That makes two of us."

The men broke apart and stood up from the table. Drake smiled. "Mr. Russo, it was a pleasure doing business with you. Send my man your account number, and I will have the money deposited."

"No. I want cash. And I want it delivered in New York."

Drake nodded. "As you wish. I will make sure it's done." He looked around and caught Hawk's eye. When Hawk nodded, Drake turned back to Russo. "We'll let our people work out the details of the exchange, shall we?"

Russo nodded. "Fine with me." He turned to go.

"One more thing," Drake said, and Russo turned back. "I may need you to attend a meeting later with Caridi."

Russo frowned and then shrugged. "Why not? Let me know where and when, and I'll be there."

"Thank you."

Russo left the room, and Drake sat down again. Mitch walked over and stood beside the table. "You want to tell me what you're thinking by inviting Russo?"

"Yes, but not here. Back up in the suite." Drake got up again and they retraced their steps to the suite upstairs.

Kathleen appeared in the hallway as they were exiting the elevator. "Is everything okay?"

Drake nodded. "Yes, part A of the plan just fell into place."

Kathleen's eyebrows went up. "There's a plan?"

Drake smiled at his older sister. "There's always a plan."

CHAPTER TWENTY-SEVEN

Spencer swore long and loud in her head as she tried to twist her wrist in the zip-tie. Pain shot up her arm. Her wrists were slick with blood, but at least she could move them a bit. Progress, however slight, but escape would not be happening anytime soon.

She tried to roll the stiffness out of her neck and shoulders. Exhaustion washed over her, and her face hurt where Eddie had hit her earlier. She twisted her neck to see into the office, but she couldn't catch a glimpse of Connor. Tony and Roberto blocked her view.

She tried to rest. She would need her strength in case an opportunity to escape presented itself. Joe hadn't tried to kill her again, which was a bonus. They'd talked about trading her, but as far as she could tell, no one had done anything about it.

She was getting antsy. She hated being tied up, but the not knowing was killing her. She tried to free up her mind and do some breathing exercises, but she couldn't concentrate. Her thoughts swung among Connor, Drake, and Kathleen.

Did Kathleen really take the money? Yes. The more she thought about it, the more likely it became. Kathleen had to choose between someone who would kill her if she tried to run and the FBI who wanted her to give them all the information to sink the Caridis and then have her hide for the rest of her life. While being pregnant. Oh, yeah, she'd grabbed some cash.

And if she knew Kathleen at all, it was tucked somewhere earning a nice interest. She smiled. Her friend was full of surprises. She was sure the money was for Connor. Assuming she didn't have to run and he would grow up in Arizona without ever knowing the truth, Kathleen would probably tell Connor it was a college fund she put aside for him that she'd invested well. All of which was true. She would just fail to tell him she stole it from his mobster father. Typical Kathleen really.

Now, however, the cat was out of the bag. The money could put her in jail. They would deal with everything when she got out of here. If she got out of here. She rolled her neck again.

The office door opened, and everyone started filing out. It was late afternoon by the look of the angle of the sun. Maybe they were going for a late lunch or an early dinner. Connor walked out of the office. She caught his eye and saw his go wide. His mouth fell open.

She frowned. Then it dawned on her. He'd only seen her after Eddie had just finished hitting her when she hadn't swollen up yet or bruised. Now both cheeks and her lips were swollen. Her left eye was also swelling, and she assumed turning black. She tried to smile to tell him she was okay, but the gag in her mouth made it impossible.

When Tony came toward her with a knife in his hand, she tensed. But he leaned down and cut her feet free and then pulled her to a standing position. She stumbled. Her feet were numb. She looked down at them. The cut on her right one had stopped bleeding but would start again once she started walking. Nothing she could do about it now. Tony gave her a small shove, and she stumbled again and fell to her knees.

"Get up, bitch!" Tony snarled.

She struggled with her hands tied behind her back, and since she was getting feeling back in her feet, pain shot up her legs. She got onto one knee and started to push her way up when a hand grabbed her arm and pulled her to her feet.

"She can't walk, idiot. You tied the ropes too tight. She can't feel her feet." Roberto helped her out to the car.

Connor tried to come to her side, but Joe put a hand on his shoulder and held Connor next to him. "You stay by me."

Roberto walked her to the trunk and helped her inside. He, the smarter of the two, had a heart of stone. There was no mistaking his flat, dead eyes. Joe was all anger and insanity. Roberto was all cold calculation. She shivered as they closed the trunk on her. Out of the two brothers, she wasn't sure which one was worse.

She curled up on her side on the gritty floor of the trunk space and listened as the rest of them climbed into various vehicles. Were they going to the meet? Her lack of sleep and the adrenaline overload made her foggy. The trunk smelled of stale salt water, and the sand was getting in her hair and eyes. She closed them and tried to relax. She might as well rest while she could.

A short time later, she woke up when they hit a large bump. She had no idea how long she'd been out, but it couldn't have been more than an hour. The car rolled to a stop a few minutes later. She heard another car stop behind it. Must be Joe's people.

She strained to listen and heard muffled voices. Everyone was still in the car, and she wondered why they were waiting.

If Joe and his people were smart, they would come early and put their guys in place. That's what she would do. Joe didn't seem all that bright, but Roberto knew how things worked, so maybe they had arrived early for the meet. She dozed off again but woke to the sound of the car doors opening and closing.

The trunk popped open. Spencer blinked against the sudden brightness. Her shoulders were hurting from having her arms tied behind her and she was a bit woozy from dehydration. Tony reached in and hauled her out of the trunk. He plopped her on her feet, and she stumbled but she managed to stay upright this time. She blinked as she looked around. They were pulled off to the side of the lane in a graveyard.

"Get moving," Tony said and gave her a not-so-gentle nudge. She bumped into Eddie, who sneered and pushed her away. She righted herself and walked gingerly across the pavement. Her heart began to hammer in her chest. Where was Connor? She craned her neck to finally spot him ahead. He was walking between Joe and Roberto. They were surrounded by security. A lot more men were here than there had been previously. Hired guns maybe?

She took the opportunity to study her surroundings. It appeared to be a military graveyard. The Punchbowl. That's what they called it, but she had no idea of the official name. The green grass, broken only by the headstones, many marked by flags, looked beautiful in the late afternoon sunshine. If she died here, she was going to be in good company. This was the final resting place of warriors. All had served in one war or another. It gave her comfort somehow.

Sounds drifted to her on the breeze. She glanced over and saw a large group of mourners gathered at a graveside. They were all in uniform. A beautiful day to put someone to rest.

"Tony?" Joe called and then gestured to the mourners.

Tony shrugged. "Some bigwig's funeral, I guess. Can't do nothing about it."

Joe scowled but kept walking. They finally came to a stop on the hill to the right of a monument by a large tree. The hired guns fanned out and took up their positions. Tony shoved Spencer up the last bit of hill, and she took the opportunity to move over to stand by Connor.

Tony had taken the gag out of her mouth, so she could finally smile at Connor, or at least attempt to, but it hurt too much to actually smile. He moved closer to her. Joe and Roberto stood on the other side of Connor.

"I don't see them," Joe complained.

"They will be here. Relax, Joey. Let me handle this, and we'll get this deal done."

Joe glared at his brother, but Roberto didn't notice. He was too busy looking at his phone. Joe started looking at his phone as well. Spencer took advantage of the distraction to edge backward a little, and Connor noticed so he did the same.

"Are you alright?" he whispered. "You look awful."

She smiled slightly. "I'm fine. It will heal. No permanent damage done." She glanced over at Tony, but he was too busy checking in with all of his guys to pay attention to her. "Do you know what's going on?"

Connor nodded, but his eyes filled with tears. "They're supposed to be trading you and me for Mom. Uncle Jamie won't let them take Mom, will he?"

"No, Connor, he won't, but she might be here. They might pretend to do that, so be prepared for anything, okay? Follow whatever your uncle or Mitch or any of them tell you to do. Trust them, even if it looks like your mom is going with Joe, don't panic. There will be a plan. You just have to have faith." She said a short, silent prayer that she was telling him the truth.

There better be a plan, and it had better be a damn good one.

She looked around again. She spotted some of Joe's men among the grave markers. The funeral had broken up, and the mourners were spreading out around the cemetery. They wandered around, looking at the other gravestones. Members of the military paying tribute to one another. It was a nice image and one that lifted her spirits.

Joe glanced over at them and scowled. The sound of tires on gravel got everyone's attention. "Who's that?" Joe demanded. "Wait, is that Russo? What the fuck is he doing here? Shit. Shoot him, Tony."

"Don't be stupid," Roberto snarled. "Tony, don't shoot anyone unless I tell you to, *capiche*?"

Tony nodded.

Roberto watched as Russo and his people made their way up the hill.

"Who are they?" Connor whispered.

"More mobsters from a rival faction." She frowned. What were they doing here? She fervently hoped this was part of Drake's plan.

"Russo, what the fuck are you doing here?" Joe growled.

Russo shrugged. "We were invited." He ignored Joe and greeted Joe's brother with a quick nod. "Roberto."

"By whom?" Roberto asked.

Vehicles arrived on the lane behind them. Everyone turned to look. Drake stepped out of the lead vehicle, followed by Logan, Dragan, and Jake. Mitch and Gage got out of the SUV behind it, along with Kathleen and two armed security men. They all started up the hill.

Spencer's breath caught when she saw Drake. He looked tired but good. Logan must have said something to him because he turned slightly, and Spencer's gaze locked with his. Drake's face froze for an instant, and his eyes went flat.

He was livid. Rage seeped out of every pore. She was surprised none of the others noticed. She was glad she wasn't on the receiving end of all that anger. It was terrifying.

With the arrival of Drake and his people, everyone formed a loose circle with Joe and Roberto and their people against the tree, Russo and his people on their left, and Drake and his entourage on their right. All the security people from all sides had their weapons drawn but down at their sides or under their coats. It wouldn't be good if the mourners spotted them. It was a lot of guns, and it all made Spencer uneasy. It only took one person to panic and fire to start an all-out war.

"Let's get this done," Joe said.

Roberto scowled at his brother and then smoothed out his features. "What Joey means to say is thank you for coming, although I'm not sure why Mr. Russo is here."

"I invited him," Drake said. His voice was icy. He was still in a rage.

"I see. Well, I'm not sure what he has to do with this. The deal is between you and us."

Joe opened his mouth to say something, but his brother nudged him. One of the mourners from the funeral walked by. "I think his grave is up here," he called to a friend who was a few paces behind. He turned and nodded at the group. Spencer coughed to cover her surprise.

Joe waited until both men had passed and said, "Russo ain't welcome. Let's get this deal done." He looked over at Kathleen. "You bitch," he snarled.

Kathleen looked pale but determined. "Nice to see you, too, Joey."

Good for her. Spencer wanted to cheer. A tough front was necessary if she was going to deal with these guys.

"The boy and the woman for the money and that bitch." Joe pointed at Kathleen.

CHAPTER TWENTY-EIGHT

Russo looked at Drake. "I thought we had a deal."

"We do. Joe here is mistaken. We haven't made a deal yet. He just yelled his demands over the phone and hung up."

Joe scowled and opened his mouth, but Roberto cut him off. "What do you mean, Drake? What deal did you make with Russo?"

Drake smiled. "Mr. Russo will be getting the money that Kathleen...borrowed from the organization, plus a decent amount of interest."

Joe yelled, "That money is mine!"

"Shut the fuck up, Joey," Roberto commanded. "So what are you offering us?"

"For you Roberto, a seat at the table of the five families in New York," Drake offered. He wanted to pound Joe into the ground and do the same with his brother after him, but he had to play the game. Had to be patient. There was no room in business for emotion. He needed Roberto to want this deal, or it all fell apart.

Joe snorted. "You don't have the right to offer that.

You're not part of the organization. Where the fuck do you get off?" He was getting worked up, waving his arms and pointing.

Drake ignored him completely. "Roberto, I spoke with Mr. Bacchi, and he agrees the idea is a good one, especially now that he owns a lovely little boutique hotel in SoHo. He needs you to keep an eye on things." He turned toward Russo. "I spoke with some of the others as well. They agree it might be better to formalize Cosa Nostra's place in New York rather than all these side deals."

Russo turned to one of his guys, and they took out a cell phone and made a call. Roberto did the same thing.

Joe glared at his brother. "What? Do you believe this asshole?"

Drake fisted his hands. It was taking every ounce of self-restraint not to beat the living shit out of Joe. He risked a glance at Spencer, but it was a mistake. His chest immediately hurt again, and rage poured through his body. Her face was swollen, and her eyes were darkening by the second. She had no shoes, and her feet where bleeding. He took it all in at a glance, but the image was seared into his soul. He would make Joe pay for that. It didn't matter if he had done the punching or not. He was the man in charge.

Drake caught a glimpse of Eddie, who was over on the other side of Spencer. He'd had Logan dig up a picture so he'd know who Eddie was. Eddie's knuckles were bruised. He was the hitter. Drake ground his teeth. He would pay, too, and pay dearly.

Russo hung up the phone and so did Roberto.

Drake waited a beat. "Roberto, as I'm sure Don Bacchi informed you, in order for this to happen, your family has to formally renounce its claim to the business on Staten Island, and you must swear to leave Kathleen and Connor alone."

"What?!" Joe shrieked. "No fuckin' way! That's my business, and that bitch is gonna be dead. She ratted on me. She don't get to live!" Joe started forward, but his brother caught him by the sleeve and pulled him back.

"Your deal is interesting, Mr. Drake. What is in it for my brother?"

"Absolutely nothing."

"What the fuck? Shoot him, Tony!" Joe pointed at Drake.

"Don't move, Tony," Roberto countermanded his brother's order quickly. "Surely, you can see the issue with this deal."

Drake shrugged. "As I see it, Joe is the reason you are all in this mess in the first place. He got greedy. Kathleen told him he was laundering too much money too quickly, and she couldn't hide it all. She warned him it would attract attention, but he didn't listen. What was she supposed to do when the FBI came calling?

“If Joe had been patient, the whole thing would not have fallen apart. This quest to reacquire the business on Staten Island is not helpful to anyone, including you, Roberto. There are other areas where you should be focusing your energy. Your brother is just going to complicate your life.”

After pausing to let that thought sink in, Drake continued, "If you make this deal, you are now Bacchi's representative in New York. You own a seat at the table. You make the deals with the five families on his behalf. It is cleaner for everyone. Your father will be very proud."

He turned slightly. "And you, Mr. Russo, will retain your piece of the action on Staten Island permanently and the cash goes back into the coffers. It is a win-win."

Roberto nodded. "And you get your sister and your nephew back with no threat to them, yes? This is the deal?"

"Roberto! What about me?" Joe yelled. "That territory was mine. Pop gave it to me. I want it back!"

Roberto turned to his brother. "Yeah, and you lost it because you fucked up! You're always fucking up. All that time in jail, and you didn't even make any useful friends! You're a waste of space, Joey."

"You're thinking of taking this deal? You would sell out your own brother for a seat at the table? Mama would never forgive you."

Roberto laughed. "Mama would be relieved. You've always been a fuck-up. All this mess over a girl. A girl, Joey! You're an idiot."

"I'm an idiot? I'll show you who's an idiot." Joe pulled out a gun and pointed it at Kathleen.

A silenced weapon emitted a small gasp, and everyone froze for an instant. Joe clutched at his chest. He dropped the gun and fell to his knees. He wobbled for a moment and fell face-first into the grass.

Drake looked around. "Who—?" He blinked. Tony was standing there with his gun pointed at Joe's body.

Roberto nodded at Tony and then turned to face Drake. "We have a deal, Mr. Drake. I have my seat at the table, Mr. Russo gets to keep his business and the money, and your sister and your nephew are no longer in harm's way."

"And Ms. Gordon. I also want Ms. Gordon back."

Roberto frowned as he looked over at Spencer. "Right. Sure."

"No." Eddie came forward. "He can't take her, Roberto. She'll sink me. I need her to be gone."

Drake's breath froze in his lungs. This couldn't be happening. Spencer was his. She was part of the deal. He was not leaving here without her.

Roberto shrugged. "Drake, do we have a deal?"

"No," he ground out. "Spencer comes with us."

Eddie wrapped his left arm around Spencer's neck and held a gun to her head with his right. "No way. She's mine."

He started backing up, and the sound of guns being cocked filled the air. Drake didn't bother looking, but Russo and Roberto did.

"Son of a bitch!" Russo grumbled. The entire group was surrounded by men in uniform.

Drake smiled a cold smile. "Sorry, gentleman, I had to be sure things went my way."

"The funeral. These are the guys from the funeral." Connor stared in stunned fascination.

"Yes," Drake confirmed.

"Jesus, that is...impressive," Roberto commented. "Well done."

Drake nodded, but his attention hadn't waivered from Spencer. Their eyes met. He willed her to know he wasn't going to let anything happen to her. She was going to be fine. He needed her to know he would do everything in his power to bring her home safe.

As Eddie started moving backward, dragging Spencer with him, she kept her gaze on Drake. He gave her an almost imperceptible nod, and she immediately went limp. She was dead weight in Eddie's arms, and because they were on an uphill angle, it threw him off balance, and he dropped her. By the time he stood back up, Hawk had a gun against the back of his head. Eddie froze. Hawk reached around and pulled the gun from Eddie's hand.

Spencer struggled to stand. Logan came forward, cut her hands free and helped her to her feet. Spencer turned and put her hand out to Hawk. He gave her Eddie's gun. She smiled and then slammed Eddie hard across the face with the butt of his own weapon. Blood spurted out of his nose as he sunk to the ground. "That's for Will." She turned and smiled at Drake.

That seemed to release everyone. Connor ran to Kathleen, and Spencer made her way to stand beside Drake. He put his arm around her and tugged her to his side. "Mr. Caridi, Mr. Russo, our deal is in place." He offered his hand to one and then the other. Roberto and Russo shook hands.

"What do we do about these two?" Hawk asked, pointing at Eddie and Joe.

Drake turned to Roberto. "I believe these are yours to deal with?"

He looked at Drake and nodded.

Drake turned to Logan. "Move everyone out of here as quickly as possible. Just in case someone changes their mind."

Logan nodded. "Or the FBI shows up. I don't want to explain any of this."

"Agreed," Drake stated. He nodded to Kathleen, who had her arms wrapped around Connor. Gage was ushering them to the cars. Logan spoke into a headset, and the uniformed men started jogging toward different vehicles.

“Who are all those men? Are they all your guys?” Spencer asked as she watched the mass exodus.

Drake smiled. “There's a Naval base here with a SEAL team. Mitch put out the call, and they all came to help. It's good to have friends you can ask for help.” He turned to Spencer. There was so much he wanted to say, but now wasn't the time. Instead, he swooped down and picked her up, putting an arm around her back and one under her knees.

"I can walk," she mumbled.

"Yes, but why would you when you don't have to? This is where asking comes in." He winked at her as he slid her onto the seat in the SUV and got in beside her.

CHAPTER TWENTY-NINE

Spencer pushed herself up higher on the sun lounger. She was enjoying watching Kathleen and Connor in the pool. They were both having a blast playing Marco Polo with another family. It was nice to see them relaxing and meeting people.

"Here is your cocktail," Drake said as he put the drink next to Spencer and kissed her on the head.

"Thank you, but you don't need to wait on me. I am perfectly capable of getting things for myself."

He sat down in the chair next to her. "I am aware of that, but I don't mind helping out. I like to watch my staff in action."

"Um hmm." She didn't remotely believe him. He'd barely left her side since the whole ordeal in the cemetery. "How's Logan doing with everything?"

"He's stressed, but Hawk is helping him. The FBI is keeping them busy since finding Joe and Eddie's bodies in the water, but he says he thinks he's managed to convince them we had nothing to do with their deaths.

"Bacchi sending a huge contingent back to New York has

been enormously helpful. The FBI is very distracted by their presence. I think the FBI is aware that a deal is in place, but as to who exactly killed the men, Logan says they don't have a clue and probably won't ever find out. He advises us to keep our mouths shut. I heartily agree. I do own an exquisite *riad* in Marrakesh if things ever look to be going south. No extradition."

She burst out laughing. "You do like your contingency plans, don't you?"

"I like to be prepared." When his phone vibrated, he glanced at the screen and then put it back on the chair face down.

She took a sip of her drink. "Did Kathleen and Connor decide what they want to do?"

Drake nodded. "She said they want to stay here on Oahu for a while. Connor made some friends at school, and he likes being here, plus he's determined to learn to surf. After everything, she doesn't want to move him just yet. She's also found a therapist for him. I think he'll be fine."

"I do, too." She smiled as Connor spun in a circle in the pool, looking for his new friend. "Did you find them a place to live?"

"A real estate agent is taking them to look tomorrow. I'm sure they'll find something they'll like." He cocked his head. "And what about you? Have you decided what you're going to do?"

She frowned. "I spoke to my boss, and we both agreed tendering my resignation would be the best course of action. No one is going to press charges, but my career is over. I'm radioactive in the community, and no one wants my bad juju to rub off on them."

"What about your parents?"

"I spoke to them as well. They weren't pleased at all, but I finally told them I didn't give a shit what they thought, and

I did what I had to do. I can live with myself, and that's the important thing. Then I hung up on them. A mutual parting of ways."

He reached over and grabbed her hand. "I'm sorry, honey."

"I'm not," she said and smiled. "When are you going back?"

"Why? Are you trying to get rid of me?" His phone sounded again, and he turned it over for a look at the screen.

"You can answer the call, you know."

"Yes, but once I start, I won't be free for ages, and I don't want to work all day."

She laughed again. "Bet you never thought you'd say that out loud."

Drake grinned. "No. It's new to me, and it's all because of you and Kathleen and Connor. I finally have people that I would rather spend time with than work. That is a nice change." The smile left his face. "I do have to go back soon, though."

"Yes. Duty calls."

He squeezed her hand. "Would you like to come with me?"

She was stunned. They'd been spending lots of time together over the last couple of weeks, but they had studiously avoided all conversations about being in a relationship. And he decided to spring it on her while they're poolside at the busiest pool at the hotel. Nice. "You want me to come to New York with you?"

"Yes. I would very much like if you would be close by. I'm finding that spending time with you is what I look forward to every day. Seeing you the last thing at night and waking beside you in the morning is now...a necessity. I don't think I will be happy unless you're with me. I haven't been truly happy in a lot of years, and now that I am, I don't want to let that go."

Her heart thudded in her chest. "Kathleen and Connor—"

"Are part of that, but so are you. You are a major part of my new-found joy as well."

She looked out over the pool. "What would I do in New York?"

"Anything you want."

"Drake"—she frowned—"I mean Jamie. It's gonna take me a while to adjust to calling you that." She sighed. "I can't sit around all day or shop or do any of those types of things. I need to work."

"What would you like to do?" he asked.

She bit her lip. An idea had been rolling around in her head. She'd even discussed it a bit with Kathleen, who had given her a giant hug and said the idea was a great one. She took a deep breath. "I would like to help other women who need to escape." She let out a breath. She'd finally said it out loud.

He frowned. "What do you mean?"

"There are a lot of women in this world who need to escape from abusive relationships, and they need help to rebuild their lives. Kathleen helped me through my time of crisis, and I helped her. I want to do that for other women.

"And sometimes they need to disappear altogether like Kathleen did, and I can help them to do that. I know how to do that. This is way outside the lines, so I'll understand if you don't want to be a part of it. I know you pride yourself on running everything above board. But this is something I really want… no, I need to do.

"Kathleen is willing to give me the money she squirreled away to help set me up. Once Connor is a bit older and off at college, she wants to help me help these women." She paused, waiting for Drake to say something. He remained silent. She finally turned to face him.

"I think it's a wonderful thing you want to do. I'll help in any way I can. Tell Kathleen to save her money. I will fund your project. The thought of other women caught like Kathleen is terrifying to me. I would be honored to help." He smiled. "I also know a few others who would be a great help to you. Did Gage or Mitch ever tell you about their girlfriends? I think you'll like them."

Spencer leaned over and kissed Drake hard on the mouth.

"So does this mean you'll move to New York and live with me?"

Her heart flopped in her chest, and a million butterflies took flight in her belly. "Absolutely. I can't wait." She knew she'd finally found the family she'd always wanted. She leaned in and sealed her fate with a scorching kiss.

The End

ALSO BY LORI MATTHEWS

Callahan Security

Break and Enter

Smash And Grab

Hit And Run

Brotherhood Protectors World

Justified Misfortune

Justified Burden

Falling For The Witness

ABOUT LORI MATTHEWS

I grew up in a house filled with books and readers. Some of my fondest memories are of reading in the same room with my mother and sisters, arguing about whose turn it was to make tea. No one wanted to put their book down!

I was introduced to romance because of my mom's habit of leaving books all over the house. One day I picked one up. I still remember the cover. It was a Harlequin by Janet Daily. Little did I know at the time that it would set the stage for my future. I went on to discover mystery novels. Agatha Christie was my favorite. And then suspense with Wilber Smith and Ian Fleming.

I loved the thought of combining my favorite genres, and during high school, I attempted to write my first romantic suspense novel. I wrote the first four chapters and then exams happened and that was the end of that. I desperately hope that book died a quiet death somewhere in a computer recycling facility.

A few years later, (okay, quite a few) after two degrees, a husband and two kids, I attended a workshop in Tuscany that lit that spark for writing again. I have been pounding the keyboard ever since here in New Jersey, where I live with my children—who are thrilled with my writing as it means they get to eat more pizza—and my very supportive husband.

Please visit my webpage at https://lorimatthewsbooks.com to keep up on my news.

Printed in Great Britain
by Amazon